G.W. Kent's books have been published in more than twenty different countries. He has written fourteen novels, a number of critically ac........ fiction books and several prize-winning televisi.......... produced hundreds of radio plays a................g organizations all over the world. As a freelance jo.......it he has written for many national newspapers and magazines. For eight years he ran an educational broadcasting service in the Solomon Islands. He lives in Lincolnshire.

ONE BLOOD

A Sister Conchita and Sergeant Kella Mystery

G. W. Kent

ROBINSON

Constable & Robinson Ltd
55–56 Russell Square
London WC1B 4HP
www.constablerobinson.com

First published in the UK by Robinson,
an imprint of Constable & Robinson Ltd, 2012

A copy of the British Library Cataloguing in
Publication data is available from the British Library

ISBN: 978-1-84901-341-3

Typeset by TW Typesetting, Plymouth, Devon

Printed and bound in the UK

3 5 7 9 10 8 6 4 2

ACKNOWLEDGEMENTS

I would like to thank coast-watchers D.C. Horton, William Billy Bennett and Joseph Supa for providing details of the search they conducted for Lieutenant John F. Kennedy and the members of the crew of PT-109 in the Western Solomons at the beginning of August 1943. For insight into the workings of the Solomon Islands Police Force in the 1960s I am indebted to Sergeant John Gina. As always, this book also owes more than I can say to the encouragement and help provided by my agent Isabel White.

The charming and gifted editorial team at Constable & Robinson, Krystyna Green and Nicky Jeanes, have added greatly to the making of this book. I am also conscious of how much I owe to Emily Burns and the sales, marketing and publicity departments for all their efforts on my behalf. My American publishers Soho Crime have been most supportive and encouraging from beginning to end.

ONE

The Japanese destroyer came out of the night at forty knots like a huge shark snarling across the lagoon. It struck the small American craft and cut it in half before disappearing into the blackness. Part of the fragile plywood and mahogany vessel sank almost at once, with two of the thirteen-man crew already dead. Sprays of gasoline were flung across the surface of the water, burning intermittently.

The young lieutenant in command of the craft had been at the wheel when the ramming had occurred. Fearing that the flames spreading across the water might reach the chewed-up remnants of the vessel and destroy them, he ordered the survivors over the side. In seconds, the crushing wake of the already invisible destroyer had extinguished the blaze. The eleven survivors, two of them badly hurt, hauled themselves back on board.

They remained huddled on the fractured, water-slopped deck until daybreak. As the sun edged over the horizon, the two ensigns and eight enlisted men looked to the lieutenant for instructions.

'What do you want to do if the Japs come out?' he asked. 'Fight or surrender?'

The remaining half of the plywood coffin began to settle in the water, almost obscuring the inscription on its splinter shield: PT-109.

TWO

'The problem is,' said Sister Brigid, loudly enough for Sister Conchita to hear above the noise of the crowd, 'when does an inconvenience transcend into sacrilege?'

Sister Conchita smiled sweetly and resisted the temptation to batter the elderly Irish nun about the head and shoulders with one of the carvings for sale on the table by the door leading to the refectory. On display were ebony walking sticks inlaid with mother of pearl, patterned pandanus baskets, vicious-looking stone war clubs and the engraved prows of several miniature war canoes, known as *toto iso*. Sister Jean Francoise should have been in charge of the stall, but Conchita could see the French nun through the open window, her habit hitched above her scrawny ankles, paddling contentedly in one of the rock pools on the white-sand beach, ignoring the visitors eddying around her. That left only Sister Johanna, and she almost certainly would be engrossed in dismantling and reassembling a piece of domestic machinery somewhere in the building.

In the reception room of the old stone building, the visitors to the mission's first ever open day surged through the doors and out into the gardens leading down to the reef and the open blue sea beyond. Behind the house, wooded foothills swelled in green profusion until they merged into the extinct volcanic mountain in the centre of the small island. Marakosi was a beautiful enough mission station; it was a pity about the three elderly rapscallions who had made up its religious complement for so many decades and who were slowly driving Sister Conchita mad.

'It's all very *modern*,' said Sister Brigid in tones that emphasized that the word was not meant as a compliment.

'Please keep circulating,' Sister Conchita exhorted the visitors, continuing to ignore the older nun. There was hardly room to move inside the house. 'The whole mission and its grounds are open to you today.'

'And don't we know it,' said Sister Brigid loudly, to no one in particular. 'There's not room left to swing a cat.'

There was no doubt about it, thought Sister Conchita, smiling until her face hurt, she would have to fetch Sister Jean Francoise back inside. The elderly French sister might be as crazy as a coot, but at least she seemed to have some influence on Sister Brigid. Perhaps she could keep the acerbic Irish nun quiet until the guests had left. It definitely was time to clutch at straws. Brigid was a sour, withdrawn woman who spent most of her time as far as Conchita could make out standing on the reef staring out at the lagoon. Officially she was in charge of housekeeping at the mission, but the layers of dust everywhere and the dreadful food they had been eating for the last month bore witness to her lack of commitment in these areas.

'Excuse me,' said Sister Conchita brightly, pushing through the throng like a very small but extremely determined running back. There were at least sixty visitors in the room and another two or three hundred scattered about the mission building and grounds. They were mostly Solomon Islanders, bolstered by a few expatriates from the nearby tiny district centre of Gizo, all attracted by the prospect of seeing what the notorious Marakosi Mission was really like. Leavening the attendance was a group of bewildered-looking American tourists who were staying at the government rest-house over at Munda, a nearby island. The Solomons consisted of a string of hundreds of beautiful and remote tropical islands, five hundred miles east of Papua New Guinea and a thousand miles north–east of Australia. The islands were difficult to reach, and the tourist trade was in its infancy.

There was a human log-jam at the door leading to the small in-house chapel used by the sisters for their private devotions. A bulky female American tourist in shorts stretched dangerously across her thighs had stopped in the open doorway and was brandishing a carved model of a turtle above her head.

'Where do I pay for this?' she demanded.

'We must all pay for our transgressions eventually,' said Sister Brigid coldly before Sister Conchita could reply, her voice rising and falling like a dagger plunging with deadly accuracy into a body. 'How and when lies in the hands of the Almighty.'

Not if I get to you first, Sister Conchita promised herself vengefully, squeezing past and emerging from the front door of the two-storey mission house on to the stone terrace leading to the beach and the calm lagoon beyond. Blocks of coral jutting out into the sea broke the force of the waves thundering against them in the distance beyond the reef and provided a safe anchorage for smaller vessels. She stopped outside, luxuriating in the sudden peace, although even here her mind was registering automatically the improvements needed. The ancient and cracked mission bell used to regulate the nuns' day with its strident summonses to matins, lauds, vespers and compline was suspended from a crossbar between two wooden posts that needed strengthening. It was tolled from the first sunrise Mass, and then regularly through the day to summon the nuns to meals and work sessions, ending with evening prayers.

Those visitors who had escaped from the heat of the house were scattered across the sand. The flower beds around the mission were overgrown and unkempt. A vegetable patch had surrendered almost completely to rough grass. Chickens and pigs wandered unchecked around the fringes of the crowd. A few dispirited yams struggled through the baked earth. It would not have been difficult to rotate the crops, with sweet potatoes following cabbage, but no one had made any effort to do so.

Conchita could not imagine why so many visitors had turned up. It might not be much, she thought, but the open day was probably the most interesting thing that had happened at the mission for generations.

There was so much to do, and it looked as if she was going to have to do most of it herself during her stay, she agonized, heading for Sister Jean Francoise, who was still paddling happily, oblivious to the strangers all around her. Like the other two nuns on the station, she would be well into her seventies now, small and bird-like in her movements, her face lined and weathered brown by the sun, but still possessing traces of the pretty and vivacious country girl she must once have been before she came to the Solomons.

'Sister Jean Francoise,' coaxed Conchita. 'We really do need your help in the mission. Do you think you could possibly spare us an hour or so?'

The French nun looked up from contemplating the smooth surface of the rock pool. She smiled beatifically, radiating an all-pervading charm.

'In the mission?' she asked with only a faint trace of an accent. 'But I am the laundry and garden sister. I seldom enter the mission except to eat, pray and sleep.' She paused, and then giggled. 'Almost literally I have been put out to pasture.'

'Even so, it is our first open day. There are so many people here. We could do with your help.'

'Open day?' Sister Jean Francoise looked about her vaguely, as if seeing the visitors for the first time. 'Oh yes, I remember something about that. An effort to modernize us, I believe. Throwing the mission open to the public. I don't understand. It is most unlike Father Karl to approve of such a thing. He is a very private man.'

'I'm afraid that Father Karl is dead,' said Sister Conchita.

An expression of sadness passed over the elderly nun's face. 'Oh yes.' She nodded. 'Now I remember. The poor man was ill for so long. You know, he got quite senile towards the end. It must be very sad, when your mind goes.' She started hopping around the pool again, sending up tiny splashes of water. 'I believe they're sending a sister from Honiara to run the mission until a new priest is appointed, some American girl with a strange name. I wonder when she will arrive.'

'I'm the new sister in charge,' said Conchita. 'I'm Sister Conchita. I've been here a few weeks now. That's why—'

'What an unusual name,' mused Sister Jean Francoise. 'Do you perhaps have Mexican antecedents? Of course, that would be nothing to be ashamed of. Perhaps you could teach the children at the school La Danza del Venado. That's where they have to imitate deer, you know.'

'I'm afraid I don't dance. As for my name, I thought originally that I was going to be sent to a mission in South America after I had finished my training,' said Conchita automatically. She had given this explanation many times since her arrival in the Solomon Islands. 'So I picked what I thought would be an appropriate name for the region.'

'And then they sent you here instead,' said Sister Jean Francoise, placing a damp, sympathetic hand on the other nun's arm. 'I really don't envy you, my dear. You're so young and we've all been here so long. I imagine that the more senior members of the staff in Honiara prudently turned down the chance to reform us and left us to your best efforts. I'm afraid we've all got rather set in our ways at Marakosi.'

You can say that again, thought Conchita, trying to be philosophical and forget the litany of slights, insults and outright insubordination that had already been her lot at the hands of her new colleagues, ever since the mission vessel had delivered her at the island.

'So, if you don't mind, Sister,' she said, indicating the mission building.

'If I don't mind what?' asked Sister Jean Francoise, wriggling her toes sybaritically in the warm water. She looked across at a school of dolphins playing out in the lagoon.

With an effort, Sister Conchita forced herself to be patient. 'I'd like you to help us inside.'

'Why, certainly,' said Sister Jean Francoise, raising an eyebrow in surprise and stepping out of the pool, slipping her feet into an ancient pair of flip-flops. 'You only had to ask.'

The French nun started to walk towards the building. A thought seemed to strike her and she looked back. 'By the way, who are you, my dear?' she asked vaguely.

'I've told you, I'm Sister Conchita.'

'Ah.' A twinkle appeared in the nun's eye. Suddenly she seemed neither aged nor abstracted. 'I expect you really want me in the mission to keep Sister Brigid under control. She can be something of a trial, I agree, and she doesn't usually take to strangers because she's so shy. She's Irish, you know, and occasionally outspoken. She has the heart of a lion, though. During the war she guided the crew of a crashed American aircraft for three days through the Japanese-occupied territory to safety. It was so sad what happened to her after that. She hasn't left Marakosi for ages. None of us have, I suppose. We must be adding a whole new meaning to the term "enclosed society".'

Sister Jean Francoise waved and walked away, nodding affably to the visitors she passed. Exasperated, Sister Conchita wondered how much of the Frenchwoman's apparent senility was an act. She prepared to follow the other nun. There was so much to do that afternoon. There were refreshments to prepare and serve to the visitors, prescriptions to be made up and bandages cut in the dispensary, plans for a proposed new boarding school to be put before the other nuns, the kiln used for melting coral into limestone for walls to be serviced, and above all the eccentric and unpredictable sisters to be supervised in their idiosyncratic endeavours.

In spite of her resolve, Sister Conchita felt very tired. Impulsively she turned and entered the mission church, a large, sprawling building with a sloping red tin roof and thin white stone walls. If she were to take her problems to the Lord for a few minutes it would help.

It was dark and cool inside. In front of the altar table were rows of wooden benches placed on an earthen floor packed hard by the feet of generations and covered with woven mats and sand. A large upturned shell served as a font. A metal candle-snuffer leant against it. A hand-carved mahogany cross hung from one of the walls. Gratefully Conchita began to yield to the ambience of calm, something in short supply since she had arrived on the island.

She saw with a start that someone else was already inside the building. He was a white man of about forty, plump and dishevelled, in white shorts and a floral shirt. He was well below average height, resembling an aggressive jockey who had ridden too many losing horses. He was kneeling in front of the altar rail, one arm extended to rest on the carved wooden cross in an attitude of supplication. Instinctively Sister Conchita turned to leave him alone, but the man heard her and scrambled clumsily to his feet.

'Pardon me,' he said in a New York accent. 'I was just resting. It's so hot outside'.

'For a moment,' smiled Sister Conchita, embarrassed at intruding on what obviously had been a private moment, 'I thought you might be claiming sanctuary.'

'Is that what it looked like?' said the man vaguely. He began to move away from the altar rail. He did not come up to Sister Conchita's shoulder. 'A lot of people would like the chance of that in their lives, I suppose. To find a safe place, set aside from normal existence, especially if someone's looking for you.'

'Certainly, if that is what you seek.' Conchita was surprised. The man looked more like a miniature hoodlum than a philosopher. She really must stop making snap judgements. 'However,' she went on, trying to marshal her thoughts, 'some claim that sanctuary is in fact the spot where heaven and earth meet. In strictly legal terms, of course, the concept of using a church as a place to claim safety was done away with in the seventeenth century.'

'That's a shame,' said the man. 'You can never find a refuge when you need one.'

'Of course,' said Conchita, 'it must be remembered that the guilty have never been protected merely by the presence of the sacred. A degree of repentance also has to be involved.'

'Oh, that old thing,' said the man. 'I'm Ed Blamire, by the way. I'm with the tour party.'

'Sister Conchita,' said the nun, taking the small man's extended hand. She hesitated, anxious to get back to her duties in the house but aware that somehow the visitor to the mission needed her. 'What do you do for a living, Mr Blamire?' she asked politely.

'Oh, I've done a lot of things in my time,' said the tourist. 'Tinker, tailor, candlestick-maker, security, pilot, tree-hugger, I even dived for pearls off Hawaii for a time.'

'Very interesting,' said Conchita. 'However, at the moment I feel that you are looking for something. Can I help?'

For a moment she thought the tourist was going to say something of importance to her. Then he shook his head and turned away.

'One thing I haven't been is a good Catholic,' he said.

'Welcome to the club,' said Sister Conchita.

'I remember one or two things though,' said the man. '*The letter kills but the spirit gives life*, is that right?'

'The Second Book of Corinthians,' said the nun. 'Very well, Mr Blamire, I shall be here at the mission if you would care to talk to me. Good afternoon.'

As she headed for the side door of the church, Blamire had turned back and was standing in front of the altar again, his shoulders slumped. Sister Conchita knelt in the aisle and prayed quickly for the other sisters at the mission, for herself that she might be fit for her new task, and for the tourist at the altar who seemed lost and troubled.

She emerged from the church to an area of the beach roped off from the rest of the mission grounds and hidden from sight of most of the visitors by the church building. A huge pile of coconut husks had been assembled to a height of ten feet above the ground. This was Sister Conchita's brainchild. She had been preparing it for most of the month since she had arrived at Marakosi, ever since she had learned that it had been a mission tradition dating back to before the war that ships visiting the station would be greeted by a blazing pyre of husks set off by the nuns.

A wooden torch soaked in oil and a box of matches lay on the ground ready for the ceremony. Sister Conchita intended to wait until dusk, just before the open day was due to end, and then ignite the bonfire to bid farewell to the departing guests. She checked that everything was in place and went back round the side of the church to join the crowd.

She noticed with satisfaction that the other attractions she had organized for the day seemed to be drawing plenty of attention. Among the outer fringe of trees, Malaitan labourers from the local logging camp, supervised by a white overseer, were felling a kapok tree with a two-man power saw, while others were stripping the branches from several felled trees with economical blows from their bush knives. On a marked-out course on the sand, islanders were racing one another over a sixty-yard distance carrying heavy bags of copra on their shoulders.

Out in the lagoon, a dozen large canoes provided the incongruous sight of members of a brass band lustily playing 'Abide With Me' on their highly polished cornets, trumpets, tubas and trombones. This was the self-styled Silver Band of the Christian Fellowship Church, a recent breakaway denomination from the

United Methodist Church of the Solomons. Its members had built a village called Paradise on the nearby island of New Georgia. The leader of the new church, the Holy Mama, who claimed to be the fourth member of the Trinity, was sitting approvingly in one of the canoes of the flotilla, waving his arms decorously in time to the music. He was an elderly islander wearing a long white robe and a shell-decorated turban. Sister Brigid and the other nuns had objected to his presence because he was reputed to have designated a dozen of the most attractive girls from his island as his personal angels. The more pragmatic Sister Conchita had felt, as the moment drew near, that her cherished open day threatened to be so lacking in entertainment that she was willing to overlook any teething troubles experienced by the CFC and the personal peccadilloes of its founder, as long as its instrumentalists could provide a selection of rousing hymns played roughly in tune.

On her way back to the mission house, Sister Conchita could not put the man in the floral shirt out of her mind. Had she ignored a cry for help? Mr Blamire had denied the fact, but perhaps she should have been more sensitive to his needs, whatever they might have been. It seemed to her that the plump man in the church had been very frightened.

By the time she arrived back inside, Sister Johanna had appeared from the recesses of the house. Tall and angular, with a face apparently consisting of little but straight planes, the German nun had a forbidding appearance. Her hands were deeply engrained with dirt and oil, brought about by years of toil as the mission's mechanical genius. There were several smudges on her face. She greeted Conchita with a chilly nod.

'So many people,' she said gutturally. 'One would almost suppose that your plan had been a success, Sister Conchita.'

Sister Brigid snorted. 'Nonsense! It's all an irrelevance. What are we to expect next? Swings and roundabouts? This used to be a working mission.'

'Not for some years, as I understand it,' said Conchita, before she could stop herself. She was at once aware from the severe expressions on the faces of the other sisters that she had made yet another error. 'I believe that you have been more of a contemplative order lately,' she said in an effort to redress the balance. 'I have never served in a cloistered mission before.'

'How long have you been in the Solomon Islands now?' asked Sister Brigid after a chilly pause.

'Six months.'

'You are surely very young to have been appointed to a position of authority,' said Sister Johanna. 'Even over us.'

The other nuns laughed. Conchita resolved that they would not trample her underfoot again that afternoon.

'As it happens, I'm twenty-six,' she said, 'but I feel that I'm growing older by the minute, Sister.'

'Twenty-six,' said Sister Johanna. 'I have habits older than that.'

Sister Brigid cackled. It was strange, thought Conchita, how protective the other two nuns seemed of her, and how quick they were to come to the defence of such an apparently graceless and unpleasant woman.

'You mustn't tease the child,' said Sister Jean Francoise vaguely. 'I'm sure she means well. She's new, that's all.'

From out in the grounds there came a sudden crackling noise. This was followed almost at once by a muffled roar, and then by screams of terror from the visitors on the beach.

The sisters looked askance at each other. Conchita was the first to guess what was happening.

'Someone's set fire to the bonfire too soon!' she said.

She turned and led the other nuns out of the house and down past the church to the roped-off area containing her laboriously prepared bonfire. Most of the other visitors were hurrying in the same direction, gathering by the ropes. The heat from the fire was almost unbearable. Thick clouds of smoke obscured the pile of coconut husks. A sudden swirling breeze parted the smoke, revealing the fact that the husks were now blazing.

One of the female tourists screamed and pointed at the side of the pyre. The other visitors took up her cry. Sprawling across the side of the blaze, almost in an upright position, was the body of a white man in a floral shirt. His eyes were open and he was staring sightlessly at the crowd. Two courageous islanders charged forward and dragged the smouldering body free of the husks. They hurled the man to the ground and beat out the flames with several of the empty sacks in which the coconuts had been collected.

Conchita forced herself to go forward. The islanders stood aside, shaking their heads dolefully. The nun knelt at the side of the man. Enough remained of his charred face and body to enable her to recognize that it was the tourist Ed Blamire, and that he was dead.

'Take him up to the hospital,' she whispered to the islanders, although she knew that it was too late to do anything for him. The two men took Blamire's body by the shoulders and legs and carried him through the now silent and awe-struck crowd.

'Ladies and gentlemen,' said Conchita, rising and facing the visitors. 'There has been a dreadful accident. I'm afraid that the open day must end at once. Will you please leave as quickly as possible.'

The crowd began to disperse in small shocked knots. Conchita saw that the other three nuns were accompanying the body back to the mission house. She hesitated, and entered the church through the side door to say a prayer for the dead tourist. Inside, the place was a shambles. The altar table had been knocked over, the crucifix had been torn from the wall, the shell font had been smashed and several benches had been overturned. Sister Conchita surveyed the carnage.

'Sanctuary!' she muttered to herself in horror.

THREE

'Bigfella long sky tokk-im long me. Himi say work-im long boat all-same Noah,' said the old islander with red betelnut-stained teeth, glaring defiantly at the men who had been threatening to kill him.

'God has spoken to you and told you to build an ark like Noah's,' translated Sergeant Ben Kella of the Solomon Islands Police Force, wearily playing for time. He was standing among the gardens on a sloping hillside outside a small salt-water village on the coast of his home island of Malaita. The small plots of earth carved out of a clearing among the trees were given over to the cultivation of sweet potatoes, yams, taro and tapioca. The taro had been watered conscientiously, but the yams grew better in dry conditions and had been left to struggle as best they could through the cracked earth. The fertile ground in which the subsistence crops had been planted had been cut and burnt out of the forest and would be cultivated intensively for several more years before the villagers moved on to begin another patch. Usually the food would be tended by the women of the area, struggling with bush knives every day to keep the *alang-alang* grass and brambles at bay, but word had gone out that this afternoon there was to be a lethal payback. This was men's work, especially if a ritual killing should turn out to be involved.

On the other side of the garden area, twenty or thirty young men from the village glowered at the old islander. They were clad only in shorts or loincloths under the blazing sun. Their faces were tattooed with the diamond lozenge marks of the *fual alite*, the nut of the alite tree. Without such tattoos a Lau man would not be admitted to a place of honour on Momolu, the island of the dead, when the time came for him to begin his long journey into the dark. Kella noticed that ominously some of the young men were carrying heavy sticks, while one elder was carefully assembling a pile of stones to throw at the ark-builder when the fighting began.

Kella sighed. So far this had been just another routine, uneventful one-man police patrol of the coastal villages, no different from dozens of others he had conducted lately. Then the government-appointed headman of this hamlet had sent for him with the disturbing news that Timothy Anilafa, an islander of unblemished reputation, acting completely out of character had spurned tradition and was defying village customs and the white man's law by trespassing on cultivated land. Normally this would be a matter for the headman, and would not involve a government policeman, but several decades before, while he was still a child, Kella had also been appointed by the Lau Lagoon pagan priests as the *aofia*, the traditional justice-bringer of Malaita, charged to maintain the traditions of the ancient gods in this part of the remote Solomon Islands in the South Pacific. It was his responsibility to settle any religious disputes on the island while attempting, if possible, to keep news of his involvement from his police superiors in the capital, Honiara.

'Is there no way that you can move your ark?' he begged humbly in the Lau dialect. He had to raise his voice to be heard above the thundering of the adjacent waterfall, hidden by the trees and bushes of the undergrowth surrounding the garden area.

Timothy Anilafa shook his head stubbornly. 'God told me to build it here,' he said. 'When the floods come, they will rise to just below the level of the gardens. This is the best place to build it to save the animals when they assemble.'

All eyes swivelled to regard the object of the controversy. The skeleton of Timothy's vessel lay sprawled across a substantial corner of the village gardens. It was a ramshackle construction consisting of roughly sawn planks bound crudely together asymmetrically with vines and creepers, to form the rough-hewn outline of a boat about sixty feet long. So far only part of the hull had been laid down and the old man had made no effort to establish decks or even to caulk with pitch the lower half of the ark. It was most definitely a work in progress. However, for the toil of one elderly islander it was an impressive enough effort. The drawback was that because of its sprawling growth over the last few months, the vessel now covered much of the fertile land that provided the village with its basic supply of food.

'The headman and elders say that in the interests of the village you must move your most interesting and well-intentioned ark,' Kella pointed out.

'But the Lord told me in a vision that I must build it here,' Timothy said triumphantly, like a card-player laying down a trump. Like most islanders, he practised Christianity in tandem with the old ways of magic, switching with ease from one to the other as the mood and needs of the moment took him. Kella could empathize with the old man. All the same, at the moment, all his tribal instincts told him that Timothy Anilafa had chosen the wrong spot for his shipbuilding project. It was out of balance with the feeling of the area.

As if to confirm this thought, the crowd of men on the other side of the garden started growling. Kella took care to remain where he was, as a token shield between Timothy and the wrath of his putative attackers. It was plain that the villagers were on the verge of destroying the vessel and sweeping the old man away with his project in the process. The problem was that Timothy genuinely believed that he had experienced a vision and would not step aside when his younger kinfolk surged forward. Desperately Kella cast about in his mind for a way of resolving the problem to the satisfaction of both sides, before the elderly villager got hurt. Somehow he had to facilitate the movement of the ark without offending its architect's jumbled religious beliefs. The persistent drumming of the adjacent waterfall seemed to grow even louder in his ears as he racked his brain for a solution.

Vague memories of his Bible lessons at Ruvabi mission school twenty years earlier, before he had abandoned the white man's religion, began to stir in Kella's mind. He remembered Father Pierre prowling up and down the rows of desks in the overcrowded bamboo classroom in his bare feet and ragged cassock. The old man had hoped that Kella would one day enter the priesthood. He must have been severely disappointed when the youth had been summoned away by the custom chiefs, the *hata aabu*, those whose name must not be spoken, to undergo the calling and cleansing ceremony among the artificial islands of the lagoon. After that, as the *aofia*, he had been lost to the white man's church for ever.

However, unbidden, one phrase from his dusty mission lessons leapt into Kella's mind.

'The springs of the great deep!' he said loudly. 'That's what the Book of Genesis says about the ark.'

Timothy looked at him suspiciously. 'When the Lord spoke to me—' he began.

'I am telling you what the Bible tells us,' Kella interrupted, gently but firmly. '*All the springs of the great deep burst forth, and the floodgates of the heavens were opened.*'

'That will assuredly happen again,' nodded Timothy, regarding the policeman intently.

'But where?' asked Kella. The villagers were edging forward, all except the one in charge of the cache of stones, who was now engaged thoughtfully in selecting the sharpest ones. The policeman spoke quickly. 'The waters of the earth rose first, before the rains came.'

'And they will once more,' said Timothy, as if speaking to a child. 'That is why I must finish my ark soon, to be ready for the overflowing of those waters.'

Actually it looked as if it would take a fair number of years for the old man to complete that particular quixotic project, thought Kella, looking at the ramshackle collection of detritus that made up the vessel's insecure and uncompleted base. 'Where will the water rise around here?' he asked rhetorically, indicating the gardens. 'There are no springs. The women have to carry water all the way from the pool at the base of the waterfall to feed these plants.' He paused for effect. 'You must locate your ark close to the waterfall. Then you will be ready to float away in glory down to the river, and from there to the sea with ease when the rains come.'

Timothy frowned. The villagers stopped advancing. Kella drove home his point. 'It was an understandable mistake,' he said. 'You have chosen the wrong place.' He pointed in the direction of the unseen thundering waterfall. 'That is where you should have built your ark, next to the cascade. Assuredly that is where the springs will erupt when the Lord decides to send his first flood before the rains come.'

Timothy Anilafa looked thoughtful. For all his zeal, he knew how much present danger he was in at the hands of his disgruntled *wantoks*. In the interests of self-preservation, he was not averse to a face-saving compromise. The village men, suddenly aware of Kella's intention, chorused their agreement, their mood lightening. Melanesians delighted in long, hair-splitting arguments to while away the empty hours. Only the solitary man in command of the stones could not conceal his disappointment as he continued to crouch over his carefully selected missiles, like a protective bird on a nest.

'The waterfall is only a hundred yards away along the track, on common land,' said Kella. 'Take the ark there and carry on with your building in peace. No one will bother you again. You will become a big man in the eyes of everyone. The waterfall is a sacred place for the gods. Perhaps they will unite with the Christian Bigfella and join with him to bless your efforts for years to come.'

It was a telling point. Nothing bore more weight in the Lau culture than an activity that obviously had secured the approval of the entire spirit world, pagan and Christian alike. Judiciously Timothy Anilafa nodded.

'There is wisdom in what you say, *aofia*,' he conceded. 'But how will I move my ark? It is large and heavy.'

'We will all help you,' said Kella, setting an example by walking forward rapidly to the mangled heap. The rest of the islanders, understanding his purpose, followed him willingly and encircled the ark. They bent and with a series of groans lifted the sagging timbers from the ground, and staggered along the path previously cut and trampled down through the undergrowth. Away from the gardens, the branches of the towering trees in the tropical coastal rainforest intertwined overhead, suddenly almost blocking out the light of the sun. It was like a journey into a fast-falling night. The calophylum trees with their white bark and shiny leaves grew next to coconut palms and mangroves. Between the trees, the vines of the morning glory and the purple flowers of the bay bean curled above the tussocks of porcupine grass, making their progress difficult.

The group of perspiring men staggered beneath the weight of the rudimentary ark as they neared the noise of the waterfall. Pieces of the vessel broke off and dropped to the ground unheeded, their descent muffled by the moss carpeting the track. Kella and the straining islanders left a trail of this debris behind them as they neared the cascade. Kella was big for a Solomon Islander at six feet in height, and had been strong enough to play professional rugby league in Australia for two seasons, but even he was feeling the weight of the shared burden by the time the party emerged again into the sunlight.

They were on a treeless plateau by the side of the waterfall, halfway down its mighty descent. Water crashed to the river a hundred feet below, while spray hurtled spitefully across the level surface, soaking everyone. At Kella's command, the villagers lowered what was left of the shattered and contorted structure of the ark to the ground and stood back. Some of them were grinning slyly. It was obvious that the new site was vastly inferior to the one that Timothy had originally selected on the village gardens. The sun beat down steadily on the flying spray, producing an eerie mist that drifted across the ground and swirled to the height of a man's waist.

Kella could see that the old man was coming to the same conclusion as the other villagers. Angrily he was beginning to react to being duped. With a sinking heart, the police sergeant realized that his problems were not yet over. In a spurt of rage, Timothy Anilafa kicked out at the ark with his callused bare foot. Now the villagers were laughing openly at him. Kella moved forward to stop the old man from launching himself at his tormentors.

Then the islanders stopped laughing. They were looking at the edge of the forest. A small, undistinguished rodent was crouching among the undergrowth, its whiskers twitching suspiciously. A beatific smile appeared on Timothy Anilafa's face.

'Emperor!' he said caressingly, almost as a greeting.

No one else on the plateau spoke. Kella moved to one side to get a better view of the rat. He could not recognize its species, but surely the old man was not right? The Emperor Rat, once indigenous to Malaita, had not been seen for the best part of a hundred years. In the 1880s, a British colonial administrator, driven half mad by loneliness and the effects of the sun, and with too much aimless time on his hands, had noted the animal's existence in excruciating detail in his notebooks. Then it had vanished on to the international registers of extinct species. Over the decades, some islanders claimed to have seen examples of the creature deep in the bush, but there were no recorded official sightings. Yet here was the villager greeting the shy, twitching creature almost as an old friend.

The Emperor Rat lurched forward and then walked steadily towards what was left of the ark. It stopped beneath an overhanging spar and looked back towards the trees. A second, smaller rat, as undistinguished as the first, emerged and scurried over to its mate. The two animals hesitated for a moment, and then were lost inside the dark recesses of the structure. Kella could hardly believe what he had just witnessed, but he did his best to take advantage of the moment.

'You have your first pair,' he told Timothy Anilafa. 'Now you must continue with your building here and wait for others to follow. It might take a long time, but the creatures of the island have taken their first steps to assist you in your venture. You have your first animals, the rarest in the whole of the Solomons.'

The old villager nodded, for once lost for words. Kella looked at the other islanders. No one was laughing any more. All were regarding the ark and its builder with sudden awe. Of such incidents were legends established. Kella clapped Timothy on his scrawny shoulder.

'*Nganwi ilana*,' he said respectfully, giving the old man the traditional title bestowed upon islanders who were not priests but who had displayed indisputable proof of being able to see into the future. For the sake of peace in the village, he hoped that the completion of the ark would occupy the remaining years of the venerable old man's life, thus giving him local prestige in his evening years, together with a sense of purpose. At the same time, fortunately for his welfare, it was very unlikely that he would ever be called upon to test the plainly unseaworthy vessel before the eyes of his peers.

All in all, it was proving a most satisfactory state of affairs. The policeman decided that it was time to bring an end to proceedings and quit while he was still ahead. He gestured to the other islanders.

'Fetch-im mary bilong you quick time,' he suggested.

The men started to hurry back through the trees to bring their wives up to continue work on their now uncluttered gardens. Kella followed them down the slope at a more leisurely pace. Overhead, hornbills crashed their wings like cymbals through the air. A sense of well-being pervaded him. The sudden appearance of the Emperor Rats had been, almost literally, a godsend as far as preserving the peace in the area had been concerned. He did not intend, however, to make any mention of the event in his end-of-tour report. It was likely to be misunderstood by his superiors in the capital. There were some matters with which it just did not pay to bother his expatriate bosses. What they did not know could not hurt them. Especially, decided Kella, when he did not fully understand them himself.

The sergeant glanced at his watch. He decided that he would spend the remaining hours of daylight walking along the beach to the adjacent village of Haarumou. He had heard rumours that an elderly carver of traditional pan pipes there was refusing to practise his craft any longer because he had been threatened by a Gossile, one of the ghost-children who dwelt among the graves of women who had died in childbirth. The Gossile were reputed to spend their time making pan pipes for the gods. Sometimes they took umbrage if a human being developed the art too well, and would move in on the unfortunate man to harass him.

Kella's sharp ears heard someone climbing the wooded hill towards him. The noise was too loud to be made by a local, but very few expatriates visited this part of Malaita. Circumspectly Kella stood behind a broad banyan tree until he could make out who the newcomer was. A few minutes later he glimpsed the portly form of Sergeant Ha'a toiling up the slope, gasping audibly for breath, giving a creditable impression of a tyre with a slow puncture. Like Kella, he was wearing the khaki shorts and shirt and red beret of a member of the Solomon Islands Police Force. Kella stepped out from behind the tree and waited for Ha'a to see him. The other sergeant wiped the sweat from his eyes and squinted uncertainly through the trees.

'I've been looking for you all damn day,' he complained when he recognized his colleague. 'You're overdoing this juju-man bollocks. You don't have to make yourself invisible just for my sake!'

Sergeant Ha'a was a rotund, amiable Western Islander with jet-black skin, a flashing white smile and a reedy tenor voice that had once secured for him a minor reputation as a singer of comedy country-and-western songs on the northern club circuit when he had attended a course in Yorkshire. His bowdlerized rendition of 'Your Daddy Ain't Your Daddy, But Your Daddy Don't Know' had once even secured him a brief spot on a BBC Radio Light Programme talent show, a taste of fame that Ha'a had relished almost to the point of obsession. As a result, he now spent much of his time applying to attend more courses, of any description, in Great Britain, so that he could return and live the dream once more. In the meantime, he was noted for his addiction to the relatively mild fleshpots of Honiara. It would have taken considerable efforts on the part of his superiors to shoehorn him out of his air-conditioned office in the capital.

'I would have thought that it would have made a nice change for you to get back to your roots like this,' commented Kella sarcastically.

Sergeant Ha'a shuddered. 'I'm from the west,' he said. 'We don't make such a big thing about fresh air as you primitive Malaitans. I'm here to take you over to Honiara sharpish. There's a government ship waiting for us at Auki. Your attendance is urgently requested at Government House. Apparently there's some sort of flap on.'

'What about?'

Ha'a shrugged indifferently. 'I operate on a need-to-know basis,' he told the other policeman. 'And believe me, the older I get, it's surprising how little I really need to know.'

FOUR

'The good news,' said Robinson, the Secretary for Internal Affairs, 'is that we have an interesting assignment for you, Sergeant Kella. He gave a wintry smile. 'The bad news, I'm afraid, is that it will take you away from your niche on Malaita.'

Kella shifted in his chair. He always felt uncomfortable in any of the offices in the administrative block of the Secretariat in Honiara, and this one was no exception. Robinson, the Secretary, was an African retread, with thirty years' overseas service behind him. On the shelves were carvings of masks and animals, evidence of long official colonial sojourns in what had once been the Gold Coast, British Somaliland and Cameroon, names that were no longer even detailed on maps of the continent in this era of independence.

'I know nothing of the customs and traditions of other parts of the Solomons,' said Kella hastily. 'I would be of no use to you outside my own island.'

'You haven't always been much use to us on Malaita,' grunted Chief Superintendent Grice sourly. 'The last time you got into trouble over there, we had to send a dozen policemen to get you out.'

The expatriate policeman glowered at Kella. The pair of them had experienced a number of run-ins over the past few years when the Malaitan had, in Grice's opinion, put his duties as the *aofia* before the administration of the law.

'Nevertheless,' said the Secretary smoothly, 'I think we can agree that Sergeant Kella's knowledge of his area, and in particular his unique position in the, er, local religious and cultural hierarchy there, have been of considerable benefit to the authorities on a number of occasions, unorthodox although his position and approach may sometimes have been.'

Kella looked out of the office window at the single main coastal street that made up the capital, with its population of three thousand people. One side consisted mainly of corrugated huts left behind by the US forces after the war and now used as shops. The other side of the road was occupied by government offices, supplemented with a few more permanent stone buildings, including the exclusive Guadalcanal Club and the ornate Mendana Hotel. Behind the offices was the sea, skirted by the finger of Point Cruz Wharf. Casuarinas added a splash of colour to the afternoon somnolence.

'Of course, if you want to put your faith in a witch doctor,' shrugged Grice, once again washing his hands of the matter under discussion.

Accustomed to such displays of overt hostility, Kella ignored his superior. Robinson looked pained. He was a thin, pinched man in his early fifties who had devoted much time and effort over the latter stages of his career to maintaining his balance on the shifting, shrinking sands of the British Empire and, unlike Grice, had learned enough at least to pay lip-service to local observances.

'We're going to send you to the Western District,' he explained. 'It's rather a delicate mission.'

Grice harrumphed through his nose at the thought of his rebellious sergeant being tactful or discreet.

'That would be the Alvaro logging station in the Roviana Lagoon, then,' said Kella. He tried to conceal the relief he was feeling. For a moment he had feared that he was going to be sent on another overseas academic course. He had almost lost count of the number he had undertaken, starting with his BA at the School of Philosophy, Anthropology and Social Enquiry at Melbourne University. Since then he had studied for varying periods of time at the London School of Economics and the University of Manitoba, as well as serving attachments with police forces in the USA, New Zealand and Fiji. In the early days he'd believed that Chief Superintendent Grice genuinely thought he was helping in the personal and professional development of his local subordinate, but lately it had been fairly obvious that it was just to keep the unpredictable Kella out of his hair, even if it did mean acting as a part-time travel agent for him.

Robinson looked surprised. 'How did you know that?' he asked. 'We've done our best to keep it quiet.'

'It couldn't be anywhere else,' said Kella. 'Most of the labourers employed there are from my own island of Malaita. Presumably that's the reason why you need me.'

'Correct,' said the disconcerted Secretary for Internal Affairs. 'Spot on, in fact. We've had reports of trouble at the station. The logging efforts are being sabotaged, people being beaten up, that sort of thing. We'd like you to look into the matter, Sergeant Kella. The Malaitans there will talk to you. You might be able to get to the bottom of the problem.'

Chief Superintendent Grice's disgruntled expression showed that he did not share the Secretary's confidence in his subordinate's ability, but he said nothing. Kella was inclined to agree with him. Sending a Lau man to investigate a crime in the Western Solomons would be akin to asking an Inuit to intervene in an inter-tribal squabble in Dahomey.

'Do you have any idea who's behind the attacks?' he asked.

'There's some talk of an independence movement being involved, said Robinson. 'Nothing concrete, though. That's one of the aspects we'd like you to investigate.'

'But carefully,' added Chief Superintendent Grice. 'The situation's very delicate in the west. There's even talk of them wanting to secede from the Protectorate. For God's sake don't go blundering in like a bull in a china shop. Show some finesse for once.'

'Even more important than that,' said the Secretary for Internal

Affairs, wincing at the policeman's bluntness, 'we want you to be very careful in your dealings with the Alvaro Company. I don't have to tell you how important their logging business is to the economy of the Solomons. Our total revenue in the Protectorate last year, including a substantial grant-in-aid from the UK, amounted to less than a million and a half pounds sterling. We need new industries in the Western District.'

'Even if they're ruining the forests there?' asked Kella. 'They used to have some of the largest freshwater crocodiles in the world on Alvaro. I hear they've all gone now.'

Like they were on Guadalcanal, he thought. But that had been due to the activities of bored US servicemen stationed on the island after the war who had spent their weekends idly taking pot shots at the creatures.

'Do you see what I mean?' exploded Grice. 'He's a loose cannon! You can't send this man up there. Who knows what he'll get up to?'

'I expect Sergeant Kella to do his duty, simply that, whatever his private views might be,' said the Secretary for Internal Affairs crisply. 'He will fly to Munda as quickly as possible, investigate the sabotage attempts at the logging camp and put a stop to them. Frankly, Mr Grice, I cannot think of anyone else in your police force capable of undertaking such a hazardous task. Are your duties clear, Kella?'

'Yes, sir,' said Kella, rising.

A thought occurred to the official. 'By the way, will you still have authority among your people when they are so far from their home island?'

Kella had been wondering the same thing. He had spent a few months in the Western Solomons during the war, but all he knew about the islands was that the women were supposed to be sexually voracious, and that in the the old days, known as the time before, headhunters had been so successful that human skulls were still being retrieved in remoter areas.

'I don't know, I've never tried,' he said. 'It should be all right.

Ramo diingana.' He translated for the benefit of the others. 'The chief is still a chief in his canoe, wherever he travels.'

'I sincerely hope you're right,' said the Secretary for Internal Affairs. 'Thank you, Sergeant Kella, that's all. Chief Superintendent Grice, will you remain behind for a moment. Good morning, Sergeant.'

'Mind you,' said Kella, stopping at the door, unable to resist a final word. 'The Roviana gods may be stronger than mine, and then the lagoon spirits will have home advantage.'

Before he could close the office door behind him, Kella could hear the voice of Chief Superintendent Grice raised in anger as the policeman argued with the Secretary for Internal Affairs. Kella and Grice had a long history of disputes and the senior officer would not be happy with any assignment that gave his subordinate such a degree of autonomy as this one, especially in territory that was virtually unknown to the sergeant and was so remote from the control of his superiors.

As he started to walk away, he heard the Secretary for Internal Affairs' voice raised decisively in a tone that invited no denial. 'That's as may be. Kella may be a law unto himself, but he's also a bloody good policeman. I don't have to remind you that there are only three indigenous university graduates in the Solomon Islands and that Kella is one of them. Like it or not, Grice, he represents the future of these islands. Let him get on with his job.'

Kella had left the building and turned right to walk to Police Headquarters, past the flame trees lining Mendana Avenue, before he heard his name being called. He stopped and turned. The tall, grey-haired figure of Welchman Buna was hurrying after him. Buna was a reserved, dignified man with an exact triangle of beard. Always smartly dressed, even in the midday heat, he was wearing a shirt and trousers with precise creases. He showed no signs of perspiring. He was one of the local members of the council advising the High Commissioner on island affairs. It was common knowledge that before long, elections would be held for a proposed Legislative Council, giving much more power to the islanders. It was also known that Buna was unobtrusively nursing the Roviana Lagoon area, his own district, and that he was a certainty for election.

Little was known about his background. Early in his life he had been picked out by the Methodist missionaries working in the Western Solomons as a pupil of exceptional promise and had been given a place at their secondary school, Goldie College. There he had confirmed his potential. With the coming of the war to the west, he had disappeared from sight. Several years later he had reappeared, almost out of nowhere, on Guadalcanal. For a time he had worked as a clerk in one of the town banks. He had embarked upon a course of study at evening classes held at the Government Primary School and had been an almost permanent resident of the Honiara Public Library in his spare time. He had been an assiduous pupil, for he now spoke perfect English, with just a faint trace of pedantic hesitation, as if he was constantly translating the language in his mind and checking it in an invisible primer.

Now that Buna was a full-time politician, his source of income was a mystery and a subject of considerable gossip. So far he had made so little impact on the Advisory Council that he was known as the Invisible Man. Kella, for one, guessed that this was not due to diffidence but a desire on the part of the ambitious Roviana man to bide his time.

'Sergeant Kella,' Buna said politely. 'How good to see you. I believe that you are going to Roviana to look into the problems at the logging camp.'

'That's right, Mr Buna,' Kella said. Buna certainly had his contacts, but so did most of the local politicians.

'You may find the situation in the west a little inflamed,' said the politician. 'I know that I can depend upon you to treat the matter with your usual common sense.'

'I shall do my best,' said Kella.

'Of course, but there's one more thing, I'm afraid.' Buna seemed to be experiencing difficulty in digging the words out. He had the appearance of a man not accustomed to asking for favours. Finally he said, 'When you return from this tour of duty in my region, I would appreciate it if you would report to me – unofficially, of course – and give me your opinion of things as they stand in Roviana. Would you do that for me?'

'Certainly,' Kella said, wondering what was coming next. He waited for the politician to say more, but Buna merely nodded and turned and hurried away. After a few yards he stopped and turned back.

'Perhaps you would be good enough to do so before you make your official report to the Police Commissioner,' he said, before turning and continuing his journey.

Kella strolled down to the wharf and looked at the cargo ships being loaded with copra. He thought uneasily about his assignment in the Western Solomons. Not only were the two cultures completely different, but while the gods of Malaita, apart from the shark-worshippers, were mainly land-based, in the lagoon the water gods held sway. They were known to be furtive. They hid in the sea itself, and in rivers and lakes. No outsider would ever know when he had placed himself in danger by trespassing in a *tambu* sacred place. Kella's *mana* would certainly be overpowered by that possessed by the Roviana ghosts.

He would need all the help he could get on this occasion, thought the sergeant. He wondered if there was any hope of it coming from one particular direction. He had heard over the grapevine that the fiery Sister Conchita had been transferred to the Western District recently. The young nun certainly had a powerful *mana* of her own, supplied by her faith. He hoped she might be persuaded to share it with him. Whether her presence in the Roviana Lagoon might turn out to be a good thing or a bad one, Kella had no means of foretelling. Almost inevitably, however, he thought with a slight lifting of his spirits, it should be eventful.

FIVE

Sister Conchita guided her narrow-draught canoe across the Roviana Lagoon, one hand on the tiller of the diesel-driven Yamaha outboard motor. Through the pellucid water beneath her she could see floating coral gardens and even the twisted outlines of several Japanese fighter planes downed during the war. The passage of time was gradually turning these into contorted, rusted artificial reefs. Thousands of tiny multicoloured fish swarmed among the transmogrified wreckage. As usual, the surface of the lagoon was calm and peaceful. Thirty miles long, it was protected from the elements by a series of coral reefs, some as much as a hundred feet high, surrounding its quiet waters.

She was skirting the deserted white beaches of the island of Munda, a few miles from the mission. Most of its inhabitants preferred to live on the other side of the island, away from the noise of the occasional charter flights from Honiara, which many considered had practically turned the area into a metropolis. There was a tin-roofed open-sided waiting room at the far end of the narrow airstrip left over from the war. Beyond that was the sprawling wooden government rest-house originally designed mainly for the use of occasional official visitors to the area. So few touring district officers had used the structure that it had been sold to an Australian tourist company, who had installed a local woman to run it.

Sister Conchita knew that she should be heading for Gizo to pick up medical supplies for the mission, but her conscience impelled her to visit the rest-house and its inhabitants. It had only been a few days since Ed Blamire, the American tourist, had died at her mission. The remaining members of the tour party might need her help.

Most assuredly Father Ignatius in Honiara would not approve of her action. Before she had left the capital, the mission administrator had summoned her to his office for an official warning. 'We are giving you a big assignment for such a young and inexperienced member of our order,' he had informed her severely. 'At times you might find it onerous. But there is a reason for sending you to Marakosi.' The priest gave his caustic, thin-lipped smile. If he were a horse, thought Conchita, he would positively be whinnying with pleasure. 'There have been times, Sister Conchita,' he went on sententiously, 'when you have rebelled against authority. By giving you a taste of leadership so early in your career, we hope that it will provide you with experience of supervising others, and also of appreciating the responsibilities and duties of command. You could get a lot from it.'

'Am I then being punished for something, Father Ignatius?'

'Certainly not, Sister; you are being given an opportunity to enlarge your horizons. You will be at Marakosi just for a few weeks, until a replacement priest can be sent there. Go with God!'

Take the bones out of that, thought Conchita. One thing was certain: for all their avowals, there would be a number of senior nuns and priests in Honiara waiting to see her fall flat on her face in her first position of any authority.

Judging her distance, she changed direction, cut out the engine and skimmed the canoe into the shallows before jumping out and dragging it up the beach. She walked across the hot sand to the rest-house. A burly Solomon Islander with a broken nose and the patchwork scar-tissue of a boxer around his eyes was caulking the bottom of an upended canoe on the beach. He looked up and nodded cautiously.

'Sister Conchita,' he said.

'How are you, Mr Dontate?' asked the nun. 'I'm very sorry about all the trouble you've had lately. I was wondering if you would like me to say anything to your tourists.'

She had known Joe Dontate on her pastoral visits when he had worked for a while as a combined barman and bouncer in the notorious Everlasting Delight Bar in the capital's Chinatown. A former competitor in the middleweight division of the South Pacific amateur boxing championships, a decade earlier he had been taken to Australia by an enterprising professional manager, who had given him the billing of Chief Joe Dontate. Over the course of a few years the islander had worked his way up to semi-windup status, supporting the main event, at the Sydney Stadium. He had saved his purses parsimoniously and had augmented his earnings with one last substantial losing purse against a touring former world champion from Puerto Rico seeking to top up his pension fund in parts of the world where he still had a reputation. Dontate had lasted the ten rounds grittily against his over-the-hill but still useful and hard-punching opponent, and at the final bell had walked expressionlessly out of the ring, without waiting for the decision to be announced, or even waving to his supporters, a section of his life over. Returning to the Western District, he had invested his ring earnings in several successful trading stores now being run for him by trusted relatives or *wantoks*. Originally there had been disputes with a number of Chinese traders objecting to the former fighter taking business from their island-hopping vessels, but after one of these ships had been gutted by a mysterious fire, the Chinamen had altered their attitudes and their routes circumspectly, to avoid Dontate's stores and thus preserve his monopoly and their lives.

'Suit yourself,' he told the nun. 'You'll be wasting your time, though. These are cold-hearted bastards. Pardon my language. If they're tourists, I'm a *tindalo*.'

Sister Conchita was surprised at the man's scepticism. A *tindalo* was the spirit of a dead man reputed to retain his power on earth after his demise. Dontate hardly ever made any reference to island traditions, but she knew that he was proud of the fact that he came from a long line of warrior chiefs. As far as she could tell, he cared for little except the accumulation of wealth. Another of his commercial sidelines lay in acting as the local agent and guide for the Australian travel agency organizing tours in the west. He had secured an arrangement with the owners allowing his tourists to use the rest-house at otherwise quiet times of the year. Plainly he was not enamoured of his current batch of clients.

'All the same, in a way I feel responsible,' persisted Sister Conchita. 'Mr Blamire died at Marakosi. I feel that I should have a word with the others.'

'Go ahead,' said Dontate indifferently, returning his attention to the canoe. 'Don't say I didn't warn you, though.'

As she approached the rest-house, Sister Conchita could hear voices raised in anger inside. She knocked on the door and went in. There were three white men sitting in basket chairs in the sparsely furnished lounge of the building, all wearing the shorts and rainbow-hued shirts favoured by tourists. They were studying a manila folder containing a number of letters and were deep in lively conversation. All three were younger and fitter-looking than the usual run of visitors, Sister Conchita noticed.

'It's not a lot of information,' said the youngest of the three men.

'It confirms the rumours about Kakaihe,' said an older man. 'It's all we've got to go on.'

The three men stopped arguing when the nun in her white habit entered the room. They regarded her with a mixture of surprise and hostility.

'Good morning. I'm Sister Conchita from Marakosi Mission,' Conchita told them. 'I was just wondering if I could do anything to help after your bereavement?'

'What bereavement?' asked one of the men blankly.

'Mr Blamire had his dreadful accident at my mission several days ago. I thought that perhaps under the circumstances you might need some sort of spiritual guidance from me.'

One of the men guffawed. The other two silenced him with glances.

'Oh, him,' said another of the tourists. 'We hardly knew the guy. He sort of kept to himself.'

The oldest of the three men stood up and shouldered his way through to the nun, taking command of the situation as if by right. He was in his early forties, hatchet-faced, with a dark chin and a receding crew cut. 'How are you, Sister?' he said, extending a hand. 'I'm Clark Imison. It was good of you to drop by. I'm afraid the rest of our party has gone over to Gizo for the market. Perhaps some of them might need your spiritual help, but none of us here are what you would call religious. Thanks all the same.'

'How do you do, Mr Imison?' said Sister Conchita, shaking the man's hand. 'I take it you didn't fancy a shopping trip?'

'Not in our line,' replied the man. He was obviously trying to be friendly, but there was a nervous edge to his charm. 'We're just here for a tour of the battlefields. We're off to Rendova this afternoon.'

'Did you serve here in the war?'

'All three of us did. The 43rd New England Infantry Division, XIV Corps, Lieutenant General O.W. Griswold commanding.'

'The district must seem very different now in peacetime.'

'Yes, ma'am; you can say that again.'

Imison nodded politely, but said no more. The other two men regarded the nun restlessly. It was obvious to Sister Conchita that she was not wanted in the rest-house. There was something not right about the three men. They were definitely out of place in their tropical surroundings, three urban dwellers transported, probably against their will, to the remote island, like toys thrown carelessly into the wrong box.

'How long have you been in the Solomons?' she asked.

'Lady, you sure ask a lot of questions!' burst out one of the younger men.

Conchita was disconcerted by the sudden display of animosity directed at her so openly and unexpectedly. Before she could answer, Joe Dontate appeared in the doorway. He arrived so suddenly that Conchita suspected he had been lurking outside in case of trouble. He regarded the three Americans with little favour.

'Everything all right?' he asked.

'Just fine,' answered Imison. 'The sister was on her way.'

'Sister Conchita goes when she wants to go,' said Dontate quietly. 'She's highly thought of in the islands.'

Imison flushed. Conchita thought he was going to object to Dontate's tone, but then he seemed to think better of it and shrugged.

'I was forgetting,' he sneered. 'You're a big man in these parts, aren't you, Dontate. High cockalorum, or whatever.'

'Have you got a problem with that?' asked Dontate.

'It's a free country, I guess. Primitive but free. You do what you're paid for and we'll get along all right.'

'Right, if you're sure I can't be of any help, I'll be on my way,' Conchita said, trying to ease the atmosphere. 'I have to get over to Gizo.'

'Then we mustn't keep you,' said Imison, nodding with obvious relief. 'I'll tell the others that you called when they come back from their trip.'

Joe Dontate walked back down the beach to Sister Conchita's canoe with the nun. 'See what I mean?' he asked, not looking at her. 'Tough cookies, all of them.'

'They didn't seem unduly disturbed by Mr Blamire's death,' Sister Conchita admitted. 'By the way, what happened to Mr Blamire's body?'

'I took it to the hospital at Gizo. The medical assistant there pronounced him dead. He thought that Blamire might have had a heart attack and fallen on to the flames. Perhaps the sight of the bonfire going up brought on the attack. Anyway, the corpse was taken over to Honiara for an autopsy.'

'Perhaps I can find out the result from Central Hospital,' Conchita said.

'Whatever. You won't be able to see the body, though. The tour operators contacted Blamire's relatives and they had it flown back to the States for burial.'

'That was quick!'

'Bizness bilong whiteman,' said Dontate, half mockingly. 'You don't leave bodies lying around for long in this climate.'

'No, I suppose not. But nobody's come over to the mission to investigate his death yet. That seems a little odd.'

'Why should they? It was just a nasty accident. There's one expatriate inspector and a local sergeant at the Gizo police station. At the moment they're both on the other side of New Georgia investigating a custom killing. I imagine that, seeing a tourist is involved, they might send someone from Honiara to look into things at Marakosi eventually. But I wouldn't hold your breath.'

'I should hope so! It might be a bit late by then.'

'Don't worry; it will get sorted. You whiteys know how to look after your own in the islands. You've had plenty of practice. By the way, there's one thing you can tell me while you're here. Just who is John F. Kennedy?'

'He's the Democratic candidate for the presidency in the USA,' said Sister Conchita, who came from Boston. 'The elections back home are being held in a few weeks' time. Mr Kennedy is running on the slogan *A Time for Greatness*.'

'Never heard of him,' said Dontate. 'Apparently he served here in the war. Those three guys back there talk about him a lot. They've hired me to take them over to Kasolo, the island where Kennedy was stranded in 1943. It's only a few miles across the lagoon.'

'That was seventeen years ago.'

'They seem interested,' shrugged Dontate.

'Do you like showing tourists around?' asked Sister Conchita.

'It's a job,' said Dontate. 'Did you know that as far back as 1910, Burns Philp ships were bringing American tourists to the Roviana Lagoon to see the headhunters? What goes around comes around.'

He gave the nun a hand pushing her canoe back into deeper water, then walked back to the shore. The engine started up at the first pull. Sister Conchita steered the vessel back towards the centre of the lagoon. As she did so, she thought about her encounter with the three Americans back in the rest-house. It was possible that Clark Imison might have served with the US Army in the Solomons as a very young man. He had certainly been quick enough, almost too quick, to recite the name of his supposed unit and commanding officer. But if his two companions had also been in the military, as Imison had claimed, then judging by their youthful appearance, they would not have been much more than fifteen at the time, a most unlikely state of affairs. Dontate had sensed something odd about the three men as well. If they were neither genuine tourists nor war veterans, what were they doing in the Roviana Lagoon? There was something wrong on the island of Munda, mused the sister, and if her instincts were to be trusted, it almost certainly had something to do with the death of Ed Blamire.

She looked back over her shoulder. Joe Dontate was standing on the beach. He was regarding the nun in her canoe with a particular intensity. It nagged at Sister Conchita that so little seemed to have been done to investigate Blamire's death. Mentally she began retracing her steps on the afternoon upon which she had met the tourist. Why had he seemed so worried, almost frightened? Had he had a premonition of his violent death? Could he have been fleeing from someone? And what had caused the signs of struggle in the church? Abruptly she tried to dismiss her thoughts. Even if the death had taken place on her station, it was not her duty to investigate. She was mindful of a second interview she had endured before leaving the Honiara mission headquarters. This time it had been with the venerable mother superior of the order in the capital. She too had been in a warning mode.

'You have many admirable qualities, and life around you is seldom dull, Sister Conchita,' she had told the young nun, her heavily lined face at odds with a slight twinkle in her eye. 'But if I may say so, you sometimes experience a desire to explore matters that, strictly speaking, are none of your concern. It certainly enlivens whichever mission you happen to be in at the time, but it can have its repercussions among the older and more settled members of our order. Most of them have had enough excitement for one lifetime. Perhaps if you were to spend less time on your self-imposed investigations into the transgressions of others and more on developing the virtues of humility and obedience, it might be the better both for you and for our order as a whole. You are an exceptionally observant young woman. By all means continue to sum us all up, but perhaps it would be wiser to keep your conclusions to yourself.'

'Yes, Reverend Mother,' Conchita had replied contritely, resolving yet again to try to make herself a more conforming member of the organization. 'I'll do my best.'

'As for Marakosi Mission,' went on the mother superior, 'it was once a byword for activity in the Roviana Lagoon. Father Karl and the sisters toiled, literally, for many years in the heat of the sun. However, for some time they have withdrawn behind their walls. See if you can reintroduce them to the world around them. It will be good for them – but be tactful!'

It was up to the authorities to enquire into the bizarre death of Ed Blamire, decided Sister Conchita. But there were no authorities in the area. She had just been told that Inspector Lammond, the Western District police officer, and his sergeant were enquiring into a crime on the other side of the lagoon. It could be weeks before they returned. In the meantime, who was there to discover the truth? Certainly not her; her natural curiosity had got her into trouble with the islands' church leaders before, and had even, on one not-to-be-repeated occasion, drawn upon her head the opprobrium of the Bishop himself.

But why had Clark Imison and the other tourists in the rest-house seemed so unconcerned about the death? Or were they unconcerned? They had certainly been arguing about some letters when she had entered the lounge. There was plenty to think about. Fortunately she had time on her hands before she reached her next destination. She set her course for Gizo and gentled her canoe across the lagoon as the sun climbed to its apex in the cloudless sky.

An hour later, she was only four miles from her destination. She was passing one of the many small and apparently uninhabited islands in the lagoon. It was about a hundred yards wide by seventy yards long, with a ring of white sandy beach and a profusion of the spiky green foliage of the tall casuarina trees covering its centre. Beautiful coral shoals surrounded the beach. Frigate birds made languorous circles in the sun. Behind the atoll were several others, equally minute, apparently joined by a coral causeway.

At the sound of her outboard motor, two islanders ran down from the fringe of trees, shouting and gesturing to her across the turquoise water. Instinctively the young nun cut out her engine and headed for the shore. Gradually she drifted closer to the two men waiting on the beach. They were young, fiercely muscled and clad only in loincloths. She could see their dugout canoe already drawn up on the sand. Presumably they had landed on what seemed to be a deserted island to fish from the reefs. Something there had alarmed them greatly.

The two men splashed out into the shallow water and pulled Sister Conchita and her canoe up on to the beach, assisting her out.

'Quick time,' urged one of them worriedly. 'Whitefella, himi sick too much!'

Sister Conchita hurried through the trees. As she moved over the rough scrub underfoot, her brain reacted like a camera, automatically taking snapshots of the bush area. She passed hibiscus bushes with scarlet and white flowers, giant ferns and tiny orchids. Coarse spiky grass grew everywhere to a height of several feet. She noticed one patch, a few yards long, which had been flattened, presumably by the weight of a canoe dragged up from the shore. They crossed several rock pools of rainwater.

The nun followed the men to a clearing among the trees a few yards inland. There the scream of cicadas sounded like humans in pain. The open area seemed to have been used as a camp. A one-man tent was pitched in the centre. There was a scoured petrol can three-quarters full of rainwater. The ashes of a wood fire smouldered close by. She noticed the charred remnants of several gutted small fish discarded among the embers. On the ground lay a long sapling fishing rod.

Sister Conchita hurried over to a sleeping bag outside the tent. A white youth lay inside it. He was perspiring freely and threshing around, muttering incoherently, in the grip of a fierce hallucination. She heard him say '*Painim aut! Painim aut!*' and then he was silent. She leant over the boy, wondering if he was dying.

SIX

Kella stopped paddling and looked ahead at the ruined logging island of Alvaro rising jaggedly out of the sea ahead of him. This is what *suulana ano asa* must be like, he thought with a shudder. The notorious bottom of the pool into which the souls of the dead sank was reputed to be a place of fire and torment where unmentionable practices were carried out and the forsaken ghosts of the dead wandered screaming in torment among the fires of the eternally damned.

The last time he had seen Alvaro had been during the war. Then it had been as beautiful as any of the other atolls in the Roviana Lagoon, and it had remained a tranquil haven for its inhabitants throughout the fighting, even if it had lain on a dangerous route, where for the best part of a year Japanese destroyers cut through the surrounding water and Mitsubishi G4M3 bombers soared vengefully overhead, seeking the small scouting American PT boats. The passage of a decade and a half had certainly changed that. Now the island was little more than a tortured scar, suppurating on the surface of the lagoon. The coral reef that had once surrounded it had been torn from the seabed, leaving only a few jagged, blackened stumps. The water surrounding them had been transformed into a slurping cauldron of hollowed-out oil-stained debris and floating mangled logs and rubbish. The narrow strip of beach was little more than a series of dumps for abandoned, rusty machinery cannibalized almost into extinction. Huge patches of discoloured diesel oil mottled the scuffed surface of the sand. Floating in the water in a large wooden pen was the business of the island: piles of logs waiting to be collected and winched aboard by the timber ships when they arrived. On the far side of the pen, a launch bobbed at anchor. Painted in white letters on its side was the inscription *Alvaro Logging*.

The coastal mangrove swamps with their slender, distorted trees, being of no commercial value, were still in place and continued to ooze stinking mud and thrust their tangled roots grotesquely into the air, like the clutching talons of drowning witches. The mouth of a sluggish river coughed gobbets of red mud into the sea where its banks had been eroded by bulldozers. Smoke drifted over the island from dozens of bush fires lit to clear land in the interior.

Most prominent of all from his vantage point was a glaring white track thirty yards wide made of compacted and rolled lump coral, crawling miles inland through the swamp forest to the hundreds of species of more valuable trees available on the slopes of the mountain in the centre of the island. These were in the process of being uprooted in their hundreds and transported down the slope by the logging company. Large rolls of black plastic sheeting littered the side of the track, ready to be rolled over the surface should the rains come and stop work.

On either side of the path inland from the beach was a contorted assemblage of tin-roofed houses, sheds, tarpaulins and canvas tents erected haphazardly for the workers on the island. To make room for this shanty town, bulldozers and excavators would have torn the topsoil from the ground, uprooted trees and demolished the huts of the islanders who had originally lived there on custom land.

Kella muttered a short prayer to the *agal I matakwa*, the sea ghosts, for his safe deliverance from his recent journey. From the bottom of the canoe he picked up a coconut that he had found lying on the ground at Munda. He hefted it in his hand and then threw it into the sea behind the dugout as a propitiatory offering to his ancestral sharks that, according to Lau custom, would have accompanied him unseen on this trip so far from his home island.

He steered his canoe into the shallows and dragged it up on the discoloured and pitted beach. He had hired the dugout from Joe Dontate at the Munda rest-house earlier that morning, after negotiating a trip on one of the irregular charter flights linking Honiara with the Western District. He had expected the usual battery of caustic remarks from the one-time boxer. His path had crossed that of the wily and truculent Dontate on a number of occasions, and despite their mutual respect, there was little love lost between them. However, the Western man had seemed too preoccupied with a flock of disorganized and vocally demanding American tourists squawking like demented chickens around him to do more than direct a virulent scowl in the direction of the police sergeant. If he had to spend more than a few days in the lagoon, decided Kella, he would pay an island craftsman five pounds to build him his own small canoe.

He picked up his rucksack from the bows and stood and surveyed the sight before him. Although his face remained impassive, he felt sick. Close up, the island seemed in an even worse state than it had done from a distance. He knew that the desecration of the interior rainforest inevitably meant that in addition to erosion, the habitats of hundreds of birds and small animals would have been destroyed, diminishing sources of food for the few remaining indigenous inhabitants. All the available coral had been removed from the reef. If the company wished to drive the track even farther into the bush, it would also be removing all river gravel suitable for bedding rock, thus further poisoning the island's main drinking water supply. He could see that no efforts had been made at reforestation. Creepers and weeds were smothering any new trees trying to sprout.

There was less noise than Kella had expected. Patched-up tractors, bulldozers and chainsaws all waited beside the track to be moved inland. The area had an oddly unfinished and temporary look. On the edge of the logging camp he could see a 350-horsepower Cummings engine still in its marked containers, and the prefabricated units of a steel barge waiting to be assembled. The whole area was so haphazardly constructed, and with such little regard for hygiene or protection from fire, that Kella instinctively stooped and smeared his arms and legs with mud from the mangrove swamp as some sort of protection against the malarial mosquitoes that he knew instinctively would proliferate viciously in such conditions of neglect.

Two groups of men were standing facing one another in the rough undergrowth at the beginning of the track leading inland between the trees. One of the groups comprised forty or fifty sullen Malaitan men in lap-laps or shorts. The other was made up of a dozen white technicians, probably Australians. With a sinking heart, Kella saw that some of the latter, for the most part weedy specimens, were carrying rifles. To make matters worse, it did not look as if many of them were familiar with the use of the weapons. None of the white men was relishing the situation. Kella had met others like them on the handful of expatriate-owned cattle farms, copra plantations and fish-canning operations among the islands. These were mostly drifters, aimless fugitives from the law and domesticity, possessing minor engineering skills meaning nothing back home in Australia but which were still sufficient to earn them a comfortable living in some Third World countries. For the most part they were unprepossessing physical specimens, but their rudimentary sense of survival, honed in many similar situations across the Pacific, was sufficient for them to know that at this moment they were in danger of being overrun by the incensed Malaitans.

Kella increased his pace towards a big white man wearing unpressed grey trousers and a once white vest, who was standing angrily a little in front of the other expatriates, expostulating with the sullen Malaitans. He was the only whitey in the group making any effort to confront the resentful islanders. He was a ruined avalanche of a man in his forties, some six feet six inches in height and broad-shouldered, but with all his physical attributes beginning to melt and sag downwards. Jowls swung from his chin like wind chimes, and a once impressive chest had slumped obscenely to his stomach. While his body drooped, the big man's face seemed to have a life of its own and had expanded sideways, although at the same time his features had shrunk to those of a carelessly constructed snowman, with two buttons for eyes, a truncated carrot of a nose and a mouth that was little more than a perfunctory slash. His head was completely bald. He reminded Kella of an extra in an Ed Wood horror movie. He glanced briefly at Kella as the policeman approached him.

'Who the hell are you?' he demanded in an Australian accent.

'I'm Sergeant Kella, British Solomon Islands Police. I've come about the vandalism on your station.'

'I'm Jake Michie, the logging manager,' said the Australian abstractedly, not taking his eyes from the Malaitans before him. 'What's the matter, don't I deserve a white officer?'

'Believe me,' Kella told him, summing up the situation, 'the last sort of policeman you want now is a white one.'

'Is that so? Well, black or white, you've chosen a bloody bad time to get here. As you may have noticed, I've got a bit of a mutiny on my hands at this precise moment in time.'

Kella looked over at the *wantoks*. They were ominously quiet. If this had been a normal work dispute, the demands, insults and accusations would have been flying through the air by now. But the islanders, most of them young and rope-muscled through years of harsh manual work, were plainly preparing for a fight. These were the itinerant labourers of the islands, with no land of their own at home, a close-knit industrial force that toured the Solomons restlessly, picking up work wherever it could. These Malaitans, and others like them, forced to leave their own overcrowded island, usually toiled hard and uncomplainingly for their meagre pay and uncaring employers. It would have taken an important matter of principle or custom for them to down tools like this. They were plainly disturbed by something that had happened. If they decided to charge, the Australians with firearms might possibly be misguided enough to pluck up enough resolution to shoot. The gods only knew what the consequences would be if that happened.

'What's the problem?' asked Kella.

'I don't have any idea. First thing this morning the bastards refused to go into the bush to saw trees down. They wouldn't give me any reason.'

'You probably didn't ask them in the right way,' said Kella. 'Wait here. And tell your men to put their rifles down. If the Malaitans rush you, they won't get off more than a couple of shots before you're all overwhelmed.'

Michie hesitated, but nodded. Without another glance at the hapless technicians, Kella walked across the sand-dusted scrub to the labourers. He had been recognized. A murmur of greeting tinged with awe reached him. He had already picked out the probable leader of the Malaitan workers, a slightly older man with greying hair and a steady gaze. He stopped in front of him.

'Hello,' he said respectfully in the Lau dialect. 'My name is—'

'Everybody knows the *aofia*,' said the older man. 'I am Zoloveke. You are a long way from the artificial islands. Have you come here to do whitey's work for him?'

These Malaitans were a particularly tough and cynical bunch. Their itinerant lives kept them away from their homes for months and even years at a time. They would treat many of their traditional leaders and authority figures with scepticism, and would not be easy to convince.

'If you know that I am the *aofia*, then you will know that my duty is to keep the peace among Malaitans,' said Kella. 'That is why I have come to Alvaro, just in time, I think, to see you preparing to chew on rifle bullets. What is the problem? Why haven't you started work yet? Are you so tired that you have decided to work the white man's hours?'

The Malaitan snorted contemptuously at the implied jibe. 'The first work party that left to go into the bush this morning met a kwisi bird,' he explained. 'It spoke only once. Do you know what that means?'

'Of course,' said Kella, comprehending the problem with some relief. The matter was serious, but not as grave as he had feared. 'I may have spent many years away from Malaita at the white man's schools, but I still remember our customs. Leave this with me.'

He walked back to the big Australian. 'They have had a custom sign warning them not to work this morning,' he said.

'Am I supposed to be impressed?' exploded the big man. 'What those *kanakas* want is a boot up the backside!'

'You don't understand,' said Kella. 'Those men are Malaitans, the fiercest warriors in the Solomons.' He raised his voice so that the technicians could hear him.

'You lay a hand on just one of them, and you and every one of your men will be dead on the beach before the sun rises further over the trees, and I'll have a hundred forms to fill in afterwards. I doubt if you're worth it.'

The panic-stricken technicians started muttering. Kella raised his voice to explain. 'The first Lau party to leave the camp this morning saw a kwisi bird flying towards them. That's a grey bird about the size of a blackbird. It's always chattering. But this particular bird cawed only once. That was the sign that worried them. With reason.'

'What bloody sign?' asked an exasperated Michie.

'A single note from a kwisi bird means "No!" or "Turn back!" It's a warning. In the old headhunting days, if a war party came upon a kwisi bird that spoke only once, they would abandon their expedition, no matter how important it was nor how far from home they might be, and turn back and refuse to fight. That still applies today.'

'Then how the hell am I going to get them back to work?' demanded Michie. 'So far this year we've been delayed by rain, mechanical breakdown, shortages of materials and a bunch of so-called skilled workers who don't know their arses from their elbows.' He glared at the unkempt white men behind him. 'I've got a schedule to keep!'

Kella took his opportunity. 'I might be able to help,' he told the Australian. 'Of course, I would expect your cooperation with my investigation afterwards.'

A gleam of reluctant respect appeared in the big man's eyes. 'You would, would you, Sergeant?' he gritted. 'All right, go ahead. Sort them out, and at least I'll give you the time of day when you've finished.'

'First I must persuade them to take me to their temple in the trees, the *faata abu*.'

'You're wrong about that, for a start. They don't have a temple,' growled the Australian triumphantly. 'I've been here eighteen months and I've never seen one.' He looked at the men behind him. 'Have any of you jokers?'

The others shook their heads.

'That's because they've never let you see it,' said Kella, walking away. 'Stay here. And leave those rifles alone.'

He reached the Malaitans. 'Do you want to go back to work?' he asked Zoloveke, the leader.

'Only if the signs are right,' replied the older man. 'We will not ignore the *faata maea*.'

He was referring to the unfavourable omen known in pidgin as *show death*. Kella nodded understandingly. 'I wouldn't expect you to. Suppose I can lift the curse?' he asked. 'Will you go back to work then?'

Zoloveke conferred briefly with the men nearest him. 'If the ceremony is performed properly,' he agreed reluctantly. 'We know that you have been given the power to do that.'

'Then take me to your *beu aabu*,' said Kella. 'Not all of you; what I am about to do is not for everyone to see. Choose half a dozen men to come with us.'

The custom temple was half an hour's walk away through the outer ring of trees. There was no path through the densely matted undergrowth, but Kella could see that unobtrusive strands of red drachmae plants had been secured to the boles of some of the trees to indicate a route already prepared through the bush. Such signs would have meant nothing to any expatriates who strayed into the undergrowth. They struggled through knee-high grass, disturbing clouds of small yellow butterflies, which scudded ahead of them.

The temple, when they encountered it, was simple, consisting of little more than a one-roomed hut of sago palm thatch lashed together with creepers, under a sloping roof supported by posts. The opening in the front of it was only a few feet high, meaning that a man could only enter on his hands and knees, thus showing due deference to the holiness of the building. In front of the *beu* was a round flat flintstone to represent the outdoor altar. Detritus of ashes and charred sticks on its surface showed that sacrifices had been made there quite recently. On the ground around the altar were scattered minor offerings of yams, taro and twists of tobacco. Kella knew that inside the place of worship would be a collection of clubs and spears, all plaited with red and yellow vines to show that they had been dedicated to the gods. Being itinerants, the labourers would have no priest among them, and would be forbidden from practising all but the most basic ceremonies before the spirit people, otherwise he would never have been shown this sacred spot. Even now, he knew that he would not be granted much time in which to lift the curse. The spirits did not like temples that did not have permanent custodians. They would not go out of their way to assist him.

Before he made his approach to the altar, Kella stopped and opened his rucksack. He took out a well-worn sacred bag containing his own holy relics and attached it by a swathe of cloth to his head. Next he brought out a handful of areca nuts from the bottom of the rucksack, moving deliberately so that the Malaitans, watching his every move intently, could see what he was doing. He was aware of their impressed gasps as he prepared to start his ritual. Only a custom priest of the highest rank and in great favour with the ghosts would be allowed to hold in his hand so many areca nuts, the favourite food of the gods, without being struck down for sacrilege.

Impatiently Zoloveke gestured to the Malaitans to stand back while Kella approached the altar and abased himself before it. He ought to make a fire and burn some of the areca nuts, so that the scented smoke would attract the spirits, but he did not have time. Reaching up, he scattered the yellow husks of the nuts on top of the flintstone. The shell of a ripe areca nut was so hard as to be almost impenetrable, reflecting the inviolate manner of their faith and the supremacy of the gods. As he did so, he chanted the names of the first *aofias* of Lau: Maruka, Vuvura, Fili'ei, Solubosi and Lauvanua.

'He is eating the ghost,' murmured Zoloveke to the others, proud of his knowledge of ancestor worship. 'The *aofia* is sacrificing to the spirits on our behalf. He is putting himself at risk for us.'

Sweat started pouring down Kella's face from the mental and physical exertion of his incantations. The kwisi bird had warned the Malaitans not to go into the deep bush. That meant that the war gods who protected these Lau people far from home were angry and must be appeased by the whole-hearted intervention of a high priest.

'*Ma ni kobu'ana hato*,' he cried, begging the gods to accept the areca nuts.

He depicted himself as being unworthy to enter the temple despite his high standing on earth: '*Toto taa'I nau.*' He praised the war gods: '*Ramo oliolita.*' He thanked them for guarding the Malaitans on the island by sending the kwisi bird to warn the working party that morning: '*Ramo vei ngwane na.*' He begged them to send a sign that it was now safe for the labourers to resume work:

'*File bare ngwane I Afeafea.*' Finally he prayed for the future of the temple, that it might stand as a monument to the war spirits for many years: '*Agalo I mae.*'

When he had finished, Kella stood up. Briefly he clutched at a tree for support, and then, when the dizziness had worn off, he walked back to the waiting Malaitans.

'What happens now?' asked one of the younger ones.

'We wait for a sign,' said Zoloveke curtly. 'Don't you know anything?'

The small group stood in the silent, gloomy clearing for a quarter of an hour. Kella was aware of the suspicious glances being directed at him by the labourers.

'We should walk back to the beach,' he said finally. 'This may not be the appointed place.'

Dubiously the men struggled in single file back through the trees. Kella wondered if something would happen. The spirits had never denied him before, but this might be his time to be rejected cruelly and shown that he was always in the hands of the higher powers.

They had been walking for about five minutes when the bird appeared. It swooped through the trees in silence, grey and plump, its wings flapping joyfully. Not until it was only a few yards in front of them did it utter a sound. Then, soaring just over their heads, it started chattering vigorously in an ecstatic concatenation of sound. It held its unwavering, fearless course until it had passed every man in the line, and then veered abruptly to one side and was lost to view among the trees.

Zoloveke turned to face the other labourers, his face lit up. 'The war gods are happy again!' he declared loudly. He signalled to two of the younger Malaitans. 'Run back to the camp,' he said. 'Tell everyone that the *aofia*'s prayers have pleased the spirits. They can enter the bush without fear again.' He turned to Kella. 'It is true what they say,' he said. 'You are the only Lau man carrying the secrets of the spirits who has come out into the real world.'

The young men sprinted away, carrying their news. With a fresh respect in his attitude, Zoloveke gestured to Kella to come to the head of the line and lead the party back in triumph to the beach.

By the time they reached the shore, the camp had already sprung back to life. Labourers were hurrying up the track through the mangroves carrying cross-cut saws on their shoulders through the initial swamp forest and then on to the higher land where the trees more suitable for logging were to be found. Bulldozers, jeeps and the mobile winches known as log-haulers driven by the Australians were following in the wake of the Malaitans, to blast away any intervening rocks and ridges and gain access to the logs higher up, which they would bring down to the piles already in the pen by the beach awaiting shipment. The drivers were noisily tearing the clutches out of their machines in their efforts to get up the ridge. Other logs were being floated down the muddy river from the interior mountains on a filthy red torrent of pollution. Some of the labourers on the shore were busily joining logs together and lashing them to empty fuel drums with cables to form makeshift rafts, which would be towed out to sea by launches when the Swedish logging vessels arrived to winch up their cargoes from the water.

Michie, the big Australian logging boss, was at the heart of the action, vigorously directing groups to their work. Already he was barking at the labourers as if nothing had ever happened. One of the Australian drivers scurried towards him with a query on his lips. Michie skewered the white man with a glare.

'Hang around, why don't you, and I'll sing you a chorus of "My Hero" from *The Chocolate Soldier,*' he snarled menacingly.

The driver flinched, thought better of his self-imposed mission, and without breaking stride turned and hurried back to his vehicle and started it up. Michie stared at Kella. 'Come for a reward?' he demanded.

'A cup of coffee will do. And ten minutes of your time.'

With a theatrical sigh, the logging boss led Kella towards his office, a bungalow built on wooden poles, with a corrugated-iron roof. Beneath the poles were sliding log skids. When the office had to be moved farther up the trail, it could be towed by a truck. Next door was the company general store, selling 4X beer, tinned food, rice, biscuits and work clothes to the loggers and any islanders with enough money to pay its exorbitant prices. The store would have a deep freeze, powered by generators night and day. Behind the store and office, on the edge of the coastal mangroves, an effort had been made to make the area look a little more attractive by planting a few coconut palms and colourful hibiscus and oleander bushes on a patch of coral-based loam. A raised wooden structure housed half a dozen water tanks in two tiers, glistening with aluminium paint. Rainwater would be stored in the tanks and then distributed to taps in some of the houses.

'Would you still rather have an expatriate police officer here?' asked Kella politely as he entered the office.

'Don't push your luck,' warned the Australian impassively, but the edge previously in his tone was now missing. 'You may have given me a hand back then, but what else have you done for me lately?'

The office was large but sparsely furnished. A desk was covered with maps and papers. A door led to what presumably passed for the Australian's living quarters. Underneath a window overlooking the camp was a bookcase filled with tattered paperbacks that looked as if they had been read. Kella could make out some of the titles; they included *The Catcher in the Rye*, *Moby Dick* and *This Side of Paradise*.

He took the chair offered in front of the desk. Michie started to pour two cups of coffee from a percolator on a side table.

'Have you got any ideas who might be responsible for the attacks on your station?' Kella asked. 'How about the local islanders you dispossessed.'

'They were paid fair and square for the logging rights before they left the island,' said Michie quickly. 'They've got no beefs.'

'They might have if custom land was involved,' said Kella. 'Or if they didn't fully understand what they were giving up.'

Michie brought the cups over and gave one to Kella before sitting behind his desk. He shifted his stomach to one side to make room. 'Everything was explained to them,' he said. 'The company even used a local boss to represent the *kanakas* on the island. A bloke called Dontate.'

So Joe Dontate was involved, thought Kella. That would make matters difficult. The Westerner was a hard man with a lot of clout in the Roviana Lagoon as a hereditary chieftain. Presumably he was making a nice profit out of any brokering deal in which he was engaged on Alvaro, and would not give up his role easily.

'These negotiations were all right with your head office, were they?' he asked.

'My head office would do a deal with Old Nick himself as long as the logs kept coming out and the shareholders got their dividends,' said Michie bitterly. 'All they want is a smooth-running operation here, even if they have to send somebody in to kick my arse every now and then.'

'I'm told there's a local independence group that doesn't think much of your presence on this island,' Kella said. 'Could they have been involved?'

'They're just a bunch of cowboys,' said Michie dismissively. 'They're even led by a sheila, for God's sake. A local *kanaka* called Mary Gui. Do you know her?' Kella shook his head. 'She runs the rest-house at Munda for Joe Dontate.' Michie scowled. 'Thinks she's God's gift,' he went on. 'She's formed this movement called the SIIP, the Solomon Islands Independence Party. It's about as effective as a chocolate teapot. Believe me, all they're good for is holding meetings and distributing pamphlets. They wouldn't attack my blokes.' The logging boss slurped his coffee gloomily. 'Gui's just come back from Aussie university and knows it all. Can you imagine that? A *kanaka* bitch with a degree!'

'As a matter of fact,' said Kella mildly, 'I have two degrees, from Australian and British universities.'

'Christ,' said Michie. 'Now why doesn't that surprise me? What have I got? *Nada*. I don't even have a certificate of good attendance from a Hong Kong brothel. Pig-ignorant jokers like me are going to have scarcity value soon. Just who the hell are you anyway?'

'I've told you, I'm—'

'I don't mean the copper shit. How did you get my men back to work so fast?'

'Oh, that. I said a prayer for them,' said Kella simply.

Michie looked at him suspiciously across the desk. 'Are you jerking my chain?' he asked.

'No,' said Kella. 'Among the Lau people, I happen to be a custom priest, as well as a police officer.'

'You mean you're a . . .' Michie searched for the phrase and then came up with it triumphantly, 'a magic man!'

'That's what they're called in this district. Guadalcanal people call them *vele* men. On Malaita, and especially among my Lau people, I'm the *aofia*, the peacemaker.'

'But you can't be,' said Michie. 'For God's sake, you're an educated man! How do you reconcile that with this spirit mumbo-jumbo?'

'Perhaps one man's mumbo-jumbo is another man's faith,' said Kella, a sliver of steel entering his voice.

Michie grunted. 'Well, what do you want?' he asked. 'Normally I wouldn't give you the time of day, but I owe you for that business at the temple that I didn't even know was there. Don't forget, though, I can have you thrown off this island any time I want.'

Kella decided that it was time to crack the whip. 'No you can't,' he said. 'You've got too much going against you on Alvaro. Your Japanese bosses expect you to keep an uninterrupted flow of high-grade timber moving out; you've upset the local islanders by uprooting them from their custom land; most of your technicians are a bunch of gutless white rubbish men on the run from one thing or another; you've upset a local freedom-fighting group, and you depend for your labour on a force of hairy-arsed Malaitans who could take over your whole logging camp whenever they wanted to.'

Michie did not reply for a moment. His face still betrayed no emotion. The man was probably a pretty fair poker player, thought Kella.

'You don't do obsequious, do you, Sergeant?' the big Australian said thoughtfully.

'Maybe I'm practising for the post-colonial era.'

'You and me both,' sighed Michie, sipping his coffee. 'You and me both.'

Kella wondered how many dependent nations still remained to give nomadic expatriates like the logging boss work, and for how long. Already most emerging countries were insisting on any new operations being placed in the hands of local overseers. Soon the rough-hewn but shrewd Michie would be as obsolete as the remaining British official administrators clinging desperately like alcoholic limpets to their tenuous positions in the South Pacific. The difference was that Michie seemed to be aware of his precarious position.

'Do you want me to show you where the attacks took place?' asked the logging boss, with little hope in his voice.

Kella nodded. Under different circumstances, he decided, he might almost have liked the crude, bull-headed Australian. Michie was a brave man. It was not his fault that he was as much in thrall to his own background and customs as Kella was to his.

'That would help,' said Kella, draining his coffee cup and standing up.

Outside, Michie led the sergeant to the piles of logs waiting to be floated out to sea. Over the last year or so there had been so much traffic across the swampy area of peat bogs running down to the sand that Kella could see coral outcrops almost masked by dying mangrove roots visible below potholes worn in the surface. He recognized some of the different kinds of felled trees in the heaps, lopped and stripped of their branches. There were towers of kesi, airate, noora and nanum. Looming over all the others were the large collections of the grey-barked kauri pines, which would be exported to be stripped, planed and turned into profitable plywood. Michie stopped in front of two piles a little apart from the others. They were shrouded in black plastic sheeting. He shouted to a gang of labourers to strip back the coverings. The sheets fell to the ground to reveal a tangle of burnt and useless gnarled tanglewood.

'There were two separate fires, a few nights apart, about a month ago,' said the logging boss. 'By the time anyone got here, they were well ablaze. We've put a permanent night guard on the timber piles now.'

'Anything else?'

'There have been a couple of attacks on drivers,' said Michie. 'Those happened at night as well. They could have been carried out by Malaitans settling grudges against the whites, though.'

Kella nodded. 'There was something else too, wasn't there?' he asked.

'How do you know that?' asked the logging boss.

'There's no signature,' said the sergeant. He saw the look of incomprehension on Michie's face and explained. 'If the raids were done by Melanesians, they would leave some sort of sign, even if we couldn't understand it. It's a tradition of the old war parties, which is still observed.'

'Yes, there was a sign, for what it's worth,' said Michie, setting off again. 'I suppose that proves that the raids were by islanders.'

'Probably. Though I never really thought they would have been carried out by a bunch of retired expatriate planters from the Honiara Yacht Club,' said Kella. 'So I can't say I'm surprised. Show me.'

Michie led Kella to a spot close to the waterline on the beach and pointed. 'There!' He indicated. 'Is that enough of a signature for you?'

Kella walked forward and knelt by a pile of drying human excreta on the water's edge. 'The attackers left this?' he asked.

'The Malaitans wouldn't crap here, would they? They're clean buggers. They've got their own latrines. They wouldn't clean up anybody else's shit, either. That's the only reason it's still there.'

Kella had seen enough. He started walking across to his canoe on the beach. 'All right,' he said. 'I'll be seeing you.'

'Is that all you're going to do?' Michie demanded.

'For the present,' the sergeant told him, not looking back.

'So now where are you going?' bellowed Michie.

'I'm going to see some old friends,' Kella told him, pushing his canoe out into the water.

SEVEN

'Item number five on the agenda,' said Sister Conchita resolutely. 'The expansion of the mission school.'

'Out of the question!' said Sister Brigid at once. 'We have our hands full dealing with the few children we already have here.'

'And we're not educated women ourselves,' pointed out Sister Jean Francoise. 'We wouldn't know how to cope with the older boys and girls who would come to a boarding school.'

'Give me an outboard motor and a spanner and I'll tear the insides out of it in a quarter of an hour,' promised Sister Johanna. 'I'm not going to stand in front of a blackboard and pontificate about things I don't know anything about.'

'That's my point,' said Conchita. 'We're having problems because it's a day school. Children have to come for miles to get here. In the end most of them give up and stop attending. We could solve that by opening a boarding school. Then the children would arrive at the beginning of each term and stay here for fifteen weeks at a time. You could teach practical engineering, Sister Johanna – to the girls as well as the boys.'

'Impossible!' said the German nun. 'It would be against custom.'

'Have you thought this through?' asked Sister Brigid in a tone that made it plain that she had little confidence in the younger nun's judgement. 'There are immeasurable obstacles to having boys and girls living on the mission. Do you realize, for example, that a woman must never live at a higher level than a man? If we built a two-storey building, for example, the girls wouldn't be allowed to study on the floor above the boys. The whole thing would never work.'

'Nevertheless,' said Conchita, 'I'm sure that a change to boarding education would quadruple the numbers on roll and give us much more teaching time. It won't be easy. We shall have to go out to the other islands in the lagoon and recruit students. Sister Brigid, I was hoping that you would lead this team and use your knowledge of the area to bring children back to us.'

'I will not leave the mission!' shouted Sister Brigid, her hands intertwined and trembling.

The other two sisters wailed in apprehensive agreement, glaring at Conchita as if she had made an indecent suggestion. Sister Jean Francoise put a consoling arm around the Irish nun's shoulder. All afternoon they had been presenting a human wall of denial and rejection. Sister Conchita put down her pencil on the table before her and tried to look optimistic. 'However,' she said brightly, 'this was only in the nature of a preliminary meeting. Now that we've broached the subjects, I'd like you to think things over and we'll meet again later in the week to go into matters in more detail.'

And a fat lot of good that will do, she thought. From the rigid expressions on the faces of the other nuns, it was plain that none of them had high expectations of a satisfactory outcome to any such encounter. Satisfactory for Sister Conchita, that was. Every topic she had brought up over the last hour had been refuted or dismissed as impracticable by the three immovable elderly women sitting around the table in the senior sister's office. No, it would not be possible to teach carpentry to both boys and girls: it was against custom. No, it would not be in order to dam the creek in order to power a wooden mill wheel to provide power for various projects: it would necessitate moving the kiln, and who knows, it might inadvertently be placed on a *tambu* spot. No, it would not do to make bricks from sun-baked mud: the islanders were accustomed to leaf buildings.

'There is one more thing,' said Sister Brigid, initiating a topic for the first time that day. 'What about that young man you've brought to the mission hospital? He's been here for three days now.'

The Irish nun made it sound as if Conchita had smuggled the youth on to the island for her own nefarious purposes, thought the younger sister. Aloud she said: 'I'm just going along to see him now. The last time I looked in, he seemed much better.'

'We don't even know who he is,' objected Sister Brigid.

'It is most irregular,' nodded Sister Johanna weightily. 'Are we even sure that he is a Catholic?'

Look who's talking, fumed Conchita inwardly. The three of you haven't adhered to proper church practices since Pope Pius XII was a little boy.

'Was he wounded in a battle?' asked Sister Jean Francoise. 'I've been in to see him several times but I can't find any signs of wounds. I didn't know the war parties were out again.'

As usual, the other sisters ignored the French nun.

'I'll see what I can do,' Conchita promised. It was time to make a stand. 'I know that I am new here and that you have grave reservations about me,' she said. 'But I have been sent to Marakosi to do a job, and I intend to do it to the best of my ability. Your undoubted talents are not being used to the full. This mission needs a boarding school, and we are going to start to build one before I leave here. Good morning, Sisters.'

The young nun walked briskly through the mission corridors, trying not to give way to the intense, racking despair she was feeling. It was quiet throughout the building. In most missions there was only a sustained hush like this on a Saturday, when the school had closed and the nuns observed a day of silence. Sister Conchita pined for the organized bustle of her former mission on Malaita. Immediately she chided herself for allowing herself to be discontented and ungrateful. She had been presented with a task, and she would do her best to carry it through, difficult though it might prove.

She looked at the statues of saints lining the walls. They would have known how to cope with Sister Brigid and her acolytes without breaking into a sweat, she thought wistfully. She passed the small chapel used by the sisters for their devotions, with its altar and benches; the back rooms divided into cubicles for sleeping; the refectory and reception room, and entered the dispensary. This was a small room, with a worn scrubbed table in the middle and a few shelves leaning crazily against the walls. It contained only basic supplies of quinine for malaria, penicillin and sulfa tablets for bacterial infections, mycozol for footrot, iodine, bandages and lint, yet still contrived to look cluttered and untidy. Conchita resolved yet again to clean the room up as soon as she found time.

She heard a faint cry from the hospital ward next door and hurried in. A ceiling fan wheezed lethargically overhead. There was space for three beds in the room. Only one of the beds was occupied. A tall, thin youth of about nineteen was lying beneath the sheets. Sister Conchita's heart leapt. He was awake. When she had picked up the semi-conscious youth from the atoll, she had brought him straight back to the mission. After a few hours of incoherent rambling, he had lapsed into unconsciousness and had lain in a coma for the past two days. It was a relief to see him coming round at last.

'How are you?' she asked, moving quickly to his side. 'Come to that, *who* are you? I'm Sister Conchita, by the way. You're in the clinic at Marakosi Mission.'

'Andy Russell,' whispered the youth. 'I'm a VSO from Gizo.'

That would explain it, thought Conchita. Voluntary Service Overseas cadets had only just started being employed in the Solomons. They were male and female, around the ages of eighteen and nineteen, spending a gap year after leaving school and before going on to university helping out with government and mission projects. Because of their youth and lack of practical skills, the scheme had not yet taken off locally, and it was being found difficult to utilize a number of them. Some were being employed in teaching and clerical work, while others were more or less neglected and were to be found hanging around their rest-house in Honiara, enduring various stages of boredom. That still did not explain why she had found this one lying close to death on the tiny island in the lagoon.

'What were you doing on that island, Mr Russell?' she asked, moistening the boy's lips from a glass of water.

'Kasolo,' he whispered. 'It's called Kasolo. They sent me there to build a leaf hut for fishermen calling in to the island. Only I imagine they forgot I was there.'

'You mean they just left you there? How long were you on Kasolo?'

'A month.'

'But what did you do for food?' asked Sister Conchita, increasingly horrified.

'They left me a bag of rice and some tins of meat, but those ran out after the first week or so. After that I managed on coconuts and any fish I could catch in the lagoon. It rained enough to fill the rock pools with fresh water. I kept hoping they'd send someone to pick me up, but no one came. Eventually, I suppose, I got caught out in the sun, and I just collapsed. I reckon I'd been lying in that clearing for the best part of a week before you found me. It was lucky that you and the fishermen came along at about the same time.'

'You've had a severe case of sunstroke and dehydration,' said Sister Conchita. 'It could have been very nasty. I think you're going to be all right now, though. However, I'm very concerned about the way in which you were left to fend for yourself on that island. I shall be having a word with the District Commissioner about it, never fear.'

'No, don't do that,' said a panic-stricken Andy. 'I probably got it wrong. I don't want to be in any trouble.'

'Believe me, you're not the one who's going to be in trouble,' said Sister Conchita. 'I'll send a radio message to Gizo saying that we've found you. In the meantime, you just lie here and rest. I'll send Sister Brigid in with something for you to eat and drink. You've got nothing to worry about now.' A thought struck her. 'By the way, what's *painim aut*? You were delirious when I found you, and you kept repeating it.'

Andy shook his head. 'I've no idea,' he said.

Conchita left the sprawling mission building and walked along the beach, trying to control her feelings. It was so typical of the easy-going attitude of the administration in the Solomons. The neglected young VSO could have died on that island; those responsible for his well-being had much to answer for, and she would do her best to find out how it had happened. She passed a blue-robed local sister and asked her to tell Sister Brigid that the youth had recovered consciousness and needed looking after.

Continuing on her way, she walked through a small village built on stilts in the shallow water of the lagoon. The walls and roofs of the houses were made of large leaves, shaped and folded over flat sticks and held in place by the bark removed from the sticks. The leaves had been shaped into overlapping panels, tied into place with more bark. Children played in the water and on the sand. Their mothers would be working in the gardens inland and their fathers would be far out in the lagoon fishing from canoes. A few old men sat smoking pipes and gossiping under the fringe of palm trees.

Idly Conchita wondered why the VSO boy had been so upset when she had threatened to report his treatment to the authorities. There had been no doubt that he had been frightened. Something struck a chord in her memory. Ed Blamire had been similarly apprehensive when she had encountered him in the church shortly before his strange death. She had felt at the time that she had let him down by not responding adequately to his unease. She was determined that she was not going to ignore a similar plea from Andy Russell, even if he was reluctant to let her know what was wrong. Could it have been a coincidence that two expatriates should have appeared at the mission within such a short time of one another, with each in a palpable state of distress? Probably not; after all, the mission was there to provide succour for the needy.

Conchita dredged her mind to remember where she had heard the name of the island of Kasolo before. Then she recalled that Joe Dontate had told her that it was where John F. Kennedy and the other seamen from his wrecked vessel had taken refuge during the war.

She saw a canoe approaching the beach. At first she could not make out who the occupant was, but then, as the craft drew closer, she thought she recognized the paddler. There were few islanders as tall or as broad-shouldered as this, and the red beret on the man's head of thick curls made identification even easier. With a sense of relief, Sister Conchita realized that the doughty Sergeant Kella was visiting the mission.

She walked down the beach and waited for the policeman to drag his canoe up on to the sand. She was always pleased to see Kella, but was already experiencing her usual feelings of ambivalence about the burly Malaita man. She simply could not make up her mind about him. She had known him for less than a year, but already he had impressed her more than any man she had ever met. The islander was perceptive and intuitive, and she knew from personal experience that he was physically courageous. But, she worried, all these things had to be balanced against the fact that he was a pagan. More than that, he was a high priest of the Lau gods, elected while only a child to this office, charged to spend his life maintaining peace among the Malaitans.

Her elderly mentor, Father Pierre, had warned her not to worry about this aspect of the dedicated police officer's character until she knew more about the Solomons and its people. There were more things in heaven and earth, he warned, than she had been taught in the seminary. If she wanted to make a success of her mission in the islands, she would have to learn much more about the local religions, and perhaps even experience their true meanings and wellsprings. It was a daunting prospect.

She waited until the Malaitan had secured his canoe, and then walked towards him, her hand outstretched. 'Sergeant Kella,' she said warmly. 'Welcome to Marakosi.'

'Thank you, Sister Conchita,' said the policeman gravely, stooping to shake her hand. The nun was aware of his sheer physical size. He towered over her. Kella was over six feet tall, with shoulders like a banyan tree.

'You certainly took your time getting here,' she said, aware of the severity in her tone. 'I'm afraid there isn't much evidence left. The visitors trampled over the ground. And any witnesses will be scattered all across the region by now.'

'Evidence of what?' Kella asked.

'Haven't you come here about Mr Blamire's death?'

'Who's Mr Blamire?'

'He's the tourist who died here on open day. They say he had a heart attack, but I'm not so sure. And how did he get as far as the bonfire if he was attacked in the church, as the signs of a struggle there indicate? Who did he fight there? It's all very confusing.'

Kella shook his head. 'Whoa!' he said. This is the first I've heard about it. They've sent me to look into some sabotage attempts at the logging company.'

'Then who's going to investigate the death here? The district inspector's on tour.'

'Not I,' said Kella firmly. 'You know how much trouble I got into the last time I investigated a murder without authorization, and that was on my own patch. If you like, I'll use the mission radio tonight and contact Honiara about it. It sounds as if the authorities are convinced that it was death by natural causes; they will have had a good look at the body in Honiara.

'Then why was the corpse flown out of the Protectorate so quickly?'

Before Kella could reply, there were shouts from the direction of the mission house. Sister Brigid and Sister Jean Francoise had emerged and were approaching rapidly across the beach. Both nuns were smiling. Conchita had never seen either of them looking quite so animated.

'Ben Kella!' called Sister Brigid as she approached, pumping the hand of the police sergeant. 'You're a sight for sore eyes!'

Kella shook hands with both elderly nuns. 'Sisters,' he said, with genuine feeling. 'This is good!' He turned to Conchita, who was looking on in amazement at the transformation of her two former tormentors. 'Sister Brigid and Sister Jean Francoise were at Ruvabi Mission on Malaita while I was at the school there before the war,' he explained. 'Sister Brigid taught me to box.'

'You were a natural,' said Sister Brigid. 'You had a left hook to die for. If you hadn't given it up to play rugby, you might have been as good as Mike McTigue.'

'Now you tell me,' said Kella. 'All you did in our gymnasium sessions was to slap me around.'

'Ben was head boy at the school,' said Sister Jean Francoise proudly. 'We all thought that one day he would be the first Lau bishop of the islands.'

'Then the custom priests took him away to the artificial islands to teach him the mysteries of the *aofia*,' said Sister Brigid without rancour. 'So naturally, we lost him.'

'But he's back now,' beamed Sister Jean Francoise. She frowned and glanced reproachfully at Conchita. 'But have you not been offered food and drink? For shame! Come up to the refectory at once.'

'The very idea!' said Sister Brigid with a frosty glare at Conchita. 'Leaving you standing on the beach like a piece of spar wood that's been washed ashore.'

Chattering animatedly in the Lau dialect, the two old nuns flanked Kella and escorted him in the direction of the mission house.

'I've come to ask you about something unpleasant,' said Kella suddenly in English. 'Crap, in fact – genuine human crap. What would it mean in Western traditional terms if you found a pile of it somewhere you wouldn't normally expect to see it?'

'That's easy,' said Sister Jean Francoise. 'It's an old Roviana custom. If a war party attacked another tribe's island, before it withdrew, the leader of the invaders would defecate on the beach as a sign of contempt.'

'Is that so?' said Kella, looking interested.

'Come on,' urged Sister Brigid. 'We want to catch up with what you've been doing lately, Ben, not discussing *caca*.'

She propelled the sergeant in the direction of the house, chattering almost vivaciously. Sister Jean Francoise fell into step with Conchita, a few paces behind the others.

'I'm worried to see Ben here,' she confided, when she had made sure that the sergeant was out of earshot. 'He should never have left Malaita.'

'Why not?' asked Conchita, trying to understand how the two old nuns could treat a pagan religion as if it was as real and meaningful as their own. She was also aware of a pang of jealousy. Kella had not been at the station five minutes, yet already the two sisters seemed to be eating out of his hand, while the sergeant had hardly said a word to her, except to dismiss her misgivings about the death of Ed Blamire.

'Because his *mana* will not be as strong as it is in the Lau Lagoon, of course,' said the elderly Frenchwoman. 'That's why the Japanese aren't winning the war; the headhunters' ghosts are stronger than theirs.'

Sister Conchita wondered if she should tell the old nun that the Japanese had left the Solomons seventeen years ago, but Sister Jean Francoise had resumed talking.

'It is very brave of Ben to come to the west,' she said.

'Why?' asked Conchita.

'Didn't you know?' asked Sister Jean Francoise. 'It's one of the legends of the Lau people, of course. If a period of fighting between Malaitans lasts too long, then the *aofia* will be deemed to have failed in his duty.'

'And then what?' asked Conchita, not really wanting to hear the answer, but impelled against all her instincts to ask it.

'Why, then the spirits will call the *aofia* back to his rightful home,' said the elderly nun sadly. 'And Ben Kella will die. That is the custom.'

EIGHT

'I'm afraid that the whole matter of the VSO, er, Russell, was just a regrettable accident,' said the District Commissioner. 'Poynter-Davies, the head of the Public Works Department, sent the lad over to Kasolo to build a leaf house as part of a training exercise. We also thought that he was making the wrong sort of friends among the natives. He was spending more time with them than he was with the expatriate community.'

'So you wanted to get him off your hands,' said Sister Conchita. 'And then you forgot all about him and left him there without supplies for a month. The poor boy was almost dead when I found him.'

'Oh, I think that's stretching it a bit,' said the District Commissioner uneasily. 'The boy survived, didn't he? You could almost regard it as a character-building exercise.'

They were sitting in his office on the ground floor of the administrative offices on the wharf at Gizo, the district centre. Maclehose, the District Commissioner, was in his forties, a bald man wearing a spotless open-necked white shirt, pressed white shorts, long white socks drawn up to the knees and highly polished black shoes. With his coppery hue, he looked so crisp that he could have been freshly baked like a gingerbread man.

'You could almost regard it as a case of blatant neglect,' Sister Conchita said, not letting up.

Maclehose pretended not to have heard her. 'Anyway, all's well that ends well,' he said, not quite rubbing his hands together.

'Perhaps you could send Andy back to us as soon as possible. We're looking forward to seeing him again.'

'He's not ready to be moved yet,' said Sister Conchita, stretching the truth a little. Once she returned the VSO to the official maw, she would have no chance of discovering what had really happened to him. In fact the youth was up and moving now; he had even been fishing with a rod and line from a reef when she had left Marakosi that morning. He had given her a cheerful wave as she had left in her canoe.

'I don't think you quite appreciate the true gravity of the situation,' she said. It was a phrase that she had always wanted to use to an official, and she relished its delivery now. The words had their effect. Maclehose's smooth, supercilious, baby-like face crumpled like a splintering window. The District Commissioner recovered his equanimity only with an effort. 'After all,' Conchita went on, 'suppose Mr Russell decides to take legal action?'

'Legal action?' Maclehose said. 'Surely not! We can't wrap these young people in cotton wool.'

'But you do have a duty of care to them. What you and your officials did to that young man could be construed as neglect of that duty.'

Although the ceiling fan regulated the temperature of the room, the District Commissioner had started sweating. 'A genuine mix-up, nothing more,' he said.

'We'll have to see what the High Commissioner in Honiara has to say about it.'

'There's no necessity for that,' Maclehose said. 'Look, I'll have a strong word with Poynter-Davies when he returns from leave. He might have been a little lacking in judgement on this occasion. Will that do?'

'Possibly,' Sister Conchita said, wondering for how long she could let the colonial official squirm before she got to the real point of her visit. 'There is something else, while I'm here.'

'Anything,' Maclehose said. 'I'm here to help,' he added unconvincingly.

'It's about the death of Mr Blamire at the mission on Marakosi. I'd like to know what steps are being taken to investigate it.'

The District Commissioner's attitude changed with the rapidity of a wet sponge being drawn over a board. His manner of eager compliance vanished and he sat bolt upright behind his desk.

'I don't know what you mean,' he said.

'It's a simple enough question, Mr Maclehose. An American tourist died in highly unusual circumstances outside our church. There were signs of a struggle inside. Could this struggle have brought about Mr Blamire's heart attack? As far as I can tell, nothing has been done to look into it. His body has been transported to the USA, and no one has been sent to investigate the events surrounding his death. What on earth is going on?'

This time the District Commissioner did not give ground. 'I don't think you quite appreciate the difficulties involved in such an investigation,' he said. 'The sheer logistics of it baffle belief.'

'I appreciate that it's not easy,' Conchita said. 'But the government's response to the death seems to be one of complete inertia. Considering that the victim was an American citizen, I find that surprising and reprehensible. At the very least, incidents like this could damage the tourist industry.'

'Sister Conchita, you haven't been in the Solomons for very long, and you've been here in the Western District for an even shorter period of time—'

'Mr Maclehose, I don't need a long service and good conduct medal to know when something is wrong. In this instance, I might even suspect some sort of cover-up. Is the death an embarrassment to the administration?'

'That's absurd! Mr Blamire's body was examined and the official finding was that he had suffered a heart attack.'

'Yet no one visited the scene of his death. That sounds very strange to me.'

'You simply don't understand the complexities of the situation,' the District Commissioner said. 'This isn't a death in the Bronx or Brooklyn, you know. Different conditions apply here in the islands.'

'A man has died in what I, for one, regard as suspicious circumstances, and the authorities seem to be making no attempt to investigate his death. Do you deny that?'

'Of course I deny it,' Maclehose said. 'You're simply not in possession of all the relevant facts. Every possible avenue is being explored. You don't know what's going on behind the scenes.'

'And you seem determined not to tell me,' Sister Conchita said, rising and heading for the door. 'Very well, I shall just have to see what I can find out for myself.'

She stopped and tried to regain her equanimity in the dusty main street running along the waterfront of the sleepy district centre. Copra boats and several visiting yachts were moored against the wharf. Along the waterfront was an open-air market selling bananas, corn, pineapples and tapioca. In the main street there were a few stores, and Quonset huts housing the government offices of the Public Works and the Post and Telecommunications departments. A Morris car and an Austin pickup truck were the only vehicles in sight. Scattered rusted wrecks of aircraft and vessels remaining from the war still had not been cleared from the beach running parallel to the street. Rising behind the village, the laterite hills, rich in iron and aluminium, were a red-brown in colour.

Conchita started walking towards her canoe. What could have been the reason for the sudden stiffening of the District Commissioner's spine? When she had pressed him over his culpability for Andy Russell's neglect, he had responded like a frightened rabbit. Yet when she had tried to use his blatant panic to make him open up about the progress of any official inquiry into the death at her mission, the official had been uncharacteristically stubborn and intransigent. To Sister Conchita's mind, there could only be one explanation. Maclehose was more afraid of the unseen influences restraining him than he had been of being exposed as an incompetent administrator. Somewhere he had been ordered to toe the official party line over the efficiency of the investigation, if indeed there was one, and he was going to do exactly as he had been ordered.

That was not good enough, decided Sister Conchita. Ed Blamire might have been claiming sanctuary at the mission, yet all the same he had died soon afterwards. This might have been an accident, or it might not. There were things to find out, and it looked as if she might be the only person prepared to investigate.

Ten minutes later, she was standing in the reception area of the medical centre at the end of the main street. It was a single-storey building consisting of a wooden frame covered with lath and plaster. It was divided into three sections: the reception area, a clinic for day patients and a small hospital ward. Serious cases were always sent on by ship or aircraft to Honiara. This morning, the centre did not seem busy. A slight, bespectacled Melanesian in his twenties, wearing a white tunic, came out of the clinic.

'Good day, Sister,' he said respectfully in English. 'I am Benedict Waqamalo, the medical assistant. How may I help you?'

'Good morning, Mr Waqamalo,' Conchita said. 'I have come to enquire about Mr Blamire, the tourist who was brought in here a few days ago.'

The medical assistant looked apprehensive. 'Mr Blamire's body is no longer here,' he said. 'It was transported to Honiara.'

'Yes, I've heard that,' said Conchita. 'I was hoping that you could tell me a little more about Mr Blamire's condition when he was brought here.'

'He was dead,' said Waqamalo.

'Yes, I'm aware of that too,' said Conchita, wondering for a moment if the imperturbable assistant was teasing her. A look at his anxiously attentive face reassured her. 'Could you tell me about his injuries?'

'I did not examine him,' Waqamalo said. 'The tourist was brought in by Mr Dontate and some white men. They told me that they would attend to everything.'

'So you didn't diagnose a heart attack?'

'No, I told you. I was not permitted near the body. It was made clear that it was none of my affair.'

'How long did Mr Blamire's body remain in your clinic?' Conchita asked.

'A few hours; then it was flown to Honiara.'

Sister Conchita performed some swift mental calculations. 'It didn't take them long to get hold of a charter plane,' she said.

'That is correct. A special aircraft was chartered within an hour of the tourist's body being brought to the clinic. Mr Blamire's body was then taken by government launch to Munda airstrip, and from there to the Central Hospital in Honiara.'

'It all seems rather odd,' said Conchita. 'Was there any official involvement in all this?'

'Oh yes. I telephoned Mr Maclehose, the District Commissioner. He said that he knew all about it and that I was to let Mr Dontate and the others get on with it. He seemed quite relieved that the matter was already in hand and that he did not need to become involved.'

'Nothing new there then, thought Conchita. Aloud she said: 'I see. You've been very helpful, Mr Waqamalo. Thank you.'

Conchita paused in the morning sunlight on the dusty road outside the medical centre. Around her the scruffy district centre lay dormant, like a neglected frontier town between takes in a William S. Hart silent Western movie. Dontate had been lying to her. Ed Blamire had not been diagnosed with a heart attack at the centre; the assistant had not even examined him. There seemed to have been some sort of conspiracy between Joe Dontate and some of the tourists to get the corpse out of the district as soon as possible.

'Excuse me, but aren't you from the mission where that poor man died?'

The voice was strident and insistent in the nun's ear. Sister Conchita turned round. Standing at her elbow was a squat, heavyset middle-aged woman in a floral dress. She had a straw hat on her head and was clutching a locally made wicker shopping basket. Conchita recognized her as the American tourist who had been blocking the doorway of the reception room on the mission open day.

'That's right,' she replied. 'You're the lady who bought a carving.'

'Oh, I love carvings,' enthused the woman. 'That's what I'm doing here now, shopping for them. My name's Lucy Pargetter, by the way.'

'I'm Sister Conchita. How do you do?'

'Hi!' Mrs Pargetter put a hand on the sister's sleeve and lowered her voice. 'In fact, that's why I've stopped you. I've fallen in love with a simply darling carving in that store over there, but you simply never know when you're being ripped off if you're a foreigner. I wonder if you'd mind coming inside and letting me know if they're asking a fair price for it?'

Conchita had been away from the mission for far too long already. She was about to make some excuse, but restrained herself. She could start her enquiries by finding out as much as she could about the dead man from Mrs Pargetter.

'Sure,' she said. 'I can't stay too long, though.'

'This won't take any time at all,' Mrs Pargetter said, guiding Conchita across the road to one of the Quonset hut stores. 'And after that, we can have a coffee.'

The store was the usual dark, Chinese-owned-and-run jumble of goods. Tins of food, wooden plates, enamel baths, fishing tackle and unopened sacks and boxes were piled high on the shelves and counters, and even on the floor. Mrs Pargetter steered a path through the confusion to a shelf against the wall where a number of carvings were arrayed.

'This one,' she said, handing it to the sister and standing back with some anxiety to see her reaction. 'What do you think?'

Conchita weighed it in her hands. It was a modern kerosene-wood dolphin, probably from one of the villages of the Maravo Lagoon. It was adequately enough finished.

'Fine,' she said. 'Let's see how much they want for it.'

They went over to a Chinese girl standing silently behind one of the counters. 'How much?' asked Sister Conchita.

'Forty Australian dollars.'

'Hey, that's not bad,' said Mrs Pargetter, reaching for her purse.

'Plenty too much,' Conchita said, shaking her head. 'Five dollars.'

'No, more,' said the affronted shop girl. An older Chinese man, alerted by the sound of bargaining, appeared from the dark recesses of the store. He was wearing a *yi*, a traditional loose-fitting upper garment, baggy pants and a skull cap. He dismissed the girl with a shake of his head and took her place. He looked firmly at his visitors.

'Forty dollars,' he said.

'All right,' said Conchita. 'You win. Ten dollars. No more.'

The Chinese man looked scandalized. He shook his head. Conchita put her hand under Mrs Pargetter's elbow and started to guide her out of the store. The owner waited until they had reached the door. 'Fifteen,' he said.

'Twelve,' said the sister, not looking back.

'Deal,' said the Chinese man.

Ten minutes later, Conchita and Mrs Pargetter were sitting in another Chinese store practically identical to the first, sipping coffee in an area marked off for refreshments. Apart from a bored Melanesian waiter, they were the only occupants of the section.

'My, that was impressive,' said the tourist, examining her purchase with pride.

Sister Conchita smiled vaguely. How much would Mrs Pargetter know about Ed Blamire? There was only one way to find out.

'Did you know Mr Blamire well?' she asked, trying to sound casual.

'Can't say that I did, honey. He seemed a nice guy, but he kept himself to himself, if you know what I mean. He was an observant sort, though. I always got the impression that he was taking a lot in and not giving much out.'

'Did he have much to do with Mr Imison and the other ex-soldiers on the tour?' asked the nun.

The plump woman grimaced. 'Sister, if those guys were soldiers, then I'm a captain in the Salvation Army. I'm an army brat myself. My father was in the Corps of Engineers, and as a kid I was brought up in camps all over the world. My late husband Wendell spent twenty years in the Field Artillery. I know the service. Imison and his guys are slick. The army ain't slick, believe you me.'

'And Mr Blamire, did he spend much time with the others?'

'Hardly any. Come to think of it, I don't believe they liked one another very much. Imison and the others used to josh Blamire sometimes, that's for sure.'

'Josh?'

'You know, hassle him a little. They seemed to think he was square, someone who didn't belong with them. Blamire took it in good part mostly. He did have a couple of rows with Imison, as I recall.'

'What about?'

Mrs Pargetter shrugged. 'The first was the usual thing, I reckon. In my experience, men only fight over women and politics. This one was politics. Imison said something disparaging about John F.

Kennedy, and Blamire took exception to it. It was soon over, though.'

'What did they argue about the second time?'

Mrs Pargetter knitted her brows in concentration. 'That was strange,' she said. 'Mr Blamire asked Joe Dontate if somebody would take him to one of the islands in the lagoon. Imison said that there was nothing there worth seeing. When Mr Blamire still insisted on hiring a canoe and a guide and going off alone, Imison got quite angry because his advice had been ignored. It all blew over eventually.'

'Was the name of this island Kasolo?' asked Conchita.

'Come to think of it, it was. I remember because that was where John F. Kennedy was washed up in the war. Imison said that it was too small to contain anything of interest, but Mr Blamire said that you never knew what you might dig up if you tried. That made Imison even angrier. Joe Dontate had to separate them.'

That would explain why Dontate did not have a high opinion of Imison and his group, thought Conchita. The tour guide seemed to have had his hands full keeping the peace among his party.

'I see,' she said. 'By the way, did your whole party come to the mission open day on the day that Mr Blamire died?'

'Every single one of us was there, honey. Even Dontate, our guide, came with us. He used the launch to bring us over, and then took us back, including the body of Ed Blamire. That was one macabre journey, I'm here to tell you. They chartered a plane to take the body back to the States the same day.'

This was an aspect of the case that particularly interested Conchita. She opened her mouth to pursue the subject, but before she could say anything, Joe Dontate himself appeared in the doorway.

'There you are, Mrs Pargetter,' he said. 'The launch is leaving to take us back to Munda now.'

The tourist picked up her bag and rose. 'On my way, Joe,' she said, walking to the door. 'I enjoyed our chat, Sister,' she said, looking back at the seated nun. 'Let's get together again soon. We're going to be staying at Munda for another few days, isn't that right, Joe?'

'That's right,' said the tour organizer, standing to one side to allow the plump woman to leave the store. 'You can't have too much of a good thing.' His voice was expressionless. Conchita stood up to follow Mrs Pargetter. Dontate advanced and stood glowering in front of her.

'I'd appreciate it if you didn't interfere with my tourists,' he said quietly.

'What do you mean?' Conchita asked.

'Haggling for the carving back at the store was out of order.'

'I didn't want anyone to get ripped off, that's all.'

'If they want to spend, let them spend. It's no skin off your nose.'

'You mean you get a cut of anything they buy in the area?'

'That's none of your business. Just keep out of my affairs, that's all I'm asking.'

'And if I don't?'

Dontate eyed her speculatively. 'I heard you could be a nuisance,' he said quietly. 'Well you might get away with it on Malaita, but this is my territory. Don't cross me again. My people have been chiefs in Roviana for hundreds of years.'

'May I remind you that you are talking to a member of a Christian order, Mr Dontate?'

'And you're a long way from home, Sister Conchita, you and Ben Kella. You know nothing about the west. Don't meddle in what doesn't concern you.'

Dontate turned and left the store. Sister Conchita let him go, and then followed at a slower pace. It had been an interesting morning, she thought as she emerged into the sunlight. On the debit side, she seemed to have made an enemy of Joe Dontate. Fortunately, Mrs Pargetter had turned out to be unexpectedly observant. As a result,

Conchita had learned that Ed Blamire had been a loner in the tourist party. Could he have been watching somebody, and if so, why would he have done that? And why were so many people interested in the tiny island of Kasolo? It was definitely something to ponder.

NINE

Kella could hear the singing while he was still some way from the village. Women's voices were joined in a tuneless, monotonous chant that cut through the dusk like a blunt knife. He tried to increase his pace, beating his way through the steaming under-growth with a stick he had cut from a nanum tree. The path before him was slippery and undulating in the last precious hour of daylight. The earth beneath his feet squirmed with the caress of water seeping from one of the adjacent rivers. The trees rising from the mud were linked up to knee height with bushes and undergrowth, making progress on foot difficult. He wondered if he would reach the village by nightfall, or whether he would have to construct a temporary shelter among the trees and then continue his journey the next morning. Fortunately he had brought a little food with him, a few grey balls from the hearts of germinating coconuts, consisting of the solidified milk of the nuts. These should keep him going.

He was approaching the end of his first day on the large volcanic island of Kolombangara. He had paddled over from Marakosi and started his trek inland early that morning. Kolombangara was a thickly forested island some twenty miles in diameter. In the centre, the still active volcano of Mount Veve rose to a height of over five thousand feet, tendrils of its smoke drifting much higher so that they could be seen all over the Western District. There were only a few bush and saltwater villages dotted about the island, which was known to its inhabitants as Water Lord, because it was divided by over eighty rivers and streams flowing in different directions. Once its lower regions had contained the bases for ten thousand Japanese soldiers, while at the top of the volcanic peak, Reg Evans, a lone Australian coast-watcher, had radioed details of their movements to the Allied headquarters at Tulagi from his precarious eyrie.

Kella thought about Sister Conchita's problem with the lack of official activity over the death of the tourist Blamire. Before leaving Marakosi, he had used the mission's generator-operated two-way radio to contact Police Headquarters in Honiara about the matter. The reply had been short to the point of brusqueness. Blamire's death had been an accident. That particular matter was well in hand. Sergeant Kella was not, repeat not, to take any part in the ongoing enquiries. Instead he was to concentrate on the important matter of the sabotage attempts at Alvaro logging camp and to report back, preferably with a solution, as soon as possible.

Well, in a roundabout way he was doing that, he decided hopefully, toiling up another mud-covered slope, listening to the squeaks and blundering wings of flying foxes moving above him. The trees were joined together by lianas, sprawling hanging gardens of mosses and ferns. He walked warily. The bush village for which he was heading had once been the centre of headhunting forays in the Roviana Lagoon. There had been no examples of these for several decades, but during the war, the Allies had turned a blind eye to ambushes on Japanese outposts that had culminated in the triumphant party returning to their homes with a number of Japanese helmets with their owners' heads still inside them.

Kella remembered with little pleasure from his wartime service in the lagoon that on this island, local traditions were still observed. The corpses of the dead were buried upright, with their legs drawn back and secured behind their bodies with vines. Their heads were left protruding above the ground until they had rotted into bare skulls, at which time they would be detached and transferred to the *aabu*, the holy temple. At the death of a chief, a funeral pyre would be built, and the dead man and all his possessions consigned to the flames. The mourning period would last until the ashes were cold, at which time the female relatives of the dead man would strip naked, daub their bodies with red clay and then prepare a great feast of pork and yams for the whole village. At the end of the feast, the naked women would offer their bodies to the new chief.

Lately the bushmen had started making tentative advances towards the other cultures in their region. They no longer depended entirely on barter for their subsistence. They had even begun to use Australian currency, rather than strings of teeth from the flying fox, in some of their internal trading ventures. A virgin could now be purchased for ten dollars cash, while a widow could fetch almost half that sum.

The chanting ahead of him grew louder, and a drum started to beat. Kella knew that he had been seen. This would be the great talking drum of the bush people, made from a tree trunk. It was seven feet long, almost three feet wide and the same in height. The only opening was a narrow slit at the top, through which all the hollowing-out had been accomplished with a stone chisel. It was beaten with a bundle of eight rods, each about half an inch in diameter. It was used to announce the arrival of strangers within the village bounds, and could be heard three or four miles away.

Suddenly the thud of the drum was dwarfed by the sound of a woman's screams. The policeman hurried forward as quickly as the thorns and bushes would allow him to push his way through the undergrowth. Scratches and weals appeared on his arms and legs. Be cautious, he warned himself, you have no *mana* here. On Kolombangara, the water gods had precedence. He did not know what their punishment for intrusion would be, but he could guess that it would most likely include a prolonged end in some river, perhaps between the jaws of one of the gigantic crocodiles of his nightmares. The gods of all the islands could be ingenious in the forms they devised for their death sentences.

He did not slacken his pace. As a result, before long he was standing on the edge of a village established in a clearing. A dozen stunted leaf houses were huddled closely together, as if for company against the dark, threatening trees. Acrid smoke from cooking fires drifted across the area. Twenty or so women were gathered around a slight figure seated hunched on a tree stump outside one of the leaf houses. The seated person was a girl in her twenties, and she was shivering and screaming in agony as some of the women held her down. Even from a distance Kella could see that she was beautiful, with a light brown skin, curly black hair and fine features. She was wearing a long cloth lap-lap falling from her waist to her ankles, her upper body naked, revealing high, firm breasts. Incongruously, blood was pouring down her back in rivulets as she sat hunched forward, writhing in agony on her seat. One woman standing behind her, frowning in concentration, was tracing a maze of patterns on the girl's soft skin with a pointed bone of a bat, while another was rubbing coloured herbs into the bleeding wounds. Both women were retaining a firm grip on the girl's shoulders with their free hands.

Kella realized that he was watching a tattooing ceremony. The women would have been singing for hours in an attempt to keep the girl awake, hoping, usually in vain, that she might fall asleep before the gruesome ritual could get under way, thus relieving her of some of the pain. After the traditional process was over, her wounds would be allowed to ooze and congeal for three days while more and more indelible pigment was infused into her cuts.

One of the women in the group saw Kella on the other side of the clearing and shouted a harsh warning. They all glared across the intervening space at the intruder. There were no men attending the ceremony; perhaps they had been excluded because watching the tattooing was *tambu*. At least it seemed to be almost over now, so perhaps the villagers would accept him as an outsider who knew no better than to interfere. Putting a good face on it, Kella walked across the clearing towards the group, hoping that the sight of his police uniform would reinforce his immunity if inadvertently he had broken any local customs.

'Hello, *olketta*,' he said. 'Mefella Sergeant Kella, mefella polis. Me lookim long this fella Mary Gui.'

'I'm Mary Gui,' said the beautiful girl who had been tattooed, looking up with an effort. She spoke in perfectly modulated English, although she was biting her lips against the pain that must have been racking her lovely body. She gazed at him coolly and without shyness, making no effort to conceal her semi-nudity. She was fighting for breath now that her ordeal was over. 'I must say, you choose your moments for your professional calls, Sergeant. It could almost be construed as voyeurism.'

Kella could not conceal his surprise. He had assumed that the girl at the centre of the ritual came from the village, and was being initiated into the ranks of young village women ready for marriage. A suitably tattooed woman was considered a considerable prize in the bush villages of the west, and would fetch a high bride price. However, he had been told that the Mary Gui he was looking for was a mission-educated young woman who had won a scholarship to an Australian university and had recently returned to the Solomons with a degree. Why was she undergoing a centuries-old ceremony in such a remote area?

'I'm sorry,' he said. 'This is hardly the moment to question you; I can appreciate that. I'll find somewhere to sleep overnight, and come and see you when you're feeling better.'

Mary shifted her position on the log stump and winced. The women behind her moved away, their task accomplished for the moment.

'At the moment I don't think I'm ever going to get better,' she said, wincing and standing up with an effort. 'They tell me that I'm going to feel like shit for the rest of the week anyway. You might as well go ahead now. It might take my mind off things. Walk with me round the village.'

'But why?' asked Kella, falling into step with the hobbling girl. 'Why are you doing this to yourself?'

'It's custom, of course. You should know all about that, Sergeant Kella. I've heard all about you, *aofia*. This is my home village. Like you, I left it to go to a mission boarding school when I was ten, and I haven't been back much since. But now that I *am* back, I don't want people to think that I'm just a rice convert. I'm one of them. I'm proud of my traditions and I wanted to go through the ceremony. Now everyone will know that I come from Kolombangara.' She paused. 'I only wish it didn't hurt so bloody much.'

'People will only know you've gone back to your roots if you walk around half-naked,' said Kella.

'I wouldn't be ashamed of that either,' said the girl with a flash of spirit. 'Although I'm sorry if my tits embarrass you. Talking of custom, you'd better take this.' She hobbled over to one of the other women and returned carrying a betelnut the size of a plum, which she handed to the sergeant. 'We'd better observe procedure as long as you're here,' she said.

Kella nodded and put the nut in his mouth. It would stain his teeth red, but would have the kick of a mild narcotic. There were many such forms of greeting in the islands. The saltwater people would give a visitor a cooked *gnarli* fish, which had the power to bring on hallucinations. By rights the girl should also have given him lime and wild pepper wrapped in a leaf as flavouring for the nut, but she could not be expected to remember everything after such a long absence from her home islands.

In fact, she was trying just a little too hard, thought the sergeant. He could appreciate the young woman's dichotomy; he had been through it himself. The girl could not make up her mind whether she was a Solomon Islander or a brown whitefella. In truth, of course, she was neither – or both. She would discover that fact as she grew older. In the meantime, much like himself, she was trying to keep a foot in both camps. A back covered in custom tattoos would make a useful rallying point if she ever wanted to further her career in local politics and canvas votes in the bush villages.

'I tried to find you at the Munda rest-house,' he said, 'but they told me you'd gone home for a week's leave, so I followed you here. I want to talk to you about the Solomon Islands Independence Party. I understand that you are its president.'

'What about it?'

'There have been accusations that some of your members attacked the logging camp in the lagoon on several occasions and destroyed a quantity of valuable timber.'

'That's a lie.'

'But you don't approve of the actions of the loggers?'

'Does anyone? Not only are they destroying the island, but they're enticing the local girls into prostitution. The Australian workers on Alvaro lure them on to the island to cinema shows and dances and then pay them for sex. After that, they're damaged goods – spoiled marys – as far as their kinfolk are concerned.'

'Do you and your organization feel badly enough about that to do damage to the logging camp?' Kella asked.

'I'm not going to talk about it,' the girl said.

'Several attempts have been made to damage stocks of wood on Alvaro. Were you or anyone you know responsible for this damage?'

'Certainly not!' said the girl indignantly. 'I'm not at all bothered if the loggers are having trouble, but I'm not responsible for it, nor is anyone else I know. I've only been back in the Solomons for a month. That's hardly time to develop a terrorist organization. When I attempt to get rid of logging in the Roviana Lagoon, it will be by legitimate means.'

'And your colleagues in the SIIP feel the same?'

'Certainly,' Mary said. 'We're a democratically elected and organized group. Nothing is done without an open vote.'

'You mean you just talk and issue leaflets, that sort of thing,' Kella said.

'We're planning for the future of the islands, especially the Western Solomons,' Mary said. She was walking with considerable difficulty now. Kella stopped.

'You'd better go and rest,' he said. 'I'll still be here tomorrow.'

The girl shook her head. 'No, walk me round another couple of times. If I lie down, the way I feel at the moment I'll never get up again. No one will harm you. Anyway, all the men have gone crab-hunting. At this time of the year the crabs migrate from the bush to the bay in hundreds. I remember that much about my upbringing.'

They resumed their walk. Most of the other women had disappeared into their huts. It was almost dark. A fitful moon illuminated the village between scudding clouds. Mary Gui gave a little cry and stopped again.

'I think I overestimated my stamina,' she admitted, putting a hand on Kella's shoulder. 'Perhaps I should rest after all.'

'Show me your hut,' said Kella. 'I'll help you over to it.'

'No, that's all right, I can manage.' The girl cried out again and clung to the sergeant for support. Reluctantly she indicated a hut on the far side of the square. Kella helped her across and took her in through the open door. He lowered her on to a bed of straw on the ground, making sure that she was lying on her stomach. Mary groaned once and was quiet. Kella was not sure whether she was sleeping or had fainted from the pain. In either case, there was nothing that he could do. A sudden shaft of moonlight illuminated his surroundings. He saw a small wooden table and a smouldering fire in the centre of the room, kept alight for warmth, light and to keep venomous centipedes at bay. A cotton dress and undergarments were scattered on the floor. Mary's attempt to live in two worlds was evidenced by the sight of several paperback textbooks abandoned on the floor by the fire, an empty Coca-Cola tin, and an open wooden box containing a variety of small shell custom trinkets, including a necklace and several rings and pendants. Kella looked more closely at the box. The jewellery was on a tray at the top of it. He lifted the tray. Beneath it were several wads of Australian ten-dollar notes. It looked as if there was at least a thousand dollars there. He replaced the box on the floor. Then quietly he turned and left the hut.

Outside in the village square, Kella thought at first that he was alone. Then he heard someone sidling up behind him. He turned, too late. Something very hard hit him with crushing force on the side of the head. Suddenly he was falling helplessly into a whirling black pit.

TEN

Sister Conchita drew her paintbrush along the side of the exterior of the church building and stood back to examine the results. There was no doubt that she was making progress. In fact, for the first time since her arrival, she was beginning to feel the first faint pangs of something approaching optimism. Early that morning at breakfast she had allocated jobs for the day to the other three sisters. To her surprise, the unruly trio had accepted her directions. Not willingly, she thought, and certainly not cheerfully, but to the best of her knowledge at this moment Sister Brigid was cleaning the interior of the church, Sister Johanna was in the grimy process of removing the engine from the mission jeep, while Sister Jean Francoise had agreed to plant some yams and sweet potatoes in the gardens on the hillside behind the house.

No doubt Conchita would pay for these decisions at the evening meal, when each of the elderly nuns in turn would direct barbed remarks over her head to one another about the vicissitudes of their new life and the glories of the old, half-remembered previous one. Nevertheless, for the first time since her arrival, everyone seemed to be working together, no matter how reluctantly.

'I've come to say goodbye, Sister Conchita,' said a voice from behind her.

The young nun turned to see Andy Russell standing on the coral path leading down to the rickety wharf. The tall, thin boy had been kitted out with a shirt and a white floppy hat from the wardrobe of the late Father Karl, and Sister Johanna had cut his hair.

He was looking in considerably better condition than he had done a week earlier when Conchita had brought him unconscious to the mission on the floor of her canoe.

'Goodbye, Mr Russell,' she said, extending a hand. 'You could stay here longer if you want to, you know. You would be very welcome. We've hardly got to know you.'

The youth shook his head. 'No, I'd better be getting back,' he said awkwardly. 'The government vessel from Gizo is almost here. Thank you for looking after me so well.'

'You're welcome.' Conchita looked over the VSO's shoulder. She had been so busy that morning that she had not witnessed the government launch steaming self-importantly across the lagoon towards the mission like a toy vessel against a painted backdrop. 'Do me a favour and take better care of yourself in future.'

'I will,' promised the gangling youth. 'I wouldn't like to go through that again. I'm not cut out to be Robinson Crusoe.'

'I should think not!' Conchita remembered that she had not yet asked Andy the question she had started to put to almost everyone lately. 'By the way, have you had anything to do with the group of American tourists stopping at the Munda rest-house? There are about a dozen of them.'

Andy shook his head. 'I'm afraid not.'

'When you get back to Gizo, will you keep your ears open? If you hear anything about them, let me know.'

'Sure thing,' Andy said. 'I'll do anything you want me to, Sister Conchita. I owe you big time.' Sister Conchita thought that there was a touch of something resembling hero worship in the boy's eyes. She dismissed the thought as being immodest and presumptuous.

'What do you want to know in particular about the Yanks?'

'I'm not sure. Anything out of the ordinary.'

The boy looked puzzled but nodded. 'Leave it to me,' he said, transparently eager to help. The launch was tying up at the wharf. He lifted a hand in farewell and walked down the slope to the water as Sister Brigid came out of the church. Typical, thought Conchita. Brigid would not say farewell to the ingenuous VSO, but she obviously cared enough for him to want to see him before he left.

'He's a nice lad,' Conchita said, trying to draw the older nun out.

'Not bad,' conceded Brigid. 'He didn't stay with us long, though, did he?'

That's a bit cool, considering how bitterly you complained when I first brought him here, thought Conchita. However, she was growing accustomed to the Irish sister's apparently innate refusal to display emotion, so she said nothing. She watched Andy reach the wharf in long, loping strides. He was the second guest to leave. Only a couple of days ago, after an overnight stay, Sergeant Kella, unusually preoccupied, had paddled off in his canoe across the lagoon without leaving any word as to when he might return.

'Sisters!' cried a tremulous voice from the direction of the mission. Sister Jean Francoise hurried round the corner of the house and across the garden area towards them. She was carrying something wrapped in a banana leaf in her hands.

'We would never have found it if Sister Johanna hadn't had a sore throat and wanted me to find some *kava* roots to ease the pain,' she panted. 'It grows right in the middle of the bush where no one ever goes. I asked a couple of the men to find some for me. When they came back, they brought this with them as well.'

'Sister Jean Francoise, what are you talking about?' asked Sister Brigid.

'Look!' said the French nun dramatically, dropping the leaf to reveal a war club.

Sister Conchita examined the weapon. It bore no signs of age, and the shell inlay had been polished until it glistened. 'It must be one of the artefacts we were selling on open day,' she said. She turned the club in her hands. The other two sisters gathered closer to examine it. With some trepidation, Conchita turned the club until the studded head was on top. Sister Jean Francoise gasped.

, pointing.

the side of the club was a slight, bristling patina of
hair and flesh. Sister Conchita felt sick.

does that mean?' asked Jean Francoise.

think,' said Sister Conchita, 'that we have discovered the way
which Mr Blamire was really killed. The poor man was struck
down with this club!'

The other two sisters gaped at her, suddenly lost and helpless.

'Somebody's got off the launch,' warned Sister Brigid, raising her
hands to shield her eyes from the sun.

The government vessel had taken Andy on board and had already
cast off and was turning to make the return run to Gizo. A tall, slim
man in khaki shorts and a white shirt was walking up from the
wharf. Sister Conchita recognized the oldest and toughest of the
group of tourists she had met at Munda.

'It's Mr Imison,' she said. 'He's an American. He says he was here
in the war. Sister Jean Francoise, will you kindly take this club to
my office and put it in one of the desk drawers there. And don't
talk to anyone about it. We'll discuss the matter later.'

Sister Jean Francoise nodded and ran off with the weapon,
carrying it gingerly. The other two nuns waited for Imison to walk
up the slope towards them. He gave Sister Conchita a wave.

'You seem to make friends wherever you go,' said Brigid.

'I wouldn't call him a friend,' said Conchita. She was aware of
the other nun looking questioningly at her, but said no more.

'Hi,' said Imison, drawing near. 'We meet again.'

'Sister Brigid,' said Conchita, 'this is Mr Imison.'

'I'm really pleased to meet you,' said Imison, shaking the nun's
hand enthusiastically. 'In fact, I've come over to see you specially.'

'Me?' said Brigid in surprise. 'What would you possibly be
wanting with me, Mr Imison? I'm just a relic from the past.'

'Well, I wonder if I could have a word with you in private about
that?' asked the American easily.

Compared with the last time Conchita had met him, Imison pulling out all the stops to be pleasant, but there was still an eleme of menace clinging to the man like a cloak. Conchita picked up he paintbrush and turned to resume her work on the church wall. Brigid looked at her in a manner that could be construed as near-panic.

'I'm sure Sister Conchita would like to hear what you have to say as well, Mr Imison,' said Sister Brigid. 'After all, she is the senior sister at the mission. I expect she will insist on being present.'

Conchita blinked at the transformation in the other nun. Where had this newly docile and eager-to-please Sister Brigid come from? She realized that the Irish sister was looking at her imploringly as she waited for a response.

'Shall we have tea in the mission?' Conchita asked.

Ten minutes later, the three of them were sitting in basket chairs drinking tea inside the reception room.

'Now, Mr Imison,' said Sister Brigid with a trepidation Conchita had not seen in her before, 'what was it that you wanted to ask me?'

'Actually, it's about the war,' Imison said.

'Sure, and that was a long time ago. The thick end of twenty years. And I don't like talking about it.'

Sister Brigid was becoming more like a stage Irishwoman by the minute, thought Conchita. It must be a sign of her unease.

'You were here during the war?' pressed the American.

'To be sure, I was posted here from Malaita in 1942, and I've been at Marakosi ever since.'

'I understand that you played a prominent part in rescuing stranded US sailors and airmen and guiding them back to safety.'

'We had our moments,' said a poker-faced Sister Brigid, refusing to respond to the visitor's charm.

'Now here's the thing,' said Imison, leaning forward in his chair. 'Were you involved in the rescue of Lieutenant John Fitzgerald Kennedy and the surviving members of the crew of PT-109 in August 1943?'

Sister Brigid did not reply. Imison remained crouched forward, like a feral animal prepared to spring.

'May I know why you're asking the sister all these questions, Mr Imison?' enquired Sister Conchita, coming to the elderly nun's assistance. Brigid looked relieved.

The American made no effort to conceal the resentment in his eyes at the interjection. He gazed coldly at the younger of the two sisters.

'Is there any reason why she shouldn't answer my question?' he asked.

'There are any number of reasons, Mr Imison. One of them is that you are a guest at our mission, not a prosecuting attorney. Another is that Sister Brigid simply may not care to respond to your rather hectoring tone or generally help you with your enquiries.'

Imison gazed fixedly at Conchita. She returned his stare and did not move. After a few moments the American seemed to relax in his chair. 'Sorry,' he said, waving his hand apologetically. 'I didn't mean to snap at you. Guess I just got too involved in the whole thing. You've got to admit, it's a fascinating story.'

'You still haven't told us the reason for your interest.'

'That I haven't,' admitted Imison. A smile as thin as the blade of a foil whipped across his face and then vanished. 'It's just that I'm covering the story for a military magazine back home. With John F. running for the presidency, there's a lot of interest in his exploits in the Roviana Lagoon. They won him the Navy and Marine Corps Medal for heroism, you know.'

'Sister Brigid?' asked Conchita.

The other nun did not respond. She seemed as far removed from the activities in the quiet room as hardly to be present. It was as if she was hoping that if she did not react, the situation would melt away. Conchita turned back to their visitor.

'Was there something in particular that you wanted to know?' she asked.

'Sure thing,' replied Imison with alacrity. 'Kennedy's PT boat was cut in half and sunk by a Japanese destroyer in the lagoon that night. Kennedy and ten of his crew escaped and spent a week hiding from the Japs on a number of small, uninhabited islands in the lagoon. Eventually they were rescued by two natives called Biuku and Eroni, who got Kennedy and the other survivors back to safety.'

'So what do you want to know, Mr Imison? You seem to have the whole story at your fingertips.'

'There's more, a whole lot more, stuff that nobody knows about, only rumours and gossip,' Imison said eagerly. 'I have reason to believe that there was a third native in the party that rescued Kennedy, one that nobody seems to know much about. His name was Kakaihe. I'm eager to find him and get his story, but he seems to have disappeared years ago, somewhere around 1943 in fact.'

'But why should Sister Brigid be able to help you?'

'She's one of the few white people still around who were in the lagoon area in 1943. She was involved in a number of rescues of American personnel. It's no good asking the natives. They either clam up or tell you a hatful of lies.' The American could not hide his resentment. 'Believe me, I've tried.' He looked hopefully at the old sister. 'That's why I'm here.'

'I have nothing to say,' said Sister Brigid, chipping out each word.

'Oh, come on,' said Imison coaxingly. 'What's wrong with loosening up and talking about it? This is old history; it can't hurt anyone.'

'I have nothing to say,' repeated Sister Brigid.

Suddenly the old Irish nun seemed almost on the verge of tears. Conchita stood up. 'You heard the sister,' she told Imison. 'She doesn't want to talk about the matter. I'm going to have to ask you to leave now. You must forgive us. There is so much work to be done here at the mission.'

Reluctantly Imison got to his feet. 'If it's a matter of a donation to the church funds . . .' he offered.

'If you please, Mr Imison; I'm afraid you've outstayed your welcome. Have you got transport back to the rest-house?'

'They're sending a canoe over for me.'

'In that case,' said Sister Conchita, bustling Imison briskly to the door, 'I suggest you go for a nice walk round the island. You'll find that it's well marked with footpaths. Sometimes kingfishers can be found by the stream on the far coast.'

She waited until she was sure that the disgruntled American had left the premises before returning to Sister Brigid. Hastily the old nun tucked a handkerchief away in the sleeve of her habit. Conchita wondered if the apparently impregnable woman had been crying.

'What an objectionable man,' she said. 'Are you all right, Sister?'

Brigid nodded. 'I'm sorry I went to pieces just now,' she said. 'I don't know what came over me.'

'You didn't go to pieces. You chose not to talk to an unpleasant visitor. Why should you bother with him if you don't want to?'

'He was talking about events that I did not wish to remember,' Sister Brigid said.

'Well, it's all over now,' said Conchita. 'I'll make sure he doesn't bother you again.'

'You're a good girl,' said Sister Brigid. She sniffed into her sleeve. 'Even if you are in too much of a hurry sometimes.'

'That's better,' said Conchita. 'That's the Sister Brigid I know.'

'What do you mean?'

'Paying a compliment with one hand and taking it back with the other.'

Sister Brigid almost laughed. She was recovering her composure. 'I'm sorry,' she said. 'I've been in the islands too long. It's no climate for a white woman. It dries you up and makes you suspicious of people.'

'Thanks a bunch,' said Sister Conchita. 'I'll try to remember that.'

A contrite Sister Brigid touched her hand. 'I didn't mean you, Sister,' she said. 'You're a fighter; you'll get things done. We saw that as soon as you came here to Marakosi. That's why we were frightened when you arrived. We thought we might get swept away by the new broom.'

'I wouldn't do that,' said Sister Conchita. 'I can't even find a broom that works around here for a start.'

'I asked you to stay with Mr Imison and me because I knew you wouldn't be intimidated,' said Brigid. 'You wouldn't have let him bully me, even if he did try to batter me down. I used to have spirit like you.'

'You still do.'

Brigid shook her head. 'No, it's all gone now. And what a liar the man is. All that malarkey about him being a writer for a newspaper.'

'You don't believe that?'

'Do you?' asked Sister Brigid scornfully. 'The only thing that man's ever written is an application for a search warrant.'

'He's a cop?' asked Sister Conchita.

'Either that or something similar. He's used to asking questions, that's certain. And accustomed to beating the answers out of people too, if you ask me.'

'How can you tell?'

Brigid's face contorted into a savage grin. 'I haven't always been a nun,' she said. 'Back home in the slums of Belfast I had six brothers. When the police came calling at the front door of a Saturday night, it was no unusual occurrence. My ma would just ask them which one they wanted this time and to kindly take their pick and leave the rest of us alone.'

'Do you want me to make an official complaint about Mr Imison's behaviour?' asked Conchita. 'I can go to the Bishop about it.'

'No, he's not worth the bother.'

'I'd better be getting back to work then,' Conchita said. 'You wait here until you're sure you're feeling better.'

'Stay a minute,' said the old nun. 'Sister Conchita, why are you so set on finding out who killed Mr Blamire?'

'He was murdered here at the mission shortly after I rejected what I now think was his plea for help. I suspect that I ignored his appeal for sanctuary. I believe that at the very least I owe it to him to try to find out what happened.'

'How do you intend doing that?'

'I don't know,' confessed the young nun. 'I can only think that his death has something to do with the tour party. Mr Blamire didn't look like a typical tourist. I think he was there to keep an eye on other members of the group, perhaps Mr Imison and his friends.'

'And do you have any, what are they called, clues?'

'Not really; I can only follow where Mr Imison leads me.' Sister Conchita paused. 'That islander Imison mentioned, Kakaihe, he seems to be the reason why he and his associates have come to the Solomons. Perhaps he knows something. Do you know where I can find him?'

'He's dead,' said Sister Brigid.

'Well, could you take me to where he used to live?' asked Conchita. 'Perhaps someone there might be able to tell me about him. We don't want Imison finding anything out first. Heaven knows what use he'd make of any information that came his way.'

'I might be able to help.' It was a fresh voice.

Conchita turned. Sister Johanna was standing in the shadows by the door. Conchita wondered how long the old German nun had been there and how much she had heard.

'No, Sister Johanna!' said Brigid desperately.

'Hush now,' said Johanna soothingly. 'Perhaps it is meant to be. Sister Conchita may have been sent to the mission for this one purpose. Who are we to question the will of God?'

'Can you take me to Kakaihe's island, then?' asked Conchita, while Sister Brigid seemed to shrink even further back into her chair.

'I can,' said Sister Johanna. 'But think carefully before you ask me to do so. It's a dreadful place! Sister Brigid has good reason to know that.'

ELEVEN

Kella recovered consciousness to the asthmatic chugging of the engines of a small boat. He was lying on top of a blanket on a narrow bunk in the cabin of a ship. His head ached and his mouth was dry. Gently he caressed a bump on the side of his head. He swung his legs to the floor and stood up. He eased his way across the confined space of a cabin to a porthole. It was clamped shut too securely to be opened. Through the thick glass he could see the placid waters of the sea. There was no land in sight. Inside the cabin there were no other furnishings, but the available floor space was piled high with stencilled sacks of Guadalcanal Plains rice.

Kella felt giddy and sat down again. At least he was alive. In fact, someone had gone to a great deal of trouble to keep him that way. After he had been knocked out in the bush village, he must have been strapped to a makeshift stretcher and carried through the bush back down to the shore, where he had been loaded on to this ship.

He took several deep breaths and picked his way over the profusion of bulging sacks to hammer on the cabin door. At the same time he started shouting loudly. At first he thought he was going to be ignored, but then he heard the light steps of bare feet outside the cabin. A key turned in the lock and the door was flung open. Two islanders carrying solid metal belaying pins in their hands stood menacingly before him. They were short but broad-shouldered. From the tribal markings on their faces, Kella could see that they were Guadalcanal men, no friends of Malaitans. Brusquely they gestured to him to leave the cabin with them.

Outside, he climbed over more sacks of rice piled untidily for the entire length of the narrow passageway. There was a second cabin next to the one he had been held in, presumably belonging to the captain of the ship. The smells of a hundred previous cargoes clung stubbornly to the walls and ceiling of the corridor; the sickly-sweet aroma of copra, the musky scent of cocoa, the dull stench of bananas and a dozen other former loads mingled with the reek of diesel oil to deaden the senses.

The two crew members pushed him to the foot of a short companionway and indicated that he should climb up on to the deck. Once he reached the top step, he saw that he was on a typical inter-island trading ship. It was small, dirty and, like many of its kind, held together with a combination of rust and hope. The vessel had a broad, clinker-built hull with a square stern. It was powered by a coughing diesel engine and was making slow progress, low in the water, suggesting that the hull next to the two cabins was packed dangerously full of cargo. There would also be several tons of pig iron stacked in the bilge to keep the vessel upright. The deck area consisted of a flat-topped superstructure beneath a tattered, flapping awning. Near the bows, behind the solitary mast, was a raised glass-topped hatch, its surface stained and cracked. The vessel was indescribably filthy. The decks were stained and pitted and the rails lurched crazily at different angles, with great gaps where sections had fallen into the sea in the past and had not been replaced.

The ship's steering wheel was raised on the deck, a few yards behind the hatch. A tall, broad-shouldered white man in his fifties, wearing shorts and a T-shirt, was at the wheel.

'Sergeant Kella,' he boomed. 'Welcome aboard! I must say, we're shanghaiing a much better quality of supercargo these days.'

'Commodore Ferraby,' said Kella, making his way forward. 'I should have guessed. You do know that you have just added kidnapping and interfering with a police officer in the course of his duties to your usual hobbies of piracy and smuggling?'

He advanced on the helmsman. The two islanders raised their belaying pins menacingly, but the white man gestured to them to go below. 'Fetch-im kaikai,' he ordered.

Reluctantly, and continuing to direct suspicious glances at the police sergeant, the pair went back down the steps in the direction of the engine room.

'Who paid you to take me on board?' Kella asked.

'Come, dear fellow,' chided Ferraby. 'You can't expect me to divulge stable secrets like that. The Jockey Club could take my licence away.'

Kella scoured the horizon. Far off to the starboard side across the glass-like surface of the water lay a faint nebulous wisp of curved coastline with a horseshoe-shaped bay and a series of low wooded foothills behind. The land was hardly more substantial than the faint clouds blowing lazily across it.

'That's Baroraite Island, isn't it?' he asked. 'We're in the New Georgia Sound.'

'Now, how on earth could you tell that?' asked Ferraby in genuine astonishment. 'Oh, of course, you were a coast-watcher here in the war, weren't you? You sailed with that rogue John Deacon and his motley crew, carrying out hit-and-run raids on Jap coastal camps all over the Western District. For God's sake, how old were you then?'

'About fourteen.'

Ferraby whistled. 'As young as that? You always were blood-thirsty. I thought I started my nefarious career young enough, but you could give me a few years.'

'I wasn't at Eton,' said Kella.

'Neither was I, dear lad, even if I do claim that on my curriculum vitae sometimes.'

The big man hummed contentedly as he studied the water ahead of him, from time to time making minute adjustments to the set of the wheel beneath his large and capable hands. His leathery, weather-beaten face was at odds with his cultured drawl. Hugh Ferraby, who preferred, with some irony, to be known as Commodore, after a brief and abruptly terminated period as the executive of the Honiara Yacht Club, was a throwback to the pre-war years in the islands of the South Pacific, when footloose amoral expatriate soldiers of fortune prowled the area in their dozens, eking a living by any means they could, prospecting for gold, trading, managing plantations and running various dubious enterprises.

Some of them married local women and then went native, idling in the sun and depending on the extended families of their wives to provide them with lives of ease in the sun. Others, like Ferraby, were not above acting beyond the law, smuggling seashells and artefacts out of the region, pulling off insurance scams with their wrecked vessels, secure in the knowledge that the insurance companies would bear their losses with resignation rather than go to the expense of sending assessors to the remote and dangerous reefs and jungles of the Solomon Islands. Occasionally a plot would go awry, and as a result Ferraby and his ilk would spend a few months in a local prison with reasonable forbearance.

The well-educated Ferraby was one of the few beachcombers to return to the Solomons after the war, which he had spent serving with some distinction in the RNVR. With his savings and gratuity he had bought his present trading vessel, extremely ancient even in 1945, and had spent the next fifteen years running cargoes around the island, living from hand to mouth on the meagre profits and any tricks he could pull on the side.

'What are you supposed to do with me?' Kella asked.

Ferraby raised an eyebrow. 'Why, treat you as an honoured guest, old boy. No worries, Sergeant Kella. I regard you in the light of a rather special visitor. I'm looking forward immensely to your company. It'll give you a chance to see how the other half lives. You work far too hard anyway, always running around and popping up in the most unexpected places, harassing and arresting splendidly innocent fellows like me. I want you to regard this voyage in the light of an extended holiday.'

'Don't piss on my back and tell me it's raining. Where are we going?' asked Kella, although he already anticipated the answer.

'Ontong Java,' answered Ferraby with relish. 'Ever been there? Marvellous place! The women have no inhibitions at all. They're Polynesian, you see, and beautiful with it. Do you know, every so often they have a ceremony where all the virgins on the island parade bare-arsed naked, hand in hand in pairs through the main village street, so that the young bucks can ogle them and take their choice. Oh, you've got a treat in store.' Ferraby rolled his eyes. 'Imagine how a ceremony like that would liven up Budleigh Salterton or Tunbridge Wells, eh?'

Kella tried not to display the dismay he was feeling. Ontong Java was an atoll of over a hundred tiny specks of islands more than 150 miles north of the Western Solomon Islands. Only a couple of thousand people lived there. Once Ferraby had skirted the edge of Santa Ysabel, he would leave the calm island waters behind him and embark on a perilous voyage across the Pacific Ocean. The seas between the Western Solomons and the distant atoll were notoriously difficult, with frequent storms. There were rich pickings for any traders brave or foolhardy enough to make the hazardous journey to such a remote spot. To make matters worse, as far as Kella was concerned, once he reached the atoll, Ferraby would probably spend several weeks cruising among the the islands, exchanging his present cargo for copra.

'What are you taking there?' he asked.

'Rice,' said Ferraby enthusiastically. 'They can't grow their own. The poor sods live on a diet of fish, taro and coconuts. For them rice is a mixture of caviare and pâté de foie gras. We'll exchange the lot for copra and bêche-de-mer. Either way, there are whacking great profits in prospect, Sergeant Kella. O, frabjous day!'

'You won't be able to spend your profits in prison.'

Ferraby's eyes widened theatrically.

'Who on earth is going to send a law-abiding citizen like me into durance vile?' he demanded. 'We found your unconscious body on the beach, rescued you, gave you a cabin to yourself and provided medical aid to the limit of our abilities. Unfortunately, we were bound for Ontong Java and limited by the tides and weather conditions, so we didn't have time to put you ashore anywhere. Still, we nursed and looked after you, as was our bounden duty. I might even apply for a good citizenship award. And anyway, it will be our word against yours.'

'Now tell me what really happened,' said Kella. 'Were you in on this from the beginning?'

'Good Lord, no,' said Ferraby. 'I never get any fun like that. To be honest, old chum, we had to leave Gizo in a bit of a hurry a couple of nights ago. Something to do with unpaid mooring bills, I won't bore you with the details. Suffice it to say we had to cast off unexpectedly, without taking enough water on board for the trip. That same night we stopped and put ashore at Kolombangara in the dinghy to refill our barrels. When we reached the beach, who should be waiting for us but . . .' Ferraby stopped and coughed. He continued. 'Well, suffice it to say someone was standing there with you, or rather with your comatose form. When I told your captor that we were heading off on a three-week voyage into the wild blue yonder, we entered into business negotiations on the spot. A very satisfactory sum of money changed hands and I agreed to take you out of circulation for the best part of a month. *Voilà!*'

'So you didn't do this to me?' asked Kella, feeling the swelling on the side of his head.

'Would we dare, old boy? To strike the *aòfia* would practically be lese-majesty in the Solomons. Only a real hard man or a foreigner would dare touch you.'

The two Melanesians climbed back on to the deck with two plates of yams and taro and two green drinking coconuts, pierced at the top. They handed a plate and a coconut each to Ferraby and Kella. Ferraby gestured to one of the islanders to take the steering wheel. The second islander crouched at the feet of the other. Both men kept their eyes warily on the police sergeant. Ferraby led Kella over to the hatch. They sat on the flat wooden surround and started to eat. To his surprise, Kella found that he was hungry.

'Are you still playing rugby?' asked the trader.

'No, I've given that up.'

'Pity. I saw you play league in Sydney about five years ago. You were bloody good, a real hard case. You must have made a mint at that game.'

'Not really,' said Kella. 'I didn't stick at it long enough. I wanted to come back to the islands and do other things.'

'Catch me giving up doing anything I was making money at,' said Ferraby. 'However, chance would be a fine thing, I suppose.' He looked reflectively out to sea. He seemed in a mood to chat. His itinerant way of life probably made it difficult for him to find fresh people to talk to, thought Kella.

'I was twenty-five when I first came out to the Solomons,' Ferraby went on. 'I'd already failed at a fair few things – university, the navy, the City, marriage. Even then I guessed that this was going to be my last chance. Well, it was, and I blew that, too.'

'There's still time,' said Kella. He stared down into the hatch. The glass covering was smeared and cracked and plainly insubstantial. Its sole purpose was to protect the cargo below from the elements. In the hold, rows of sacks of rice were piled on top of one another to a height reaching only a few inches below the hatch cover.

'I begged, borrowed and stole every dollar I could to buy that rice,' said Ferraby, following his gaze. 'I suppose you could call it the last throw of the dice on my part.'

'Quite a gamble,' said Kella.

'I've staked all I had on plenty of those in my time,' said Ferraby.

Kella drained the last of the milk from his coconut. Casually he strolled over to the ship's rail and tossed the husk into the water. Ferraby and the two Melanesians watched him alertly. Kella put a hand on the rail. As he had thought, the iron stanchion was rusted and loose in its socket, worn away by years of wear. He tested it reflectively in his hand.

'Right, old boy, I think it's time you took your food down to your cabin,' said Ferraby sharply. 'We'll bring you up for another run this evening, all being well, if you behave yourself.'

Kella nodded and turned as though to obey. Suddenly he seized the stanchion with both hands and used all his considerable strength to tear it from its socket. He staggered back, his shoulders and biceps aching with the effort of dislodging the section of rail.

Ferraby and the islander who had been sitting on the deck leapt to their feet, while the helmsman looked on helplessly. With a couple of strides Kella leapt back to the hatch and balanced on top of it, holding the iron rail threateningly in the air.

'Hold it!' he ordered. 'If any of you takes one step towards me, I'll smash this glass cover to pieces.'

Ferraby hesitated and then gestured to the two Melanesians to stay where they were. 'Now why would you want to do something like that, old son?' he asked in an aggrieved tone.

Kella did his best to balance on the swaying glass roof. 'You'll be leaving the lagoon and sailing out into rough seas in the next twenty-four hours,' he said. 'If I've taken the hatch glass out, the first big waves you meet in the Pacific will pour into the hold and ruin your consignment of rice. You can't go back to Gizo or Honiara for a replacement hatch cover because there will be a warrant out in both places for your arrest for non-payment of harbour fees. You might be able to get a tarpaulin over the hole, if you have one on board, but any big wind will dislodge it in no time. Face it, Commodore. If this glass is gone, so is your cargo. You won't be able to sell sodden, swollen rice, even in Ontong Java. You might as well throw it over the side.'

Ferraby's face was red with fury, but he did his best to speak quietly. 'You won't be able to stay up there for ever,' he said.

'I don't intend to. If you haven't done as I say in the next five minutes, I'm going to crack this glass and then take my chances in the sea.'

Ferraby started to edge forward, surprisingly lightly for a big man. Kella lifted the stanchion high above his head.

'What do you want me to do?' Ferraby asked, halting.

'Change direction and get me close enough to land for me to be able to swim ashore.'

'There are sharks in the lagoon,' Ferraby said.

'I'll risk them. Didn't you know? I belong to a shark clan.'

Ferraby hesitated. Reluctantly he barked orders to the helmsman. Obediently the Melanesian swung on the wheel and began to head towards the coast. Kella did not take his eyes off the other three. Ferraby would almost certainly have a rifle in his cabin below, but unless he could get hold of it, there was little he could do to get the policeman off the hatch.

'Just take it easy,' Ferraby said. 'That's all I ask. Nobody's going to rush you.'

'Too true they're not,' said Kella grimly.

For over an hour the tableau on deck did not move. All the time the coast was edging almost imperceptibly closer. Once the helmsman tried to jerk the wheel abruptly in order to dislodge Kella. The sergeant raised the stanchion and Ferraby howled at the Melanesian to keep on course. After an hour and a half, Kella could make out the trees and sandy beach of Baroraite Island. Another hour crawled by. Now he could see islanders on the beach. They were gathering in a puzzled crowd on the golden sand; they were not accustomed to seeing a trading vessel pass so close to their village.

'This will do,' said Kella.

'I always knew you were a resourceful fellow,' said Ferraby, 'but did you have to prove it on my watch?'

'Goodbye, Commodore,' said Kella.

He sprinted across the deck to the gap in the rail and dived into the sea. Ferraby's ship would be too cumbersome to pursue him, and in any case, if it went any closer in to the shore, there would be a danger of grounding on a shoal. Kella could already see canoes putting out from the shore to pick him up. The islanders had recognized the danger of his situation and were utilising every form of canoe waiting on the beach. Some were graceful, with curves at the prow and stern, others were balanced with an outrigger, a few were long and heavy, with carved figureheads. The men in them were banging at the surface of the water to drive off any lurking sharks. Swimming economically, Kella headed for the leading canoe.

TWELVE

'Not that I'm complaining,' said Sister Conchita, 'well, not much anyhow, but why did you decide to bring me here? It's hardly holiday-brochure stuff, is it?'

'If you think you've got problems, spare a thought for mine,' panted Sister Johanna, her chin tucked on her chest, not looking back. 'This is my first venture outside the mission for ten years. It was time, that's all. I've been worried greatly about Sister Brigid. For years that woman has been trapped in a hell of her own making, with her own private demons, and she won't let anyone help her. Father Karl tried while he was alive, but even he had to give up in the end. It was time to make her confront her past. You were the first new member of the mission since the war. Perhaps your arrival at Marakosi was intended to bring Sister Brigid release.' The old German nun started to chuckle unexpectedly, but the sound turned into a dry, racking cough. 'You have certainly shaken us up enough in other directions.'

'Have I been that bad?' asked Conchita.

'Indescribably worse! You are a typhoon, my dear, a veritable human typhoon. Which is probably just what we needed. But how far can you go? All right, so you may be able to transform the physical face of the mission, but can you confront the secret torments of Sister Brigid? None of us has ever been able to do that.'

The two nuns were making their way laboriously along a muddy coastal track running parallel to the sea on the island of Kolombangara. They had come over in the mission canoe from Marakosi first thing that morning. Sister Johanna had directed the younger nun to the nearest safe landing place close to the village they were seeking. Kolombangara was not like any other island that Conchita had seen in the Roviana Lagoon. While all the others had been sun-kissed and sparkling, this was a dank, inhospitable place. Where they were walking, the cliffs rose so close to the shore that they had been forced to follow a winding track inland and then turn at the top of the cliffs and begin a long, sloping descent. The sound of many rivers running down to the sea from the mountain was so loud that they could hardly hear themselves speak. They were picking their way through stunted trees across a mangrove swamp. Every time they reached a patch of comparatively dry ground, their progress was impeded by mounds of slimy dead leaves and branches. There were occasional fallen trees to be circumnavigated, and stones that had rolled down from farther up the mountain. Occasionally their path would take them close to the edge of a precipice overlooking the sea, a route made all the more dangerous by the slippery mud beneath their feet. There was an overall stink of death and decay.

'This island has a dreadful history,' said Sister Johanna. 'Traditionally it was a place where headhunting parties would bring their captives and kill and eat them. During the war, the Japanese brought a group of British prisoners of war here to build a coral airstrip. They treated them so badly that all the prisoners died of malnutrition or disease. Then the Allies bombed the island and killed most of the Japanese garrison. No wonder the islanders don't have much time for visitors.'

Conchita wondered if she had made a mistake by bringing the frail, elderly sister with her. Johanna was walking purposefully enough at the moment, but she was stopping increasingly often for breaks. When Conchita suggested that they sit down for a longer rest on a log, the German nun shook her head vigorously and plodded grimly onwards.

'I don't know if I'm going to be much help to you,' said Sister
Johanna suddenly, breathing deeply and turning to face Conchita.
'All I know is that whatever happened in 1943 started here, when
Sister Brigid picked up her guide Kakaihe at the Catholic village
we're going to now. This island of Kolombangara was the
headquarters for the chief coast-watcher in the region, Mr Evans.
He was up near the volcano, while the Japanese were stationed
around the coast. He had sent out an urgent radio message asking
everyone to watch out for eleven American seamen who had been
marooned somewhere in the area after their vessel had been sunk.
I urged Sister Brigid not to go. I said there were plenty of young
islanders who could do the job better than she could, but she
wouldn't be told. She reached this island at night, picked up
Kakaihe and set off, heaven knows where, in a canoe. The next
thing we heard was that Kakaihe was dead and dear Sister Brigid
was in a state of catatonic shock. Some islanders brought her back
to Marakosi. She wouldn't say a word for months, and to this day
she has never told anyone what happened on that final trip of hers.'

'Will anyone at the village we're going to be able to help us?'
Conchita asked.

'Possibly not, but you've got to start somewhere. For some
reason, the American Imison seemed to think that Kakaihe and
Brigid were involved in something strange together. I doubt if any
of the islanders will tell him anything about Kakaihe, so you might
have a head start if you can get to his village first.'

'And Sister Brigid has never spoken to anyone about the reason
for her silence?'

'The subject was obviously far too painful for her, so after a time
Father Karl and I stopped bringing it up. The poor woman has
never left the mission grounds since, and that was seventeen years
ago. That's why I'm hoping that you've been sent here by divine
providence to put an end to the whole thing. I only wish that it
wasn't this village we have to visit.'

'Why is that?'

'You'll see for yourself directly,' said Sister Johanna with a shudder. 'It's the most squalid place imaginable.'

Twenty minutes later, they entered the village. It was hardly more welcoming than the track had been. There was an air of neglect about the huts. The ground was ankle deep in mud. Even the boles and branches of the trees surrounding the handful of huts were grey with slime. The few villagers present seemed lethargic. There was no attempt made to welcome the sisters, only sullen and indifferent glances from the doorways of the huts.

'Do you see what I mean?' whispered Sister Johanna. 'I don't wish to appear irreligious, but this must have been one of the last places that the good Lord ever made. I'll see if I can find the headman, not that he'll be much help.'

Now that she had safely negotiated the path to the village, Sister Johanna seemed to have been affected by the general lassitude of the village and to have lost much of her customary energy. She hobbled off towards a group of unwelcoming women and addressed them in what Conchita assumed to be the local dialect. Finally one of the women detached herself unwillingly from the group and slouched off to a hut bigger but no more prepossessing than the others. After about five minutes, a fat islander in his fifties emerged from the hut, rubbing the sleep from his eyes. He was wearing a scruffy, unwashed length of cloth around his waist, reaching to his knees. He eyed the nuns without enchantment, but walked slowly over to them. Sister Johanna began to address him in dialect, but the fat man stopped her with a wave of his flipper-like arm.

'I speak English,' he said curtly. 'My name is Matthew Pironi. I am the headman.'

'You speak very good English,' said Conchita.

The compliment had no effect on the headman. 'I was a mate on a Chinaman's trading boat for many years,' he said. 'What do you want in my village?'

His tone could hardly have been less welcoming, but neither sister gave any sign of being deterred by it. Conchita guessed that his spell on the trading vessel would have accrued him enough money to throw a number of feasts on his return home, which would have secured him the position of local chief.

Sister Johanna walked over to a log placed by a cooking fire and sat down gratefully. Conchita joined her. Matthew Pironi followed them with ill grace and stood facing the pair.

'We want to talk about the time before,' said Sister Johanna, using the pidgin phrase for the past. 'We want to know what happened when Kennedy was lost in the lagoon.'

Matthew did not look surprised. When he replied, it was as if he was using a speech he had uttered several times before. 'Many people used to come here and ask that,' he said. 'We told them that we don't know. So they stopped coming. Now you have come back again after many years. We still know nothing. The time before is over. We want you to go now, before the young men grow angry with you. We don't want strangers here.'

'We will go as soon as you answer a few questions,' said Conchita. 'Were you here in 1943?'

'Yes, I was a young man then.'

'I want to know about a man from this village called Kakaihe.'

'Kakaihe is dead. He died many years ago. There is nothing to say about him.'

'Just tell me about Kakaihe and we will go and not come back to your village, I promise you.'

The headman stood thinking. He nodded. 'Ask quickly, then,' he muttered.

'What sort of a man was Kakaihe?' asked Conchita.

'He was a rubbish man,' said the headman, as if speaking from the heart for the first time. 'He was very young at the time. He was about eighteen or nineteen, no more. Kakaihe was very proud and headstrong, always boasting about his bloodline. He would quarrel with people and become offended easily. He was not an experienced coast-watcher, so he was not given an important part to play in searching for Kennedy. That was why Sister Brigid found him still here and was able to use him as a guide.'

'So he wasn't a full-time coast-watcher for the Americans?'

'No, sometimes he did that,' said Matthew warily. 'At other times he did other things. He spent much time wandering about the island. There was a lot happening in the lagoon all that time ago. It is hard to remember everything.'

'But when the search was on for Lieutenant Kennedy, Kakaihe guided Sister Brigid to some of the islands to look for the American seamen?'

'We did not want Sister Brigid here,' said Matthew. 'It was very dangerous. The Japanese were just along the coast. But Kakaihe was most eager to go. Even though he was not Sister Brigid's usual guide.'

Probably because the reward for retrieving a lost American serviceman was a sack of rice, thought Conchita.

'Do you know where the pair of them went?' she asked.

Matthew shook his head. 'All I know is that a few days later Sister Brigid returned at night with the dead body of Kakaihe in her canoe. He had been stabbed to death. Sister Brigid was weeping and crazy in the head, and would say nothing that we understood.'

'Stabbed? But if they had encountered the Japanese, wouldn't they have shot at Sister Brigid and Kakaihe with guns, and not used knives?'

'Me no savvy,' said Matthew. 'All I know is that Kakaihe had six stab wounds in his body and had lost much blood. Sister Brigid would not say what had happened. We knew and trusted her, so we made sure that she was taken back safely to the mission at Marakosi. We told her not to come back to Kolombangara. They say that to this day she has never left the mission again.'

'Can you guess what happened to Kakaihe after he left this island with Sister Brigid?'

'No,' said Matthew. After a pause he added: 'There is only one man who might know that, and nobody would dare go to him and ask about it.'

'Who is that?' Conchita asked.

'Teiosi, the magic man, who lives in the bush,' said Matthew reluctantly. 'He does not come down to the saltwater villages often, but when Kakaihe was brought back to the village, he visited us and sat alone with the body on the sand for two days, listening and talking to him.'

'How could he listen to a dead man?'

'Custom,' said Matthew simply. 'We keep the body of a dead man above the ground for as long as possible, so that members of his bloodline can get here in time to say goodbye. Until the body is buried, it is not regarded as being dead. That means that it can still talk to the special people, the magic men, if it has something important to say, or some last confession to make. When the body is being buried, the soul will come out through the dead man's throat. Then it will go down to the coast and wait for the next boat to the other world. That was the time when Teiosi listened to Kakaihe.'

'And you think that Teiosi the magic man left this village with information that Kakaihe had given him?'

'It is known to be so,' said Matthew. 'He told us that before he left. The spirit of Kakaihe spoke to Teiosi and the magic man went back to the bush with the knowledge that the spirit had given him. He has guarded that knowledge ever since.'

'Is there someone who could guide us to this magic man?' asked Conchita.

Matthew shook his head firmly. 'My people do not go to see Teiosi. It would be *tambu* for us to do so. His mother was an islander and his father was a wild boar. It would be death for any of us even to look upon him. The women leave food for him on the track outside the village and then run away. That is all I want to say. Now you must go!'

The headman turned and waddled away. Other men were coming out of their huts and gathering in small groups, looking malevolently at the nuns.

'Come, Sister Johanna, my dear; I think we may have outstayed our welcome already,' said Sister Conchita.

They retraced their steps along the path leading up into the bush. After half an hour, Sister Johanna stopped and sat on an uprooted tree. While the main track continued along the clifftop, a smaller, barely discernible path branched off up a steep slope towards the interior of the island.

'Are you tired? Would you like a rest?' asked Conchita, concerned.

Johanna shook her head. 'No, I just want to think,' she said. 'Do you really believe that Mr Blamire was murdered with the war club at our mission?' she asked. 'And then his body was thrown on the bonfire, as if it was a funeral pyre?'

'I'm convinced of it. Why?'

'It is another sign,' sighed the old nun. 'You coming to the mission to change us, Mr Blamire being murdered; they're both omens that it is time for Sister Brigid's long silence to be ended.'

'But how can we do that?'

'We must follow the indications that we have been given, of course. The American has pointed us towards Kakaihe. Mr Imison may not be a good man, in fact I think that he is probably a very bad one, but the Lord could still be using him as an instrument to help us.'

'How?'

'I wasn't going to tell you this, but I think I know where the magic man might be,' said the old nun, standing up. 'Many years ago, Father Karl and I came here to inject the babies on the island against yaws. Father Karl had heard about the magic man and went up to his lair to try to find him in case he needed help or supplies. I stayed here on the main track. Father Karl did not see the magic man on that occasion, but when he returned, he told me of the path he had taken on his search. I think I can remember his instructions well enough, even after all these years, if you would like me to take you up to it.'

'I certainly would,' said Conchita, 'but you're in no state to make a detour like that.'

'It will have been a wasted journey if we don't try it,' Johanna said. 'Sins of omission are as bad as those of commission. I'm not as feeble as I may look, Sister. Follow me; I'll go at my own pace.'

The two sisters toiled at a snail's rate up the slippery incline. The trees grew so thickly here that their tops almost blotted out the sky, leaving the track in perpetual gloom. Eventually Sister Johanna stopped, exhausted. 'It should be somewhere here,' she said.

Conchita looked around hopelessly. The jungle looked no different here than it had at any other stage on their struggle up the mountainside. The undergrowth reached almost up to their waists, while the branches of the closely packed trees intermingled to provide a profusion of false roofs above their heads.

'Do you think there really is a magic man up here?' she asked dubiously.

'There's someone here, certainly,' Johanna said. 'He won't be the offspring of a woman and a boar, of course, as the headman believes. Most likely many years ago some poor unmarried pregnant girl was ejected from her village and cast out into the bush up here. She gave birth to a baby boy in isolation and died while he was young. That boy grew up alone to be the magic man.'

'What a life!' said Sister Conchita.

Johanna was studying her surroundings. 'Father Karl told me that the hermit had a home up here in the side of a large banyan tree. He had a bed of sorts on the ground. It was where two large rivers met and flowed into one another. We can hear those rivers, I think.' She pointed to the north. 'They're over there somewhere.'

Twenty minutes later, the bedraggled, sweat-stained nuns came out of a ring of trees into a large clearing on a plateau. Here the two rivers converged and swept down to the sea with a roar. The huge banyan tree stood alone on the nearest bank of the newly formed river. A hole about six feet in diameter had been cut in the side of the tree. Creepers hanging from one of the lower branches had been trained to serve as a makeshift curtain over the entrance.

'Do you think he's inside?' asked Sister Johanna in hushed tones.

'There's only one way to find out,' Conchita said.

With a confidence that she was not really feeling, the nun walked across and entered the lair. Inside, it was stiflingly hot and oppressive. A bed of leaves occupied one corner. No one was lying on it. Sister Conchita took a look round and left the room, shaking her head.

'It's empty,' she said.

It was then that she saw the rope ladder. It was long and frayed, hanging from the branches halfway up the banyan tree. She tugged the lower rungs tentatively. To her surprise, they did not come away in her hand.

'Perhaps he's up there,' she said to Sister Johanna, looking up at the higher reaches of the tree.

'You mustn't!' gasped the German nun. 'That ladder has probably been there since the war. It would be dangerous even to try to climb it.'

'I don't weigh very much,' said Sister Conchita. 'I'll be careful.'

'This is taking parish visiting to extremes,' moaned the other nun in an agony of apprehension, watching Sister Conchita begin her difficult ascent.

At first the rope ladder swayed and swirled, swinging the sister from side to side. Encumbered by her flowing cotton habit, finally Conchita got the hang of adjusting her balance as she went up, step by laborious step. Branches scratched at her hands and face, and heavy vines draped themselves over her shoulders, trying to force her back down. Often she stopped for a rest, struggling for breath.

She forced herself to continue the climb, setting one foot doggedly above the other as she went up the huge tree. Slowly her limbs grew almost accustomed to the strain she was placing on them. Finally her head cleared a ring of branches and she found herself inching up an expanse of cleared bark where the branches had been lopped away and kept trimmed close to the trunk of the banyan. Just above her head, about a hundred feet above the ground, was a huge fork in the tree. Across this fork had been laid a platform of wooden planks nailed together, wide enough to allow three or four people to stand in comfort. The rope ladder ended here, fixed to the side of the platform.

Transferring her weight carefully, Conchita scrambled from the ladder to the platform. She stood, balancing her weight, and stared out over the island. There was a marvellous view of much of one side of Kolombangara and the placid green waters of the Roviana Lagoon beyond. Coast-watchers must have stood here to study and report on the movements of the Japanese in the war, she thought.

There was a bed of leaves close to the trunk of the tree. Conchita walked over to the bed and knelt down. The emaciated form of an elderly islander was lying on it. The man was scarred and naked. Flies were crawling over his face. He had been dead for some time. The magic man must have made the long climb from the ground to die up here where he could see the island that had treated him so cruelly in his lifetime.

Sister Conchita stood up. She looked around the platform. The magic man had few possessions. There was a rusty old bush knife and a few coconut shells that had been carved into the shape of bowls. In one corner was something wrapped in a banana leaf. Conchita picked it up and opened it. Inside was a circle of turtle shell affixed to a larger white seashell. The outline of a frigate bird was carved crudely on the central circle.

Clasping the shell, the sister hesitated. The old magic man had died alone and untended. By tradition he needed the farewell incantation of a custom priest to send him on his final journey. But no custom priest would come near the corpse of this outcast. Sister Conchita would have to take his place. She bowed her head.

'*The Lord bless thee and keep thee,*' she intoned. '*The Lord make his face shine upon thee and be gracious unto thee: the Lord lift up his countenance upon thee, and give thee peace.*'

Conchita made the long descent to the ground and showed the carving to the waiting Sister Johanna.

'What is it?' she asked, brushing aside the elderly nun's expressions of concern and solicitude.

'It's a *knap knap*, a Roviana carving,' said Sister Johanna, examining the piece of shell. 'It has different meanings depending on the subject of the carving.'

'What does a frigate bird represent?' Conchita asked.

'That's a strange thing,' replied Johanna, frowning. 'It's a sign of peace from the old days. Sometimes when two tribes called a truce in their fighting, men designated to negotiate the peace would travel through enemy lines with the sign of the frigate bird strung around their necks or affixed to their foreheads. That allowed them safe passage. What would a magic man be doing with one of those?'

'I don't think it was his,' Sister Conchita said. 'My guess is that he took it from the body of the dead guide Kakaihe. When he told the villagers that Kakaihe had spoken to him after death, he meant that Kakaihe had given him a sign – that of a frigate bird on the *knap knap*. And Teiosi knew what that sign represented. It meant that in 1943, someone in the Roviana Lagoon wanted peace, perhaps even to stop fighting altogether.'

'Why on earth would Kakaihe want to discuss peace terms with anyone?' asked Johanna.

'I don't know,' said Conchita, 'but I've got a bad feeling about this place. I think we had better get back to our canoe.'

The two nuns began retracing their steps down the slippery track. Rain clouds darkened the sky. Soon it began to rain steadily. There was a rumbling noise further up the track. At first Conchita thought it was thunder. She looked round. A large boulder was hurtling with enormous velocity down the path.

'Jump!' shouted Conchita.

The nuns threw themselves off the path into the undergrowth. The boulder crashed past them, increasing in speed and crushing everything in its path. Soon it was lost from sight, but they could hear it continuing its descent. The sisters picked themselves up, mud-splattered and shaken, but unhurt.

'Did someone dislodge it deliberately?' asked Sister Johanna.

'I don't know,' answered Sister Conchita, 'but let's find that canoe as fast as we can!'

THIRTEEN

Kella followed the rest of the audience out of the Point Cruz cinema on Mendana Avenue at the end of the single performance for the evening. Expatriates and islanders alike began to scurry away to their parked cars or to their homes in the labour lines designated for government workers just outside the town.

Kella stood against a wall and let the others pass him. He was feeling tired. A few hours earlier, a Melanesian mission ship had deposited him at Point Cruz wharf. He had been lucky. The islanders on Baroraite had taken him by canoe to a mission station on Santa Ysabel, just as the *Selwyn* was preparing to leave. The voyage back to Honiara had taken two days. He had walked from the wharf to his hut in the fishing village on the outskirts of the town, washed and changed, packed another knapsack and walked back to ascertain that there was room on the charter flight leaving for Munda the following morning. He had booked a one-way ticket and then, unable to settle and not wanting to go home straight away, he had noticed that an American B Western was supporting the main feature at the Point Cruz cinema, known variously among the expatriate population of the capital, for obvious reasons, as the Flea Pit and the Bucket of Blood.

Kella loved all low-budget cowboy films, except the ones in which the hero sang to his horse. This evening's production had lived up to his expectations, as it had starred the Hollywood actor Wayne Morris, who in real life had flown a Hellcat in the Pacific during the war and who always looked to Kella to be that rarity among screen actors: a man big and ugly enough to handle himself in a genuine fight.

The only interruption to his enjoyment in the cinema had occurred after Morris's leading lady had been shot on screen and had tumbled gracefully to the ground. The ambience of the moment had been spoiled by the interjection of a Guadalcanal government clerk sitting at the back, who had shouted to the heartbroken hero in perfectly articulated English: 'Go on, whitey, shag her while she's still warm!'

This had aroused the ire of a bunch of Malaitans from the labour lines who had been sitting nearby. Objecting on principle to a man from another island raising his voice in their presence, they had started a fight with the Guadalcanal man, forcing Kella to climb over the backs of several rows of seats and slap a few heads with his open hand before a semblance of order could be restored.

Rather than risk the scuffle continuing during the interval, the projectionist had then gone straight into the newsreel. For once, the events being depicted were only a few months old. It showed scenes of the ending of the Mau Mau uprising in Kenya, Sputnik 4 being launched in Russia and a young Elvis Presley returning from army service in Germany. There was also coverage of a fresh-faced presidential candidate, 42-year-old John F. Kennedy, canvassing for votes among coal miners in West Virginia.

Kella studied the shots of the smiling young candidate with interest. The man seemed full of energy, although he was supposed to be suffering from a long-term back injury exacerbated by his experiences in the Roviana Lagoon. The announcer declared in passing that Kennedy's forthcoming campaign against the Republican candidate Richard M. Nixon seemed too close to call at the moment. Afterwards Kella sat through the main attraction, an American cop movie, with massive patience, then left the cinema.

'Hey, Kella, did you really stand me up on our last date?' asked

Mary Gui, coming out of the theatre behind him. She was wearing a floral print dress that clung to her trim figure.

'I got called away from Kolombangara unexpectedly,' said Kella.

'You mean some boy brought a telegraph all the way up the volcano to you? I hoped you tipped him well, going to that trouble.'

Kella smiled and started walking through the night crowds. Mary fell into determined step beside him. 'What did you think of the film?' she asked.

'Kirk Douglas had it made. Every time he needed information, he only had to make a telephone call from his precinct. I sometimes have to travel three days between witnesses. Plus he had a compassionate buddy and a tough but understanding lieutenant.'

'Ah,' said Mary, 'but were there any black detectives in sight?'

'No, just a black patrolman who Douglas ordered out of the way before sacrificing his life in an act of heroic folly for the good of his men.'

'You see,' said Mary. 'You've got some advantages. You haven't been asked to do that yet. When was the last time a white detective ordered you to step back on the edge of some volcano and let him justify his star billing.'

'Chance would be a fine thing. You don't find too many white cops on top of Mount Mahimba.'

'Exactly, so count your blessings.'

In spite of himself, Kella laughed. Mary took his arm. 'Buy me a drink,' she said impudently.

Kella looked around. They were opposite the almost sacrosanct elite Mendana Hotel. 'Are you kidding?' he asked lightly. 'Whitey doesn't like natives cluttering up his *tambu* spots, unless they're washing the dishes.'

'You-me nofella native,' said Mary, not moving. 'You-me first generation indigenous educated islanders.'

'And if we go into the Mendana, that's just what they might be putting on our gravestones.'

'I thought you were supposed to be brave,' Mary said.

Kella studied the girl's determined face. She seemed to be in deadly earnest. 'Do you really want to go in there?' he asked. 'I don't think you'll like it.'

'Sure I do. There's got to be a first time for everything. Come on.'

'But why?' asked Kella.

'Because,' said Mary, 'to the African retread, a permanent and pensionable colonial official now languishing in the South Pacific, in that hotel, I'm still just one generation away from being a jungle bunny, and I'm a lot more than that, don't you agree, Sergeant Kella?'

'Of course I do,' said Kella, feeling himself being propelled against his will by the sheer force of the girl's personality. 'As long as you're sure about this.'

'I say it's prejudice, and I say stuff 'em,' said Mary, crossing the road in the direction of the hotel.

'If you're certain it's not going to be a problem,' said an impressed Kella, following her.

'I didn't say it wasn't a problem,' said Mary seriously. 'It's probably going to be a hell of a problem, but if you and I aren't going to go in there, who will? Incidentally, afterwards I shall want full credit for my brazen and devil-may-care attitude.'

'You'll get it,' said Kella.

Mary took the policeman's arm again and they stepped into the quiet foyer of the Mendana Hotel. They walked past the reception desk with its clerk goggling at them, and out into the large, roofed but open-sided paved veranda running down to the sea. There were exotic potted plants around the edges of the dining area.

At this time in the evening, the dining room was busy. Expatriates in pairs and foursomes were sitting eating at the tables. There was a buzz of conversation, which died away when Kella and Mary appeared. They ran a gauntlet of disapproving looks from the white diners around them as they took their seats. At first Kella thought they were not going to be served. Then, from the knot of waiters in their long white lap-laps, one emerged and crossed the dining room towards them, shouldering the other waiters out of his way. He was a Lau man, squat and ugly in comparison with the handsome, light-skinned Western Solomons men who made up the rest of the serving complement.

'*Aofia*,' he said. 'What can I fetch you?'

Kella ordered a bottle of beer for himself and a Bacardi and Coke for Mary. Slowly the other diners resumed their conversations and started eating again, continuing to direct cold glances at the unfamiliar sight of the two islanders at their table.

Kella wondered if he should have allowed Mary to bring him to this white bastion. He would not have inflicted the embarrassment on any other local young woman, but he was interested to see how the newly returned Western girl would react to the colonial ambience. He suspected that not only would she rise to the occasion; she might even enjoy it. He had detected a vein of steely, single-minded ambition in Mary, but there was also an element of recklessness that she could probably trace back to her marauding forebears.

'What are you doing in Honiara?' he asked.

'It's my last day of freedom. Tomorrow I fly back to Munda to take up my job as warden of the rest-house. I'm staying with *wantoks* at Matanikau tonight. Now tell me, what really happened to you on Kolombangara? I looked for you when I got up the next morning, but there was no sign of you.'

'Was anyone else from the SIIP in the village with you?'

'Hardly. I was well off the beaten track, wasn't I? You know full well why I was up in the bush. I was getting the custom markings tattooed on my back from arse to shoulder. Why all the questions, Sergeant Kella? Did you bring me here to strike a blow for independence, or just to interrogate me?'

She stared at him defiantly. The Lau waiter brought their drinks. Kella paid him, and added a generous tip. The waiter grinned appreciatively and left.

'What are you going to do now that you've come home?' asked Kella. 'I don't suppose you're going to spend the rest of your life running the rest-house. You're one of the Solomons' first female graduates; you could practically write your ticket in the government service.'

'And sit on my pretty backside behind a desk for twenty years? No thank you. I'm going to climb the pole quicker than that, thank you very much.'

'You're a determined young lady. There's always politics.'

'Certainly, but not just yet, I fancy. The west is a very traditional district. Welchman Buna has got the Roviana seat sewn up for the next five years. I'll let him make his mistakes before I move in and challenge him.'

'So what does that leave?'

'You could say that I'm exploring my options,' said the girl evasively.

The drunken female voice that Kella had been half expecting since their arrival cut through the dining room imperiously.

'They're getting everywhere these days. The bloody people will be fox-hunting next,' it said, icy with condemnation. There was a peal of forced laughter from the others in the party.

Impassively Kella glanced across the room. He recognized a group of six at the next table. There were three administrators from the Education Department, stick-thin men, their faces a jaundiced yellow from the persistent injections against tropical diseases they had taken over the years in a variety of depressing dependent tropical territories. Their bored, upholstered wives were uniformly over-bosomed and fat-bottomed. Mary looked expectantly, almost gleefully, at Kella. He sighed, pushed back his chair and walked over to the table. With surprise and obvious alarm, the six expatriates saw him coming and sat up, stiff-backed. Two of the western waiters began to shuffle forward reluctantly. The Lau waiter sent them back effortlessly with one sweep of his arm. The room fell silent again as everyone waited and listened for what was to come.

Arriving unhurriedly at the table, Kella surveyed the occupants in silence. When he spoke, he pitched his voice so that everyone in the dining room could hear what he said.

'If you lot get on my tits again, I shall climb down from my tree in the jungle and come and live next door to you,' he said. 'So watch it!'

The six expatriates stared fixedly at the tablecloth before them. No one met Kella's eye. The policeman waited for a minute or two, and then nodded pleasantly and returned to his table. Mary Gui lifted her glass to him in a silent toast. The administrators and their wives started conducting a vehement conversation in hissed undertones. One of the wives stood up and stalked in an offended manner to the lavatories by the reception desk.

'Excuse me,' said Mary, standing up and slipping after the large woman.

The hotel manager, a lugubrious middle-aged Scot apparently beaten into a permanent state of submission by decades of dealing with arrogant colonial administrators around the world, appeared in the entrance, apparently summoned by the waiters. For years he had refereed the international rugby union matches regularly held on Lawson Tarma outside the capital. He wore a shiny dinner jacket and a permanently dejected expression, like a man who quite enjoyed and almost relished his secret sorrows. Kella wondered if he was going to be asked to leave. He saw that the Lau waiter was following the manager across the room. The manager noticed him and waved him away.

'I'm hoping that the rest of the customers will think I'm reprimanding you,' said the Scot, sinking into Mary's chair. 'So if you don't mind, I'll remain here a minute looking stern and exasperated. Is that all right with you, Sergeant Kella?'

'Be my guest,' said Kella.

'Actually, I've been thinking about that time you played wing forward for the Solomons against the New Hebrides. If you remember, on that occasion I sent you off for unnecessary violence to their French scrum-half. Since then we have had the honour of entertaining three separate French trade delegations in this establishment. I've changed my mind. How the hell can you be unnecessarily violent to a Frenchman?'

'A fair point,' said Kella. '*Vive l'entente cordiale!*'

The manager turned to the Lau waiter. 'Phillip, give the sergeant and his guest a drink on the house.'

'I won't, if you don't mind,' said Kella. 'I have a feeling that we might be leaving quite rapidly at any moment.'

'Point taken,' said the manager, rising. 'In that case, I shall withdraw to the sanctity of my office while I still have the chance. Phillip, call me when it's over.'

The Scot walked away, nodding affably to the rest of his patrons. The Lau waiter winked conspiratorially in Kella's general direction and went back to the suddenly agog group of waiters. Kella waited patiently, finishing his beer and draining Mary's glass for good measure.

There was a scream from the direction of the lavatories. The woman who had left the neighbouring table rushed out and stood, distraught and gibbering, at the entrance of the dining room. There was a large wet stain across the lower half of the back of her expensive dress. The other two wives at the table hurried over to her in clucking consternation. Once again the diners lost all interest in their meals and stared across in fascination at the tableau. The first woman was panting for breath and in a state of some shock, pointing back in the direction of the lavatories. When she could finally speak, she gasped:

'Someone leant across from the next stall while I was sitting down, and pulled the chain! My dress is soaked!'

The slim, demure form of Mary Gui slipped past the big woman, frowning concernedly. Kella stood up and walked across the room. He met Mary in front of the bewildered but appreciative waiters.

'Into each life a little rain must fall,' she said composedly.

'Sometimes quite unexpectedly,' agreed Kella.

On their way out of the hotel, they walked past the scandalized women, who had now been joined by their dithering husbands. None of them looked at Kella and Mary as the couple left.

'I should send for a policeman,' Kella advised them sympathetically, without stopping. Mary nodded her agreement.

The manager erupted from his office like an overstuffed bird popping out of a cuckoo clock. He bowed gravely to the departing couple.

'Sir, madam,' he said, straight-faced. Then he winked. 'If you keep coming here, they'll be charging me entertainment tax soon,' he said.

They undressed by the light of the oil lamp in Kella's hut in the fishing village just outside Honiara.

'This has been one of my more interesting evenings since I got back from Australia,' said the girl, pulling her dress over her head. 'Thank you for taking me to the Mendana. I've always wanted to go there, but you were the first islander with the guts to take me. I hope I didn't shock you.'

'I'm recovering,' said Kella.

Her dark, beautiful and unadorned figure ghosted past Kella. She lay naked on the bed, legs apart, staring up at him with anticipation.

'Let's hear it for a full and total recovery, Big Man,' she said.

'Flattery will get you anywhere,' Kella said, lowering his rigid body on top of her.

Mary moaned in grateful acquiescence. Then she gave a sharp scream and sat up abruptly.

'What's the matter?' asked Kella.

'I'd forgotten how sore my bloody back was,' groaned the girl, squirming from beneath him. 'Roll over; you'd better let me get on top.'

Kella rose early the following morning and washed and shaved. He dimly remembered Mary Gui getting up and leaving while it was still dark. It was a sign of her independence that she had probably walked all the way back to her relatives at Matanikau. He thought about the curious events of the previous night. Somehow he felt that both at the hotel and in bed afterwards, Mary Gui had been testing him. He ate a plate of taro and drank a bottle of water before putting on a change of uniform. Then he set out to hitch a lift to the airport at Henderson field.

After a few minutes on the almost empty road, a battered Ford stopped to pick him up. He climbed into the front seat with a word of thanks, to discover that the driver was the council member Welchman Buna, as smartly dressed as usual, this time in a tan safari suit.

'Well met, Sergeant,' said the politician. 'You can give me your preliminary report as we drive.'

Kella tried to give the other man a concise account of the events of the past few days. Buna listened in silence as they passed the Central Hospital on one side and the playing fields and the open-sided Anglican Melanesian mission cathedral on the other, until they reached the almost deserted wartime airstrip built by the Japanese. The two men walked into the departure lounge of the single-storey building in time to check with the Australian charter pilot that there was room for them on the waiting Piper Apache, and that they were scheduled to take off on time. The pilot left them with a wave to make his last-minute checks on the engine. Buna and Kella sat on one of the benches in the almost empty lounge. Next door, the transit lounge for incoming and waiting passengers housed only a solitary bored customs official.

'You've had a busy couple of days,' commented Buna.

'Frustrating mostly,' said Kella. 'And slightly embarrassing.'

'I go back to Roviana every month,' Buna said, as if the other man was due an explanation for his presence. 'The Legislative Council elections will be held in a few months; I have to canvas for votes.'

'Not easy to do when most of your constituency is water,' said Kella. 'How do you work that out?'

'Feasts,' said the politician simply. 'I go to every feast being held in the district. That's the Roviana custom. Being visible during kinship events is very important. How else would people get to know me? It may get me the votes, at least I hope it will, but it plays hell with my digestion.'

Kella wondered if the other man was joking, but Buna was not a humorous man. 'You'll walk in,' he said. 'You haven't got any opposition worthy of the name.'

Buna shrugged. 'I hope to be successful,' he said, 'but it's a long time since I lived in the west. I came to Honiara fifteen years ago. At least I don't think I've offended anyone back home yet. That's my best hope. I'm not a charismatic man. I just work hard for my district.'

Even in the heat of the noon sun the council member looked cool and composed. He sat very erect, not relaxing.

'May I ask you a few questions?' asked Kella.

'Certainly, Sergeant.'

'What do you know about the Solomon Islands Independence Party?'

'Not very much,' said Buna. 'It is based in my district, mainly at Munda and Gizo. It's comparatively new and not very influential yet. It consists mainly of local graduates returning from overseas universities, usually teachers and junior administrators. They sit around and have debates, pass motions, that sort of thing. They're not into direct action, if that's what you're thinking. I suppose that one day they will run a candidate to oppose me. A modern, educated progressive against an ignorant old bushman, you know the sort of thing.'

'Their candidate will have to eat a lot of pig at a lot of feasts before he whittles down your lead. And Mary Gui is their leader?'

'I believe so.' Buna smiled thinly. 'She is something of a firebrand, but she would never lead a raid on the logging camp, nor indeed leave a pile of excreta behind. At least I hope not. She has her principles, though. She refuses to take a post in government service. She earns a living by running the rest-house at Munda for Joe Dontate. Do you think she had a hand in knocking you unconscious on Kolombangara?'

'I'm not sure. It happened outside her hut. Her back had just been slashed to pieces by the tattooists, so she wouldn't have been in any state to attack me, or drag me back down to the beach. She might know who did it, though. I haven't made up my mind.'

'Doubtless you intend to get together with her?'

'I've already started work in that area,' said Kella.

'And you're going back to Munda to complete your investigations?'

'By rather a roundabout route, as it happens,' said Kella with feeling.

'I suppose one day Mary Gui and others like her will present a problem to me at the elections,' Buna said. 'Not yet, though. They are regarded as too callow and inexperienced. Whereas I lived in a saltwater village for the first twenty years of my life. I wouldn't have left even then if I hadn't been forced out by the war.'

'Did you fight in the west?' Kella asked.

'Not to your level of distinction, Sergeant Kella,' Buna said vaguely. 'I did my best to help out locally. Incidentally, I'm concerned about the part played in all this by the white man Ferraby. That man is a throwback to the 1930s when expatriates expected us to call them all master. He belongs in a museum. Will you arrest him?'

'What for? I can't prove anything.'

'Hmm, that's a pity. After the next elections, the elected members are going to have a lot more influence. I think as a matter of urgency we ought to look into the status of expatriates like Ferraby. They've outstayed their welcome in the islands. So you haven't made much progress with your investigations at the logging camp? That's disappointing – and not like you.'

'I'm going back there tomorrow to try again,' said Kella, shaking his head.

'You're persistent, Sergeant Kella; that's an admirable trait in a police officer.' Buna hesitated. 'That's another change we must make in the near future. We must fast-track the better men we already have in government service. If you handle this logging business efficiently and tactfully, it will be remembered in the right quarters, I can promise you. And I don't mean in Whitehall; I'm referring to here in the islands where all the decisions will be made before long. Find out who's launched this campaign against the loggers, and do so without upsetting anyone influential.'

'Would you like me to form a silver band to entertain the loggers at the same time?' asked Kella.

Buna showed no sign of recognising the levity in the other man's tone. 'And the attack on you at Kolombangara,' he asked, 'could it have been carried out by one of the islanders with a grudge against the police?'

'I doubt it,' Kella said. 'I was attacked by either a European or an islander with plenty of money.'

'What makes you think that?' asked Buna.

'Whoever knocked me out paid Ferraby in cash to hold me on his ship for a few weeks. None of the islanders on Kolombangara could have afforded that. I was taken down to the beach by someone with ready cash on him – or her.'

'Of course,' said Buna slowly. 'I hadn't thought of that. Are there many expatriates in the west at the moment, apart from the government workers at Gizo?'

'There's only an American tourist party stopping at Munda. I'm going to question them too, and Mary Gui, if she's come back.'

As he spoke, the girl entered the departure lounge. She was wearing a white blouse and a long floral skirt. Kella made as if to get up and walk over to her, but she shook her head almost imperceptibly and took a seat on the other side of the lounge, where she stared composedly ahead.

A voice over the loudspeaker announced the imminent arrival of the Fiji Airways flight from the New Hebrides. At the same time an official police car driven by a local officer pulled up outside the arrival and departure lounge. To Kella's horror, Chief Superintendent Grice, dapper in full uniform, got out of the back of the car and started walking towards the single-storey building. Presumably the superintendent was about to meet some dignitary from another police force. If he saw the sergeant, he would be sure to demand an explanation as to why Kella was setting off for Munda for the second time in just over a week. Like Buna, he would also ask for a progress report, which Kella, true to form, would be unable to provide.

'Excuse me,' said Kella, and dived for the Gents'.

He lurked inside for ten minutes until he had heard the two-turbo-prop-engined Fokker Friendship from Fiji land and discharge its maximum of forty-four passengers. He gave it another ten minutes for luck, and then emerged cautiously from the toilets. Chief Superintendent Grice and a uniformed chief inspector from the New Hebrides police force carrying a suitcase were walking towards the exit, talking animatedly. Grice saw his sergeant. He stopped talking and his eyes widened. Providentially, the loudspeaker then announced the departure of the local flight to Munda.

Kella sketched a desperate salute in the general direction of his superior officer and ran for the charter aeroplane waiting on the tarmac. As he did so, he noticed that Mary Gui had left her seat and was now sitting next to Welchman Buna and talking sedately to the Advisory Council member.

FOURTEEN

There were three men sitting in the office of the Secretary for Internal Affairs in Honiara. Robinson, the Secretary, was sipping a cup of tea behind his desk. Chief Superintendent Grice was sitting bolt upright in front of him. Occupying the third chair was a tall, stooped, grey-haired man in a lightweight suit.

'The Chief Secretary has asked me to convene this meeting,' said Robinson, 'while the Police Commissioner has designated Chief Superintendent Grice as his representative. I am also delighted to welcome Mr Sanders of the US State Department to Honiara.'

The grey-haired man bowed slightly. There was a sympathetic glint in his eye, as if he could recognize an example of the buck being passed when he saw it.

'Good afternoon, gentlemen,' he said. 'It's good to be here.'

'The purpose of the meeting,' continued the Secretary for Internal Affairs, 'is to correlate certain activities taking place in the Western Solomons and to ensure that we have covered our bases, if that is the expression, Mr Sanders.'

'Covered our arses, more like,' said Chief Superintendent Grice.

The Secretary for Internal Affairs winced. Sanders ignored the interjection. 'Exactly right, sir,' he said in a courtly fashion. 'As you both know, the whole affair is a delicate one and we need to make sure that we are on top of it at all times.'

'Buggered if I know what's going on at all,' said Grice. 'My department has been left pretty much in the dark.'

'Then I hope that matters will become clearer to you as the meeting proceeds,' said Robinson acidly. He nodded to Sanders to continue.

'I must apologize to you, Chief Superintendent Grice; there was no intention to leave you out of the loop,' said the American official. 'It was just that events started moving very quickly in the Roviana Lagoon and we had to react to them with equal rapidity before we all went to hell in a hand-basket. Anyway, I shall try to bring you up to date now. The body of Ed Blamire has been examined at an autopsy in Washington and it has been confirmed that he was killed by a blow to the head with a blunt instrument.'

'Murdered, you mean?' asked Grice.

'Oh yes, no doubt about that, no doubt at all.'

'Good God!' said Grice, aghast at the thought. 'A white man murdered in the Solomons.'

'I don't wish to appear too mercenary about this, but the cost must have been horrendous,' said the Secretary for Internal Affairs uneasily. 'Private chartered flights, autopsies, and all the rest of it.'

'I can set your mind at rest there, Mr Robinson,' said Sanders. 'The tab has been picked up by Mr Blamire's employers.'

'Who are they?' asked Grice.

'I'm afraid that has to remain classified for the moment,' Sanders said. 'What I can tell you is that their identity came as a bit of a surprise to my department. We weren't expecting intervention from that quarter.'

'What quarter?' asked Grice.

'Shall we say the private sector,' said Sanders. 'Still, we've been in touch with them and everyone seems happy. Or as happy as possible under the circumstances.'

'Please carry on, Mr Sanders,' said Robinson. 'We are anxious to ascertain whether there might be any repercussions from the death of this man Blamire.'

'I think we're fairly safe there,' said the official. 'He was a freelance. Ed Blamire had no official connections whatsoever, absolutely none. Nothing can be traced back to any of our sources.'

'That's a bit of luck,' said Robinson, brightening.

'But do you know who he was working for?' asked Grice.

'Oh yes, once we had his body, we were able to trace his background.' Sanders looked rueful. 'We may not have been able to keep Batista in power in Cuba last year, but we're still good for some things. We tracked down his employers and had a long and in the end satisfactory talk with them. As a result, we have a clearer idea of what is going on in the Roviana Lagoon at the moment. Again, I can't go into details.'

'Are you going to share any information with us?' asked Grice.

'I'm afraid that for the time being we have to proceed on a need-to-know basis,' said Sanders. 'I can assure you that this has been cleared at the highest levels between our respective governments, is that not so, Mr Robinson?'

The Secretary for Internal Affairs nodded but said nothing. Sanders continued. 'Of course, the people who sent Blamire to the Solomons will have to pour a few buckets of cash over his dependents, but they've done that in a number of similar cases in different parts of the world and can well afford it.'

'Quite so,' said Robinson.

Grice looked at the other two men and tried to nod sagely. He had heard of the phrase parallel universe and he wondered if he could be groping his way through one at the moment. Robinson and Sanders seemed to be having a perfectly normal conversation, yet he could hardly understand a word of what they were saying. He tried to think of an intervention that would give the impression that he was in touch, without betraying his complete ignorance of the situation.

'So where does that leave us at the moment?' he heard himself saying.

'That's a very good point, Chief Superintendent Grice,' said

Sanders approvingly, with no trace of irony in his voice. 'As you have just correctly implied, matters are still very much in the air in the Roviana Lagoon. There are some dangerous and ruthless characters floating around down there at the moment. We know from experience that they will kill without compunction, and we don't want that to happen.'

'Why don't we just deport the lot of them?' exploded Grice.

'If we did that, the political fallout would be drastic,' said Robinson, sounding shocked. 'It would be like knocking down the first in a row of dominoes. That's why we expedited the departure of Mr Blamire's body, to avoid any such reaction.'

'Quite so,' said Sanders. 'If it's any consolation, if anything's going to happen, it will occur in the next week or two.'

'What makes you think that?' asked Grice.

'Because of the date of the elections, of course,' said Sanders. 'Back home we go to the polls on the eighth of November. That's ten days away. If the people we're watching are going to come up with anything, it will almost certainly be in the next week.'

'What elections?' asked Grice.

'Why, the US presidential ones,' said Sanders, looking hard at the police officer as if wondering if he was serious, while Robinson squirmed. 'JFK against Dick Nixon is going to be a close one. Both sides are going to come up with all the dirty tricks they can muster. It's just unfortunate that they seem to have spread as far as the Solomon Islands.'

'It's difficult to comprehend that something as important as that might be influenced by what goes on in such a remote spot in the Pacific,' said the Secretary for Internal Affairs, shaking his head.

'Are you trying to tell me,' asked Grice, beginning to understand, 'that we have a bunch of murderers roving about in the Western District and we've done nothing to apprehend them?'

'That's the last thing we want to do,' said Sanders vehemently. 'We've got to find out what they're up to first and then stop them.'

'Exactly,' said Robinson.

Chief Superintendent Grice shook his head and closed his eyes, at a loss for words.

'That's why we've got to keep a close eye on things,' said Sanders a little more calmly. 'We think we've got a guy in place down there, but we can't be sure how effective he's going to be. We've had him there in readiness for a contingency like this one, but we've never had to use him before.'

'What about the native fellow, Dontate?' asked Robinson. 'By all accounts he's very close to Imison and the others.'

'Best we can figure it out, Joe Dontate's just a hired gun,' said Sanders. 'He's linked up with the others because they're paying him.'

'We could arrest him and take him out of circulation,' offered Chief Superintendent Grice.

'No!' said Sanders sharply. 'Our man down there has investigated him. Dontate's not just an opportunistic thug. He's what they call a Big Man in the Roviana area. He comes from a long line of warrior chiefs and headhunters, both matriarchal and patriarchal. If you move in on him, you could have an armed uprising among the locals.'

'You think?' asked Robinson in alarm.

'That's our best information. I suggest you watch Dontate but leave him alone,' said Sanders. 'It's complicated, I know. By the way, who have you got down there?'

'Where?' asked Grice.

'In the Roviana Lagoon, of course,' said Sanders. 'That's what we're talking about, isn't it?'

'Of course,' said Robinson quickly. 'We've had someone in place for a few days. Don't you remember, Chief Superintendent Grice? You gave Sergeant Kella his briefing in this very office?'

'Kella? Yes, of course,' mumbled Grice.

'You've only got a sergeant on the job?' frowned Sanders. 'This operation will take more weight than that, believe me.'

'He's our top Solomon Islands policeman,' Robinson assured him. 'He's unorthodox, but he can infiltrate places where no white officer would dare set foot. Isn't that right, Mr Grice?'

'Oh yes,' said Grice, speaking with conviction for the first time that afternoon. 'It never ceases to surprise me where Kella gets to and what he does when he gets there.'

FIFTEEN

'Has anyone seen Sister Brigid?' asked Conchita.

She was sitting at the evening meal in the refectory with Sister Johanna and Sister Jean Francoise. Brigid had not joined them at the table, a most unusual occurrence for her. So far the simple meal had been conducted in silence, with each nun occupied with her own thoughts. Earlier that evening they had listened to the local news programme on the Solomon Islands Broadcasting Service. That had been followed by a recorded episode of a Paul Temple thriller supplied by the BBC Transcription Service. Unfortunately the series had been supplied on half a dozen separate discs, an occurrence almost guaranteed to confuse the various local announcers on duty each night. Over the last five weeks the episodes had been played in the order of one, four, two, one again and three, a pattern which so far had rendered a fairly simplistic story positively labyrinthine, and had even led to a number of Honiara's expatriate community sending a delegate to the studios to request that the serial be started again from the first episode. ·

'I thought I saw her on the beach looking out at the lagoon earlier,' said Sister Jean Francoise.

Conchita folded her napkin and stood up. 'Excuse me,' she said. 'I'll just make sure she's all right.'

It was a cool, refreshing night out on the beach. Earlier in the day it had rained, and the leaves of the trees and bushes gleamed like unsheathed swords in the half-light.

Sister Brigid was standing on a small escarpment of rocks with the placid water lapping at her bare feet. She nodded as Conchita joined her.

'It's beautiful here,' she said. 'Who would think that the lagoon has suffered so much bloodshed and misery?'

'Are you all right?' Conchita asked.

'Why should I be anything else?'

'I was hoping that you would tell me that,' Conchita said.

Brigid looked away. 'I can't,' she said. 'I know that that doesn't make me a good nun, or even a good woman, but I can't talk about it.'

'It must be something very painful,' said Conchita.

'You don't know how painful,' Brigid said.

'Suppose I tell you what I have put together about what happened seventeen years ago,' said Conchita. 'Mr Evans, the coast-watcher on Kolombangara, put out an all-points radio message that an American patrol boat, the PT-109, had been sunk in a collision with a Japanese destroyer in the Roviana Lagoon. No one knew if there were any survivors. In fact, Lieutenant John F. Kennedy and ten of his crew, some of them wounded, had managed to swim to the island of Kasolo. Later they swam across to a larger neighbouring island called Olasana, which had more food. Evans asked for all available coast-watchers and their helpers to scour the area to find Kennedy and his men, before the Japanese got to them. Soon the area was buzzing with activity. At that time, the Japanese occupied Gizo, Munda and Kolambangara, while the US forces were preparing to launch a campaign to dislodge them. In the middle of all this, eleven American seamen were trying to hide from the Japanese and contact the Americans.'

'It was chaos,' said Sister Brigid. 'There were ships and aeroplanes everywhere, and you couldn't be sure which were American and which belonged to the Japanese.'

'You had been taking incredible risks helping to smuggle crashed

American airmen back to the Allied lines ever since you had arrived at Marakosi mission.'

'Wasn't I the feisty one?' said Sister Brigid indifferently.

'You heard over the mission radio schedule that Coast-watcher Evans was recruiting everyone he could get his hands on to rescue Kennedy and his men, and you wanted to join in.'

'I'd left it a bit late,' said the Irish nun. 'I'd only been at Marakosi for a year or so, and I didn't know the lagoon too well. By the time I got myself organized, most of the islanders I'd worked with before had scattered all over the place in their search. I needed a guide, and I was told that the only ones left who knew the area were on Kolombangara.' The nun shuddered. 'It was a dreadful place. I knew as soon as I got there that I'd made a terrible mistake. That island was evil incarnate.'

'But you found an islander willing to guide you.'

'Kakaihe, yes. He was very young, but he seemed keen. He begged me to let him paddle us both across to Olasana. That was the first island in the area that we chose at random.

'So you actually landed on Olasana while Lieutenant Kennedy and the others were there?' asked Conchita.

The other nun ignored her question. 'I was in such a hurry to get away from Kolombangara. You see, when I arrived there, I discovered that a detachment of Japanese soldiers had been stationed on the other side of the island. I think the islanders had invited them; I wouldn't put it past that treacherous lot. So I picked up Kakaihe and we paddled away for dear life.'

'And three days later you brought his dead body back home.'

'The Japanese had left by then, recalled to defend Gizo. I helped with the poor boy's burial service and came back to Marakosi.'

'You were in a pretty awful state by then,' said Conchita. 'What happened during the three days that you were away looking for Mr Kennedy?'

'I can't tell you that.'

'You mean you won't tell me.'

'Put it that way, if you like. Things were told to me during those three days, and I made promises myself. I shall keep those promises until my death, no matter what.'

'You're protecting someone, aren't you?' asked Sister Conchita.

'If it were only that, I wouldn't give a damn!' said Sister Brigid with a flash of feeling. 'But it's much more. I have been charged with saving a man's soul!'

SIXTEEN

Michie, the logging boss, had done something to improve security at the camp since Kella had last visited the island of Alvaro. Two of the improvements were heading in his direction now. As he stepped out of his canoe in the shallow waters of the lagoon, two large middle-aged white men strolled down the beach to meet him. They were wearing shorts and shirts and were unshaven. They walked with the confidence of men who hit other people for a living and did not get hit back very often.

'Hold it right there, mate,' said the leading man. He was distinguished from his partner mainly by the fact that he was the balder of the pair. He was probably balder than any man in the Roviana Lagoon, thought Kella, studying the expanse of naked skull drawing ever nearer like a polished battering ram. The man did not stop walking until he was very close to Kella. His breath stank.

'I'd like to see Mr Michie,' Kella said.

'No chance,' said the bald man. He started to edge forward, thrusting out his ample belly, in an attempt to force Kella back towards his canoe by sheer momentum.

'You don't understand. I'm Sergeant Kella, of the Solomon Islands Police Force. I'm here on official business.'

'No, it's you who doesn't understand, mate. We don't care if you're the fairy on top of the birthday cake,' said the other man, approaching Kella from the side.

The second man was taller than his partner. A faded, mottled scar ran down one side of his face, and his front teeth were broken and discoloured. Like his companion, he spoke with an Australian accent.

'We've got our orders,' said the bald man. He had been unable to dislodge Kella, so he had stopped shoving. He looked annoyed about the fact. 'No unauthorized visitors are allowed on the island. Things have changed since we arrived. We run a tight ship here these days. So go back where you came from.'

'Why should I? Have you thought that it might be nicer here?' said Kella mildly. 'Perhaps I prefer it.'

Both men looked disconcerted. They did not seem easily able to handle people who answered them back. The bald man put a hand on Kella's shoulder and pushed him. Kella sighed. Normally he was an equable man, but over the past few days he had been sandbagged from behind and press-ganged on to one of the most evil-looking and smelling cargo boats in the South Pacific. He had also met a girl who puzzled him, and Kella did not like being puzzled. He did not want such cavalier treatment to become a habit. Keeping his eyes innocently on the bald man's face, he jerked his elbow viciously into the stomach of the scarred man. The scarred man grunted and doubled up. At the same time, Kella took a step backwards and kicked the bald man in the groin. The bald man fell to his knees in the water with a splash. The scarred man straightened up and threw a roundhouse swing at the sergeant. Kella ducked beneath it and hit the scarred man in the stomach again, this time with a right-hand uppercut. The scarred man sat down abruptly in the lagoon and bent forward, retching. The bald man started to struggle to his feet. Kella let him move into a crouched position, and then brought his knee up in a parabola under the bald man's jaw. The man grunted, fell backwards and lay motionless, blood trickling down his chin. Kella looked down at the two men.

'When you get sent back home,' he said, 'and judging by your performance just now, that will be sooner rather than later, I should seek work in tougher pubs. You need the workout. You guys have got soft.'

The bald man lay where he was, moaning softly, but the scarred man started groping in the air, trying to drag himself up. There was a rush of oncoming feet, and a dozen or so Malaitans who had been dragging tree trunks across the beach charged over. Some were bearing sticks. At the sight of them the scarred man groaned and dropped back into the water. Kella waved the islanders off.

'Leave them alone,' he told them in dialect. 'Just make sure that no one disturbs me while I'm in with the boss.'

Michie was waiting for him in his office. The Australian was looking defiant, but he had backed off to the furthest wall.

'No more arsing around,' Kella told him. 'What's been happening? Why have you beefed up security, if that's the right phrase?'

'Orders from head office,' Michie said sullenly. 'I knew those two cowboys weren't worth a shit as soon as they arrived.'

'You just can't get the right sort of hired muscle these days,' said Kella unfeelingly. 'They're all too busy entering bodybuilding contests. But why did your head office in Japan decide that you needed more protection?'

Michie did not answer. Kella dropped into a chair. He was hungry. His plane had landed at Munda airstrip only an hour ago, and he had paddled straight over to the logging island.

'If I tell the Malaitans on this island to stop work for a week and to prevent your technicians from working as well, they'll do it. You know that, don't you?' he asked.

For a moment Michie looked defiant. Then his shoulders sagged and he sat down behind his desk. 'You'd do it, too, wouldn't you?' he asked. 'What sort of a copper are you?'

'Unusual,' said Kella. 'What's happened since I was last here to make you pull up the drawbridge?'

'There was a radio message from head office,' said Michie. 'They were afraid that local activists might be stepping up their operations against the island. So they sent those two so-called hard men over from one of their operations in Papua New Guinea to keep the place secure. A waste of space, the pair of them.'

'And?' prompted Kella.

'They said they were taking additional precautions at a higher level. They wouldn't tell me what that meant. That's all I know. You can tear the camp to pieces, I still wouldn't be able to tell you any more. Now will you kindly sod off? As if I haven't got enough on my plate, I've had orders to show a bunch of visitors round the place.'

Reflectively Kella walked back down to the water's edge. He had the feeling that many things at the logging camp had changed since his last visit to Alvaro. Fifty yards offshore, a launch was coming to a halt. Its distinctive appearance marked it as the fifty-two-foot-long vessel with a steel hull and an aluminium superstructure belonging to the Australian tourist company.

A dozen canoes propelled by Malaitan labourers were heading out to the ship. The Malaitans remaining on the beach had allowed the two big Australians out of the water to sit on one of the logs littering the beach. The bald man's jaw was swollen. The scarred man was hunched forward, holding his stomach. Kella paid no attention to them. He saw Zoloveke, the older Malaitan who had taken him to the temple in the bush on his previous visit, and beckoned him over. Zoloveke came forward grinning, followed by a few more islanders. He jerked his head in the direction of the two stricken white men.

'The next time you decide to do that, tell me first so that I can come and watch,' he said happily.

'Have there been any other visitors here since I last came?' Kella asked.

'You think I spend all day on the beach like a Chinaman waiting for customers?' asked Zoloveke. 'How would I know? I'm a working man.'

'I saw someone a few days ago,' said a younger islander in Lau, coming forward. 'I was working here on the beach when he arrived.'

'What were you doing on the beach?' asked Zoloveke. 'Were you licking whitey's arse again?'

The young man ignored the older one. There was an undercurrent of animosity between them. Perhaps Zoloveke suspected that the younger islander had ambitions to challenge his leadership among the Malaitan labourers on the island.

'What did you see?' Kella asked, before a quarrel could develop between the two men.

'Boss Michie came down to the beach to meet him. This made me think that he was a big man. He spent much time in Boss Michie's office.'

'What was this visitor like?'

The young islander bit his lip with the effort of concentrating. Zoloveke jostled him impatiently to hurry the young man up. The islander refused to be rushed. 'Blackfella,' he said after a while. 'A Roviana man, but I see him often in Honiara as well.' He abandoned his native language which did not contain the words he was seeking, and broke into pidgin. 'Plenty talk-talk long bigfella house. Himi luluai.'

'Luluai,' Kella said. 'He was a talk-talk man, a politician?'

'Him now,' said the young islander triumphantly. 'Politisen!'

'What did he look like?'

The young islander was in full flow now. He seemed eager to display his knowledge of pidgin, while Zoloveke stood frowning disapprovingly in the background.

'Hair bilong himi grey. Himi gottim mouthgrass. No catchim tuhat,' he said.

'A politician with grey hair and a beard, who did not sweat,' said

Kella. There was no doubt about it, the young islander had just described Welchman Buna.

The canoes were returning from the launch. Each one contained a white man or woman sitting behind the islander paddling. When they reached the shallow water, the Malaitan jumped out and signalled to his passenger to climb on to his back. Galloping through the spray, the islanders carried their white passengers piggyback and deposited them gently on the warm sand. Kella noticed Joe Dontate following behind the others, walking unhurriedly through the water. This must be the American tour party from Munda that he had heard about, he thought.

'Welcome to Alvaro logging camp,' boomed Michie, walking down the beach. 'If you folks will just follow me to the company store, refreshments will be waiting for you, and then I'll give you a conducted tour of the island. This way, everyone.'

Chattering animatedly, the tourists straggled up the beach after the logging boss. Most of them cast curious glances at the battered security guards slumped on the log. Michie ignored the two Australians.

'I see that you've been doing your bit for community policing again,' said Joe Dontate, stopping and indicating the two guards.

'It's a dirty job, but somebody's got to do it,' said Kella.

Michie was ushering the tourists into the company store. The Malaitans were dragging their canoes up on to the beach and dispersing to their jobs. Dontate did not move. He was wearing shorts and flip-flops. The long, smooth muscles of a professional athlete rippled effortlessly across his bare torso.

'When are you going to stop picking on amateurs and see what you can do against me?' Dontate asked.

'Whenever you can fit me into your busy schedule,' said Kella. 'They tell me you're too concerned with getting rich at the moment.'

Dontate grunted and turned away. He followed the tourists into the store. Kella watched the former boxer go. Dontate was right.

One day the pair of them would clash. In the meantime, like Dontate, he had more important things to do. What had Welchman Buna been doing at the logging station? There were no votes to be garnered here. Kella also wondered about the tour party. It seemed to be turning up all over the lagoon. The visitors would have an excuse for being almost anywhere. There were still too many loose ends to be put together.

He pushed his canoe down the beach into the lagoon. Next he would look for Welchman Buna and ask the politician what he had been doing at the logging camp just before Jake Michie had increased the security arrangements there.

SEVENTEEN

The airstrip at Munda was crowded for so early in the morning when Conchita tied up her canoe at the wharf and walked up the slope. Eight or nine American tourists were waiting for the flight to take them back to Honiara. Joe Dontate was helping a couple of islanders to bring their luggage from the rest-house and take it down to the beach. Later it would be rowed out to a launch to follow the tourists to the capital. Clark Imison and his two partners were sitting on the ground in a semicircle apart from the other Americans, talking earnestly and ignoring the bustle. An attractive, self-assured Melanesian girl in a white dress walked across to Conchita with a welcoming smile.

'Good morning, Sister,' she said. 'I'm Mary Gui, I supervise the rest-house. Were you looking for a room?'

'No thank you,' said the nun. 'I've just come over from Marakosi to pick up a consignment of quinine for our clinic on the morning flight. You look busy. Is everyone leaving?'

'Most of the Americans are flying back to Honiara,' said the girl. 'Just a few are staying on for a couple more days.'

'Let me guess,' said Conchita. 'Mr Imison and his two friends are remaining in the west.'

'That's right; how did you know?' said Mary. 'They must like it here. They've hired Joe Dontate to give them a special tour of the lagoon for the rest of the week. They want to go to Kasolo and Olasana in particular. I can't think why, there's nothing at either place, not even a village.'

The too offhand way in which she pronounced the islander's name made Conchita wonder if the girl's feelings for the former boxer were more than casual.

'I believe that they are two of the islands where John F. Kennedy was stranded in the war,' she said.

'Really?' asked Mary, in a tone that expressed her lack of interest in the subject. 'The war's been over a long time.'

'The past is important to some people,' said Sister Conchita. 'The time before can mean a great deal.'

'Not to me,' said Mary. 'That's the trouble with this place. Too many people are living in the past. Still, it's good business for Joe, running his tours.'

That should be fun, thought Conchita, remembering how Dontate had expressed his low opinion of the three Americans the last time she had visited the rest-house. Still, the islander would do almost anything for money, and presumably Imison and the others would have a plentiful supply of dollars.

'I'm sorry about your open day,' Mary said. 'It was going really well until that dreadful accident.'

'Were you there?' asked Sister Conchita.

'Sure, who wasn't? We don't get many social events in the lagoon.'

'You've been busy this week,' said Sister Conchita. 'This can't be an easy place for a woman to run.'

'It's hard enough being a woman anywhere in the world,' said Mary. 'In the Solomon Islands it's like pushing a pea uphill with your nose.' She stopped, as if she had said too much. She looked at her watch. 'I'd better go and make sure our guests haven't left anything in their rooms,' she said. 'Excuse me.'

The girl walked back into the rest-house. She was tough-minded and independent to a degree far beyond that of the usual Solomons woman, thought the nun. She could not make up her mind if she liked Mary Gui on such short acquaintance. She certainly had a strong personality. It would probably depend upon whether she was on your side or not. Glancing through the open door of the rest-house, the nun took in the layers of dust everywhere and the frayed and stained woven mats on the floor. Whatever her other qualities, Mary Gui did not seem to rate good housekeeping highly among them.

Conchita stood unobtrusively in the shelter of the eaves, looking on at the bustle of events around her and missing little. Mrs Pargetter, the plump tourist, saw her and waved. The nun waved back but did not walk over.

'Good morning, Sister Conchita,' said a voice in her ear.

Conchita turned. Welchman Buna had stepped out of the rest-house. As usual the politician was immaculately dressed. His khaki drill trousers were pressed to a knife-edge and he was wearing a white shirt that refused to wilt in the sun.

'I'm beginning to think that if I stay here long enough I'll meet everyone I've ever known,' said Sister Conchita, shaking the man's offered hand.

'The rest-house does indeed tend to be an obligatory focal point for visitors to the Roviana area,' agreed the politician.

'Something like Purgatory,' said Conchita.

Before she could say anything else, Mrs Pargetter left her group and fluttered over to them. 'Sister,' she said. 'Come to see us off? That's might gracious of you.' She turned her attention to the Advisory Council member. 'Mr Buna, how nice to see you again! This is almost like having an official delegation to bid us goodbye.'

Buna looked politely puzzled. Mrs Pargetter shrieked with affected laughter. 'Why, you naughty man,' she chided. 'I do believe you've forgotten me already. We met at the open day at Sister Conchita's mission. We were in the church and I asked you a question about the carved crucifix on the wall. You were very gracious and told me all about it.'

'Yes, of course,' said Buna. 'How could I forget?'

'I didn't know you were at the open day,' said Conchita. She seemed to be learning something new every minute this morning.

'It was very crowded,' said the politician dismissively. 'I didn't stay long. Now, if you will forgive me, ladies, I must be on my way. I have a number of villages to visit on foot on the island today in my perennial search for votes. Glad-handing, I believe you Americans call it. Then I have arranged to meet the estimable Sergeant Kella and the District Commissioner in Gizo tomorrow afternoon to discuss the annoying raids on the logging camp. No peace for the wicked!'

He nodded and walked towards the fringe of trees at the far end of the airstrip. He stopped when he reached Imison and the two other American men, and sat down cross-legged in their circle, talking earnestly for some minutes. Then he stood up, nodded and continued on his way.

Joe Dontate saw him and left the pile of luggage he was guarding, in order to greet the politician. They spoke urgently in undertones for a few minutes. Buna seemed to be pleading with Dontate, while the ex-boxer was shaking his head obdurately. Buna put a placating hand on the other man's shoulder. Dontate shook it off angrily. Buna shrugged and continued on his way. Soon he was out of sight among the trees.

'Mr Buna is such a nice man,' said Mrs Pargetter, oblivious to what had been going on by the trees.

'That's right,' agreed Conchita absently. 'Tell me, when you were in the church with him, was Mr Blamire there as well?'

'I believe he was,' said the tourist, screwing up her face in concentration. 'I think he was sitting on one of the benches by the altar rail. I guessed he was probably praying, so I didn't disturb him. That was odd really. I'd never taken Ed Blamire to be a religious man. Perhaps he had problems. My husband used to say that there were no atheists in the trenches, though how he knew that I don't know, because to my certain knowledge Wendell never went near a trench in his whole service life. A few bars, certainly, but trenches, never. It could be, I suppose, that if we're in trouble, the most unlikely of us turn to God as a last resort. No offence, Sister. Oh, there's our plane. I must be off. It was nice meeting you. If you're ever in Baltimore, look me up.' Mrs Pargetter indicated Imison and his companions with disfavour. 'And keep away from those three. They're bad medicine, I can tell. Snake-oil salesmen with attitudes, that's all they are! So long, honey.'

The lumbering twin-piston-engined de Havilland lumbered over the lagoon, steadily losing height. It taxied to the end of the runway and stopped. The only passenger to descend was Andy Russell, the VSO. He was carrying a box with a hospital green cross on the lid. A young pilot who did not look as if he could possibly be much more than twelve years old began to supervise the waiting passengers on to the aircraft. Dontate and the two islanders came back from piling the luggage on the beach. Andy reached Sister Conchita in a coltish jumble of long legs and handed her the container with a shy grin. He was as lathe-thin as ever, but he was looking much better than he had done the last time the nun had tended him at the mission clinic.

'Good morning, Sister,' he said. 'They asked me at Number Nine if I'd bring these medical supplies back for you.'

'Thank you, Andy,' said Conchita, accepting the package. 'Have you been ill?'

'No, I'm fine. The DC sent me over to Honiara for a check-up after I got back to Gizo from Marakosi, but you'd already fixed me up great. I hitched a flight back here on the charter.'

So her representations to the District Commissioner had had some result, Conchita thought. At least the official had been concerned enough to make sure that Andy was all right. Number Nine was the sobriquet of the Central Hospital just outside the capital, so-called because it had been established on the site of the ninth field hospital in the Solomons during the war.

'I don't know if they've sent a boat to take me back to Gizo,' said Andy, looking hopefully in the direction of the wharf. 'What the heck, I've been stranded in worse places than this.' He caught Conchita's eye. 'Sorry! Constant flippancy can be annoying, can't it? It's just a defence mechanism.'

The de Havilland wasted no time. It began to taxi along the airstrip and then took off economically with its crew of two and load of tourists. Soon it was just a dot across the lagoon. At the last moment Mary Gui came out of the rest-house and perfunctorily waved the passengers off. Dontate walked back from the wharf, dismissing the two islanders who had been helping him, slipping some notes into their hands. As he passed Mary Gui, he put an arm around her waist. She shook it off expressionlessly. Dontate looked aggrieved and sat down with Imison and the two remaining Americans.

Conchita wondered how many other people she knew had been present at the mission open day besides Welchman Buna. And how many of them had encountered Ed Blamire as he sought sanctuary in her church? She turned back to Andy Russell. She decided that she needed to swallow her pride and ask for help. It was something she should have done earlier.

'I'll take you back to Gizo in my canoe,' she said. 'You'll have to wait for half an hour while I write a letter, and then we can go. There's a favour I'd like you to do me as well. Is there anywhere around here where I can get some writing paper and an envelope?'

Andy opened his holdall and took out some creased paper and an envelope. He rummaged in the holdall again and produced a stump of a pencil and gave it to the nun.

Then nodding without any visible signs of curiosity, he headed for the shade of the rest-house. Mary Gui grinned at the VSO and went back inside with him. Conchita saw Joe Dontate glaring across at the building. It looked as if Miss Gui was capable of playing the field, thought the nun. However, she would probably be ill advised to trifle with the volatile ex-boxer's affections. She looked at the writing paper Andy had given her. It was unused, and bore the printed heading SIIP.

As she started to compose her letter, the nun wished that she could turn to Father Pierre for help, but he was back at Ruvabi mission on Malaita. Conchita knew that there was only one other person with the experience to help her, and that was Ben Kella. She would have to hope that he had forgotten how coldly she had treated him on his last visit to Marakosi because he had seemed so much at home in the company of the other nuns. Her pencil travelled quickly over the paper as she described the events of the last ten days, ever since the open day at the mission. She described Ed Blamire's terror as he waited in the church for death to arrive, and the stories of the quarrels he had had with Imison and the other Americans. She wrote of Imison's interest in the dead scout Kakaihe and of the rumours of the latter's connections with the young Lieutenant John F. Kennedy. She depicted Sister Brigid's traumatized state and her refusal to discuss the last fateful journey in the Roviana Lagoon that had resulted in the scout's death. She went into some detail about the shell *knap knap* with the picture of the frigate bird that she had found among the dead magic man's possessions. She mentioned the discovery of the war club with the tissues of blood and hair embedded in it. She tried to leave nothing out, including the refusal of the authorities to take any interest in the affair. Discarding all reticence, she begged the police sergeant to advise her on what she should do to bring the killers of Ed Blamire to justice.

Conchita sealed the letter in the envelope, said a little prayer and sat patiently waiting for Andy Russell to emerge from the rest-house.

EIGHTEEN

'We won't stop here long,' said Sister Conchita reassuringly, noticing the VSO's growing unease. 'I'd just like to see the island properly. I've heard so much about it.'

Andy nodded but did not turn round. He was hunched in the prow of the canoe, staring across the water of the lagoon at Kasolo island. Not a happy bunny, decided Conchita.

Perhaps she should not have asked the boy to come with her, thought the nun contritely. Obviously he had bad memories of his enforced sojourn on the island, forgotten by the authorities. However, he would know the place thoroughly, and should be able to guide her across it. It would do him no harm to spend another hour on Kasolo.

'I'd just like you to show me the island,' she said. 'There's nothing like having a personal guide.'

'All right, but this place gives me the creeps,' said Andy. 'What's so special about it?'

'This was where John F. Kennedy took refuge during the war.'

'Who's John F. Kennedy?'

'Some people think he's going to be the next president of the USA.'

'Sounds like he's got better job prospects than I have,' said Andy gloomily. I don't think the DC is going to give me much of a reference when my time's up here.'

'Believe me,' said Sister Conchita confidently, 'Mr Maclehose will give you an absolutely glowing testimonial. I guarantee it. What are you going to do when you get back home?'

'I've got a place at Cambridge,' said Andy.

'So you couldn't manage Harvard? No, really, I'm impressed. What made you want to come to the Solomons for a year?'

'It sounded exotic.'

'The islands are that all right, if you don't die of sunstroke or snakebite or fever first.'

Andy laughed. Sister Conchita cut out the engine. The VSO picked up a paddle and steered the canoe through the sharp rocks of the lagoon. He stepped out into the shallow water and dragged the canoe up on to the beach, then stood looking about him without enchantment as Sister Conchita got out of the canoe.

'I never thought I'd come back here,' he said with a shudder.

'I'm sorry; it must have real bad memories for you. I promise you we won't stay a minute longer than we have to. I just wanted to see what all the fuss was about.'

'I didn't make a fuss,' said Andy indignantly.

'Of course you didn't. I was referring to Kennedy and the other ten men from the PT-109.'

'What's the PT-109?'

'Stop it; you're making me feel old! I'll explain it to you later. Do you want to give me the full tour of the island?'

'Sure, it should take all of twenty minutes,' said Andy.

In the event, it took just over half an hour. Conchita retraced her steps over the route she had taken when she had first gone ashore to Andy's aid. Even after such a brief time, most of the signs that either of them had been there had vanished, a sign of how fragile human incursions into the island were. The trampled grass had sprung back into place. The fire upon which the VSO had cooked his fish was now only a heap of cold ash. Only his tent remained in the clearing.

Andy led the way through the trees and took the nun from one side of the island to the other. Conchita could see no indication that Kennedy and his crew had ever landed on Kasolo. If most signs of the VSO's habitation had disappeared in a few days, what chance would there be of finding any references to the crew of the PT–109 seventeen years earlier?' After all this time, it would have been foolish to expect to discover anything. The whole visit was turning into an anticlimax. She had been looking forward to visiting Kasolo, but it was just one island among hundreds like it.

Conchita was about to apologize to the VSO and suggest that she take him back to Gizo when she heard the sound of an approaching engine out in the lagoon. With Andy at her shoulder, she made her way through the trees until she could see the water. The tourist launch was a few hundred yards away, getting closer. It was being steered by Joe Dontate, with Imison and the two other American tourists behind him, staring ahead at the atoll.

'What are they doing here?' asked Andy.

'Hush!' said Sister Conchita. 'Let's wait and see.'

The launch could not get as close as Conchita had been able to with her canoe. Dontate was forced to approach from another direction and stop the vessel some way out. He lowered a small anchor and jumped over the side. The calm water came up to his chest. Imison and the other Americans joined him and started wading ashore, taking care to avoid the jagged edges of the coral reef. One of them was carrying a small box wrapped in greaseproof paper. He held the container high over his head to avoid contact with the water.

Sister Conchita watched intently as the four men reached the beach. The three Americans stopped on the shore, but Dontate continued to walk inland until he reached the trees and was then lost to sight. Imison issued orders to the other two men, and they opened the box. There seemed to be a number of small objects inside. Imison pushed the others to one side and selected one of the objects, putting it in his pocket. Then he spoke curtly to his companions, and the three men started walking towards the trees. One of them picked up the box carefully and took it with him.

'Sister Conchita,' said a voice from the trees. 'The praying Mary spying on others? For shame! What will the Bishop say?'

Conchita and Andy turned to see Joe Dontate surveying them with caustic enjoyment. 'I saw your canoe from the trees,' he said. 'You were so busy, you didn't hear me coming up behind you.'

Dontate called out. After a few minutes, Imison and the other two men blundered into sight through the undergrowth. None of the Americans looked pleased to see the nun and the VSO.

'What the hell are you doing here?' asked Imison.

'I wanted to see what all the fuss was about,' said Conchita, trying to sound casual. 'I've heard so much about Kasolo that I asked Mr Russell to show it to me.'

'They must have seen us,' said one of the Americans, a slim man who looked as if he had to shave twice a day.

'There was nothing to see,' said Dontate quickly. 'You came ashore in a properly constituted touring party, with a well-known local guide. What can anybody make out of that?'

'Too many things are going wrong,' said Imison. 'We're not tidying up as well as we're supposed to. Maybe we should make a start.'

'That would be overkill,' said Dontate. 'This is a small place. Things get noticed. Don't do anything hasty.'

'I don't like it,' said the dark-chinned American. His companion grunted assent.

'Lot of things I don't like,' said Imison. 'Being stuck with you two, for a start. Nothing I can do about it.'

'Well, we've had our little excursion,' said Sister Conchita as nonchalantly as she could. 'I think we should be on our way now, Mr Russell. A lot of people are expecting us.'

'Are they?' asked Andy.

'Oh, yes; I have to take a consignment of medicine back to the mission hospital, and the District Commissioner is waiting for you to get back from Honiara today. We'd both be missed. Very quickly, too.'

'Oh, I see what you mean,' said the VSO eagerly. 'Yes, that's right. A lot of people at the airstrip must have seen me get off the plane this morning.'

Imison gnawed at his lip, trying to come to a decision. Finally he nodded to Dontate.

'Best be getting back to your fan clubs, then,' said Dontate to Conchita and Andy. 'We wouldn't want any broken hearts on account of you being missing.'

The islander stood to one side to allow the nun and the VSO to walk away down to the beach. Imison and the other two Americans looked unhappy about the situation, but made no effort to prevent them from leaving.

Conchita said no more until she and Andy had pushed their canoe back into the water and she had started the outboard engine and was steering them back towards Gizo.

'What was that all about?' asked Andy.

'I'm not sure,' said Conchita.

'It was almost like they were going to stop us leaving.'

'Surely not,' said the nun. It would not do to alarm the boy, but for a few moments back on the island it had looked to her as if Imison and his men had been contemplating killing the pair of them in case they had seen anything untoward. It was only Joe Dontate's intervention that had saved them. Sister Conchita knew that inexorably she was getting out of her depth. It was time she brought in the bigger guns. She opened the briefcase at her feet and took out the letter she had written at Munda. She handed the envelope to the VSO.

'When you get back to Gizo, I'd like you to look for Sergeant Kella, the policeman. You'll find him at the District Commissioner's office tomorrow. Please give him this.'

NINETEEN

Kella could hear the man's voice raised in anger as he walked up from the beach towards the plantation house on the hill. He had seen the motorized barge at anchor some way out in the lagoon, and had guessed what was about to happen. He hoped that he had arrived in time to prevent bloodshed.

The path up from what was left of the wharf veered sharply. Round the bend, Kella saw an emaciated middle-aged man menacing with a shotgun two larger, younger and definitely uneasy white men.

'Take it easy, Dad,' said one of the younger men.

'I'm not your dad,' snarled the emaciated man. He lifted the shotgun, his finger curling speculatively round the trigger.

'Easy!' shouted Kella.

He reached the group and placed his hand on the barrel of the gun, forcing it down until it was pointing to the ground. At first the emaciated man struggled, but then he relaxed, the fight running out of him like sand in an egg timer.

'The old bastard was going to shoot us!' shouted one of the younger men, emboldened by the emaciated man's obvious sense of defeat.

'If he wanted to shoot you, you'd both be dead by now,' Kella told him. He nodded to the older man. 'Hello, Mr Hickey. Seeing off the scrappers again?'

'Thieving sods,' muttered the emaciated man. Suddenly he looked very tired.

'I'm Sergeant Kella, Solomon Islands Police Force,' Kella told the two younger men. 'I take it you're scrap-metal merchants from Brisbane?'

'We came ashore to make the owner a genuine offer for his war relics,' said the younger man who had done all the talking so far. 'He charged out of the house and waved that bloody blunderbuss at us.'

'Liars!' snarled the middle-aged man. 'They were walking straight past the house to start loading up without my say-so.'

'When we saw the house, we thought it was abandoned, so we went on,' said the younger man. 'Well, look at the state of the place! It was a perfectly genuine mistake.'

'That's enough,' said Kella. 'This plantation belongs to Mr Hickey. Nothing on it is for sale. Go back to your barge and move on. And be careful how you behave in the lagoon. I shall be putting out a radio message warning people to keep an eye open for you.'

'Sod him, he's only a *kanaka* policeman,' sneered the man who had not spoken so far.

'That's true,' said Kella. 'But I think you'll find that this is a *kanaka* country, if you live long enough.'

The two men slouched away down the track to the beach. Hickey stooped and picked up his shotgun. He aimed it in the air and pulled the trigger. The noise of the explosion sent birds wheeling and screaming. The two scrap-metal dealers broke into an undignified run, sliding down the path to the beach. Hickey started to climb the steps into his house.

'That's telling 'em,' he said. 'Come inside, mate. Long time no see.'

They entered the living room of the planter's house. The building was raised on top of four hardwood piles on the side of a hill five miles along the coast from Gizo. A large veranda occupied the front of the house, with a sweeping view of the sea below. The building had a galvanized-iron roof and large windows with

171

wooden shutters. Efforts had once been made to surround the house with a lawn, but it was now a neglected and overgrown sprawl of kunai grass and weeds.

'You'll probably remember this place when it was at its peak,' said Hickey bitterly. 'Changed a bit, hasn't it? Drink?'

'It's a little early in the morning for me,' said Kella.

'It's never too early,' said Hickey, refilling his glass. He was a slight, narrow-shouldered man in his fifties, bare-chested and wearing long white shorts and scruffy sandals. He had not shaved for several days.

'When were you last here?' he asked.

'Not since the war,' said Kella. 'That's what I want to talk to you about.'

'You're a bit young to be writing your memoirs,' said Hickey. The planter was not drunk, but his speech was beginning to sound slurred. 'Did you pick up any mail for me in Honiara?'

'There wasn't any.'

'Sod it!' Hickey indicated a bamboo table covered with handwritten sheets of paper. 'You'd think that Government House would reply to at least one of my bloody letters.'

'What are you writing to the High Commissioner about?' asked Kella, although he already knew the answer to his question. Hickey's vendetta with the government was common knowledge.

'What the hell do you think I'm complaining about?' said Hickey, indicating the view of his plantation through the open window with a sweep of his arm. 'Compo, mate, that's what I'm after, compo! I'm due a bagful and it's well overdue. I've been asking for it for donkeys' years. Do they pay me a blind bit of notice? Do they buggery!'

'Haven't they paid you any compensation at all yet?' asked Kella. 'That's bad.'

'Bad, it's a bloody tragedy! How am I expected to live? Planters in Papua New Guinea have been repaid in full for war damage done to their estates. Those of us unlucky enough to live in the Solomons have had zilch! Come with me and I'll show you the state the place is in.'

As they walked out of the room, Kella noticed a box containing half a dozen sticks of dynamite stored carelessly under the table. It was possible that the planter was using the explosive to make structural alterations to his grounds, but it was more likely that he was employing the sticks to stun dozens of fish at a time in a local river or lake and thus accumulate enough to send to the market at Gizo. Hickey followed his gaze.

'Going to lock me up, Officer?' he asked.

'Not if you give me what I've come for,' Kella said.

He followed the other man out of the house. It had been more than fifteen years since he had last visited Hickey's home, but the change certainly was staggering. Once the Australian's plantation had been a byword for order and efficiency. Regimented rows of carefully tended palms had been spaced with scientific precision to allow coconuts to be harvested and the copra extracted with a minimum of fuss. The drying sheds for the copra meat had been painted. Now the area was an expanse of raw and gutted wasteland. The trees had been felled and their roots torn out by bulldozers so that the whole area could be transformed into a Japanese army camp. The camp had gone in its turn, leaving only the debris of its former occupants.

To one side of the campsite extended an airstrip of crushed coral, running the entire length of the plantation. The rest of the ground area was covered with flat concrete slabs, which had formed the bases for barrack rooms and administrative buildings. The few palm trees that had been left around the fringes of the camp had been neglected. Coconuts had been allowed to fall from the trees and lie in rotting piles on the ground.

'The Yanks didn't even bother to invade the place in 1943,' said Hickey. 'They just bombed it to smithereens and then starved the

Japs out over a period of months. This is what they left – the few who were still alive.'

Scattered over the ground were the rusted, twisted remains of military hardware. There were rusted shell casings, searchlights, barbed wire, bloated rubber wheels and gas cylinders. They had all been crudely hacked with saws and axes so that the more valuable parts of the metal could be wrenched off and loaded on to barges.

'The Japanese didn't leave much of any use to you,' said Kella.

'That wasn't the Japs, that was the bloody scrappers,' said Hickey. 'As soon as the war ended, they sailed up from Australia and swarmed over the place like vultures. By the time I got back here, all the good stuff had been loaded and taken, and I was left with this useless rubbish.'

Hickey plodded on ahead, shaking his head at every fresh piece of evidence of depravations to his estate. He had had an eventful war. When the fighting had reached the Western Solomons in 1942, he had climbed into the hills behind Gizo. From there he had reported on Japanese troop, ship and aircraft movements over a cumbersome three-hundred-pound teleradio, operated by storage batteries but capable of transmitting for a range of four hundred miles. He had been so good at his job that he had been smuggled out to Townsville in Queensland to monitor and correlate all the incoming coast-watchers' reports from the Solomon Islands. After that he had joined the Australian army and served as an infantry officer in New Guinea. He had not returned to his plantation for two years, by which time it had been reduced to its dilapidated present condition. He had been affected so deeply that he had made no effort to return his grounds to their previous effective state. Kella had no idea how he had been scraping a living ever since.

'Anyway, what did you want to know?' Hickey asked, examining the shattered fuselage of a Japanese floatplane.

'I want to know what really happened in the search for the crew of PT-109,' said Kella. 'You know better than anybody what went on.'

'What are you asking me for? You were here at the time.'

'Not in August,' said Kella. 'We were looking for a Japanese landing barge off Rendova for the first two weeks.'

'Deacon and the rest of you ragged-arsed cutthroats always were a law unto yourselves,' said Hickey. 'We never had any idea where you were.'

'We weren't too sure ourselves half the time.'

'You went ashore with the Marines at Segi, didn't you? That was a bloodbath.'

'My sense of self-preservation kicked in,' said Kella. 'By the time it was over, I was running faster than the bullets they were firing at me. What can you tell me?'

'I don't know,' said Hickey doubtfully. He turned over the remains of a searchlight with his foot. 'There's the Official Secrets Act to consider,' he said. 'I'm sure I signed it.'

'When the new Legislative Council meets for the first time, the elected members will have a great deal of power,' said Kella. 'Personally I think they should take up the matter of compensation to planters for war damage.'

'Are you pulling my pisser?' asked Hickey, hope flickering in his eyes.

'I'm not promising anything, but I'll talk about your plantation to some of the politicians I know,' said Kella.

'Suit yourself,' said Hickey, trying not to display his elation. 'I'd appreciate that.' He started walking across the littered terrain again, a little faster this time. The endless hunks of abandoned metal before him made the landscape look like the aftermath of a battle between robots on some distant planet.

'Kennedy's disappearance caused a right shebang,' he went on. 'Those PT boat captains were the elite, a bit like the Prussian cavalry. They were only young sprogs, but many of them were Harvard or Cornell graduates. That meant that their families had influence. And young Kennedy had more influence than most. I'll say he did! His daddy was old Joe Kennedy, for God's sake; one-time ambassador to England and as rich as Croesus. Mind you, he blotted his copybook a bit early on when he told Franklin D. that Britain had no chance of winning the war.'

'So your orders were to find young Kennedy quickly?'

'It was a case of panic stations. Only it wasn't as easy as that. At the time, the Yanks had invaded New Georgia and were in the process of taking five thousand casualties. In the week that Kennedy went missing, the Yanks attacked and took Munda from the Japs. In response, the Japanese from Rabaul were bombing the coast-watchers on top of the volcano on Kolombangara and everything else they could see that moved in the Roviana Lagoon.'

'Difficult to divert people to look for one PT boat crew in the middle of all that,' commented Kella. 'Kennedy was on Kasolo by then, wasn't he?'

'It was like this. The PT-109 had been patrolling at night in the Blackett Strait,' said Hickey. 'A Japanese destroyer ran it down and cut the boat in half. The PTs weren't the most substantial of craft. They had a complement of three officers and fourteen men and operated mainly at night. After the collision, the ship caught fire. Kennedy swam to Kasolo with his surviving crew members from the wreckage. He even towed one badly burnt seaman on a rope held between his teeth. Apparently he'd swum the backstroke for Harvard.'

'Not a complete waste of a privileged education, then.'

'Seemingly not. They soon decided that there wasn't enough food on Kasolo for eleven men, so Kennedy started swimming around the lagoon looking for a bigger island, while keeping out of the way of the Japs. That took some guts. Eventually he found Olasana a couple of miles away. It was a much bigger island, and thickly wooded to give them shelter in case there were Japs there as well. After that they moved on to Naru, but the coast-watcher scouts were closing in on them by this time. They found Kennedy and his crew and got them back to safety. That's your story.'

'Right,' said Kella. 'Then what?'

'What do you mean?'

'What you've told me so far tallies with the generally accepted account, as far as it goes. But there's more, isn't there? There always is.'

'Rumours,' said Hickey disgustedly. 'Rumours and gossip that don't amount to anything.'

'But that don't always reflect well on Kennedy?'

'Not if you believe them. I don't.'

'And you know what was being said because you heard everything at Townsville. Everything passed through your receiver. Tell me about them.'

Hickey skirted a line of Japanese foxholes and stopped abstractedly to admire some ground orchids growing through a skein of barbed wire.

'Why do you want to know all this?'

'It might have some bearing on an investigation I'm conducting.'

'Look,' said Hickey. 'Everything factual that I've heard about the story makes Kennedy look good. He did everything right and he showed that he was a brave bloke into the bargain. For God's sake, Kella, the guy could be president of the USA in a few weeks. Leave it alone.'

'Good luck to him and all who sail with him,' said Kella unfeelingly. 'What were the rumours?'

'Once you get your teeth into something you don't let go, do you?' The planter started walking again. Kella went after him. 'You know what it's like. Every time somebody starts to make a name for himself, other blokes try to run him down. If you must know, there were stories that the authorities were considering court-martialling Kennedy for negligence in allowing a Japanese destroyer to ram him, but it all blew over and they decorated him for heroism instead.'

'What else?'

'Christ, you're a nosy bugger! It goes with the job, I suppose.' They had travelled in a wide arc and were walking along the sandy beach. Hickey studied with simulated interest an old pontoon bridge half-submerged in the water.

'The other rumours seemed to centre round a native called Kakaihe. There were stories that he discovered Kennedy before the other scouts did. All we knew was that Kakaihe was stabbed to death in his search for Kennedy and that his dead body was brought home by a nun, who would never say what had happened.'

'What sort of rumours were spreading at the time?'

'You're going to talk to the politicians about my compo? Put in a word for me?'

'I promise you. Go on.'

'Well,' said the planter, 'it was all very confused and I was hundreds of miles away, but the gist of it was that Kennedy was mightily pissed off because he'd seen no signs of any rescue attempt. The story was that he might even have been considering surrendering to the Japs.'

Some frigate birds flapped heavily overhead. Waves lapped against the beach. A small leaf frog hopped ahead of them and then hid under a length of pipe. Somewhere among the trees on the hills a cockatoo screamed.

'It would be hard to work that into an election slogan,' Kella said. 'Unless you happened to be Benedict Arnold. Where does Kakaihe come into this mix?'

'There was speculation, and it was no more than that, mind,' Hickey said slowly, 'that a panic-stricken Kennedy or one of his men might have stabbed Kakaihe in case he got back and spread the story that the Yanks had been in the act of surrendering when he found them.

'I see what you mean,' said Kella after a long pause. 'Dangerous stuff. Who spread this story? Was it Kakaihe himself?'

'He would have had to be quick; he was dead.'

'Perhaps he told the nun who brought him home. She might have been with him before he died.'

'We asked her. She couldn't or wouldn't tell us anything. Then the Catholic hierarchy in the islands ordered us to lay off, so we did.'

'Doesn't do to upset the bishops.'

'Like I said, there's not an atom of proof to support that supposition,' said Hickey. 'At the time, we were all too busy. Nobody knew where anybody else was. We just had to wait until the smoke cleared. Afterwards Kennedy was given command of another PT boat, Kakaihe was dead and the nun, who seemed to be the only person who knew what had really happened, wouldn't say a word to anyone. I'm sorry I can't be more helpful. Do you want to spend the night? There's plenty of room.'

'No thanks,' said Kella. 'I've got to answer a letter.' Before the puzzled planter could ask him what he was talking about, he said: 'Can I ask you something else? Why haven't you made any attempt to get your plantation working again – until you get your compensation, that is?'

'To tell you the truth, I just can't be bothered,' said Hickey. 'I'm too old and too bloody tired. Now let me ask you something. Just what is this case you're investigating anyhow?'

'I'm not sure. I'm supposed to be putting a stop to attacks on a logging camp, but another case keeps getting in the way. Perhaps they're connected.'

'And perhaps they're not,' said Hickey.

'In my culture there is no such thing as coincidence,' said Kella. 'Everything is related to everything else. All things happen for a purpose. It's just a matter of finding the right links.'

'And what are the links in this case?'

'Everywhere I look, a group of American tourists seems to crop up. These tourists appear very concerned about John F. Kennedy's time in the Roviana Lagoon. To be honest, I've only got two leads at the moment.'

'What are they?'

'Well,' said Kella dispiritedly, 'to put it bluntly, it seems to be a matter of finding out who crapped on the beach at Alvaro and who smacked me behind the ear on Kolombangara.'

'Good luck,' said Hickey. He shook his head. 'I wonder if this bloke Kennedy ever realized just how many islanders risked their lives to save him when his boat went down. What's the pidgin for a close relative or a special mate?'

'One blood,' Kella said.

'Well, if you ask me, Kennedy had a lot of one-bloods he'd never heard of looking out for him in the Roviana Lagoon.'

TWENTY

'Bloody nuisance, this logging-camp business,' said Maclehose, the District Commissioner. 'That company has got a lot of influence in Whitehall. If we can persuade them to expand their timber industry in the west, we might even come close to balancing our budget one day.'

'They bring plenty of problems with them too,' said Welchman Buna. 'I'm getting a lot of complaints about their Australian workers.'

'The price of progress,' shrugged Maclehose. 'They come to Gizo on benders most weekends, but they spend a lot of money here.'

'There's the environmental aspect as well,' said Kella. 'The loggers have turned Alvaro into a hellhole. It's only a matter of time before they move on to other islands and do the same there.'

'I'm sure the authorities have that in hand,' said Maclehose. One of his eyes twitched. For the last hour he had been undergoing an unexpected grilling from the politician. The so-called Invisible Man had been all too visible and audible at their meeting, and the District Commissioner was beginning to look punch-drunk. For an impressed Kella, it was like watching a butterfly emerging from its chrysalis. The normally retiring Buna had been interrogating the official fiercely on every subject he had brought up about problems in the Roviana Lagoon. The islander must be pretty confident about getting elected to the Legislative Council, thought Kella. If his conduct over the last hour was anything to go by, the new assembly was going to be more than a mere talking-shop. Maclehose, another African retread, was probably recognizing the symptoms, which would account for the twitch.

'What about the tourists?' Kella asked. 'Do they give you any trouble?'

'Apart from getting murdered like that man Blamire at the mission open day?' asked the District Commissioner. 'One or two of them practically live in this office. There's a woman called Mrs Pargetter. So far she's been in to complain about the dirty state of the rest-house, the slowness of mail to reach the Solomons from the USA and the fact that there is no television service in the islands. And there's an American called Imison. He keeps coming in to ask me about the islands John F. Kennedy hid on while the Japanese were searching for him. I've told him everything I know about the man, but it doesn't seem enough to satisfy him.'

'What about the one who died – Ed Blamire?' asked Kella. 'Did he ever come in about anything?'

'Just the once,' said Maclehose. 'What was that about? Oh yes, I remember. The fellow wanted to know if I had the power to arrest anyone.'

'What did you tell him?' asked Kella, interested at once.

'I said that was the duty of the police.'

'But Inspector Lammond and Sergeant Jomanu are away on New Georgia.'

'I wasn't aware of that at the time,' said Maclehose.

'Did he say anything else, like who he wanted arrested, and for what reason?'

The District Commissioner bowed his head in concentration. He looked like a man at prayer.

'There was something,' he said. 'It was something about needing to find the letters before he could be sure. Yes, that's it. He said he would find the letters and bring them back here as evidence.'

'Evidence of what?'

'He didn't say,' said Maclehose.

'Do you have any idea what he was talking about?'

'None at all, old boy. You'd be surprised at the amount of twaddle I have to sit and listen to in this office.'

Twenty minutes later, Kella and Buna were walking down the dusty main street together.

'Where are you going next?' asked the politician.

'I'm hoping to find Joe Dontate,' said the sergeant.

'That's somebody else we will have to keep an eye on after independence,' said Buna. 'I'm all for learning from other countries, but that young man picked up far too many tricks of the wrong sort during his stay in Australia. You would think that with his background, he would have more respect for the traditions of the islands.'

'I think he does,' said Kella. 'He has to balance that against his desire to make money as quickly as possible.'

'Much of that is due to his girlfriend, Mary Gui,' said the politician. 'She's the one pushing Dontate to get involved in all these dubious ventures.'

Buna raised a hand in farewell and hurried away. Kella walked up the hill leading out of Gizo. Soon the bitumen road had faded into a mere track. Halfway up the hill, he came to the radio shack. It was little more than a large windowless shed with half a dozen aerials sprouting from the roof. Kella knocked on the door and went in.

There were two men inside the shack. They were both Melanesians. One was fat and somnolent, with a pockmarked face. The other was small and wiry. The fat man was asleep on top of a pile of sacks. The wiry man was sitting at a large radio receiver-transmitter that ran the full length of one side of the room. He looked up and saw the sergeant.

'Hello, Kella,' he said in Lau. 'Do you want to buy a rifle?'

The wiry man's name was Raesohu. During the war he had been a radio operator on the launch raiding Japanese stations in the Western District. He had been noted for his habit of swimming ashore at night and stealing rifles from sleeping Japanese troops before cutting their throats. Few of the weapons had been handed in to the authorities in 1945. Seventeen years later, the Malaita man was still selling them at thirty dollars apiece to all comers.

'Hang on to it; you may need it when you start your own revolution,' said Kella. 'Do you keep records of the signals you send out?'

'Of course.'

'When the white man died at Marakosi Mission recently, his body was brought here to Gizo for a few hours. Did another white man come up here to send a radio message to Honiara?'

The fat man on the pile of sacks snored. Raesohu stood up and walked over to a heap of files on the floor. He extracted a flimsy piece of paper and handed it to the sergeant. Kella read it and copied the contents into a notebook that he took from his pocket. He handed the message back to the wireless operator.

'Thanks,' he said, heading for the door.

'When I start that revolution, whose side are you going to be on?' asked Raesohu.

'Wouldn't you like to know?' said Kella. 'How's the planning coming along?'

'Just fine,' said Raesohu.

'Holding meetings and passing resolutions?'

Raesohu looked contemptuous. 'That's the last thing I need,' he said. 'When I decide to act, it won't be after a committee meeting, believe me.'

'No, I suppose not,' said Kella. 'Would you give me the names of some of the other men who think as you do in Gizo?'

'Why on earth would I do that?' asked Raesohu. 'So that you could take the list to whitey?'

'Do you think I would do that?' asked Kella. 'I want to talk to these men. If you give me their names, it may stop an innocent man going to prison.'

Raesohu looked at the police sergeant for a long time in silence. 'It's a good job I know you, Kella,' he said. 'If any other man had come to me with a request like that, his body would have turned up floating in the lagoon.'

'I know,' said Kella. 'Three or four names will do.'

'Lohmani,' said Raesohu, 'Otalifua, Dara and Tavo. Will that do you?'

'If you say so,' said the sergeant.

Kella walked back down the hill. He knew that he was getting nowhere with his investigations, and he knew why that was so. He was far from home, and in such unfamiliar territory that so far he had been conducting his enquiries like a white man. The policeman who had been sent to the Roviana Lagoon had been Sergeant Ben Kella, BA, MPhil, writer of dissertations and attender of courses. He was facing his usual problem of trying to exist in two worlds at the same time. Ever since his first Christian mission teachers had marked him out as a potential high-flyer, which, coincidentally, had been at about the same time that the old custom priests had called him to start his training as the *aofia*, he had been struggling to assimilate two different cultures. It was time to forget the white man's influences and concentrate on what he was good at. What was wanted here was some good, old-fashioned bush-tracking.

He spent the next hour visiting the four men whose names he had been given at the radio station. In a small place like Gizo, it was not difficult to track each one down. They all gave him the answer he had been expecting. Then he occupied an exasperating hour in searching without success for Joe Dontate. Gizo was little more than a glorified village, with only a few hundred permanent residents, although the occasional tourist party and the crews of visiting vessels made up the numbers at various times. All the same, although Kella had tried most of the bars and cafés by noon, there had been no sign of the former boxer. It was shortly after midday that he reached one of the less salubrious waterfront drinking dens, an open-sided, thatched-roofed building with a bar consisting of beer crates piled on top of one another and a suspicious-looking Melanesian pushing bottles of Australian 4X beer to thirsty patrons. He directed a glare at the sight of Kella in his police uniform, but said nothing as the sergeant stood in the entrance on the wharf surveying the bar's patrons. There were islanders from all over the Solomons, most seamen on Chinese trading vessels: dark-hued Melanesians, big, handsome light-skinned Polynesians and even a few spare, lithe Gilbertese uprooted from their own islands to their settlement at Wagina.

Kella saw a group of Lau seamen sitting on crates drinking in a corner, and made his way over to them. They shifted up respectfully to make room for the *aofia*. One of them offered him a swig from his bottle, but Kella declined with a grunt of thanks.

'I'm looking for Joe Dontate,' he said in the Lau dialect. 'He's a big man in Gizo.'

'Or thinks he is,' said one of the seamen, to general laughter.

'True,' nodded Kella. 'Sometimes a lizard thinks that it is a crocodile. Does anyone know where I might find him?'

The others shook their heads placidly. One of them, a young man with his hair dyed blond with lime and wearing a dirty T-shirt with the inscription *Elvis the King*, raised a hand, like a schoolboy at the back of a classroom, and asked:

'Why don't you make him find you?'

'How do I do that?' asked Kella. A fight between a Tikopian and a Choiseul man broke out in the doorway, but no one in the group paid any attention to it. The sergeant noticed that the Choiseul man was swinging huge, flailing blows, while the Tikopian was ominously compact, nuzzling his opponent's chest with his face as he delivered straight short-arm punches to the other man's ribcage.

Kella's money was already on the Tikopian. The Lau men, connoisseurs of bar-room brawls, waited with puzzled attention for the blond youth's response to Kella's question.

'Plenty of things going on Joe Dontate doesn't want the police to know about, in plenty of different places,' suggested the youth. 'If the *aofia* goes and waits in one of them, Dontate will soon hear about it and come running to get rid of the evidence.'

The other seamen guffawed and slapped the blond boy on the back in appreciation of his animal cunning. Kella reached into his back pocket and produced an Australian five-dollar note, which he handed to the preening boy.

'Good thinking, *wantok*,' he said. 'Buy your friends a drink. Can any of you suggest which place will draw Dontate to me the soonest?'

The Lau men conferred in undertones. Again it was the blond youth who addressed Kella first.

'Place bilong kina,' he said. 'Dontate has something strange going on there this week. I saw him take some whiteys in there a few days ago.'

'The shell house?' asked Kella.

'Behind the Joy biscuit factory,' said the blond youth.

'Thank you, you keep your eyes open. Your captain should make you a lookout,' said Kella, standing up.

'That's what we do when we rob the Chinese,' said another Lau man.

The seamen were still laughing as Kella left the bar. As he did so, he stepped over the body of the already recumbent, groaning Choiseul man in the entrance.

The shell house was a long tin shed on a piece of wasteland behind the biscuit factory, which supplied Gizo with fresh bread three times a week. Kella kicked heavily on the door of the shed, making a booming noise. Somebody inside shouted at him in pidgin to go away. Kella kicked harder, making a dent in the door. The door was unlocked and inched open to reveal a pair of eyes.

Kella kicked again, as hard as he could. The door flew open, sending the man who had unlocked it crashing backwards. Kella stepped inside.

'Good morning, *olketta*,' he beamed at the workers inside the shell house.

There were about a dozen of them, all Melanesians, few of them young, sitting at long tables littered with carving implements, different types of wood and dozens of seashells. They looked up with apprehension as the sergeant made his dramatic entrance. The man he had knocked over picked himself up and slammed the door shut, lumbering towards Kella. He was a big New Georgian islander with impressive biceps and a chest like a black iron trunk. He came to a halt when he saw Kella's red beret and khaki uniform.

'Just a routine inspection,' said Kella, smiling benevolently and starting to patrol up and down the tables. 'There's nothing to worry about. Treat me as if I wasn't here.'

The first table he passed at a leisurely pace was devoted to shell carving. The Melanesians stared at their work as if they found it fascinating, not looking up at the policeman. Kella could recognize cowries, mussels, conch shells, thorny oysters, cones, clams, turtle shells and a dozen others. The tools being used with contemptuous ease by the carvers allowed them to cut, pierce, polish and engrave. They handled and discarded saws, drills, knives, hammers, files and pumice stones.

Unfortunately, the work they were producing was of a shoddy standard. Kella looked at the mounds of beads, necklaces, bracelets, decorated boxes and pendants being dropped into boxes at the feet of the carvers. These were cheap and nasty imitations of genuine carving work and were designed only to fool unsuspecting tourists.

The same could be said of the wooden carvings being produced at another table. They were inferior copies of traditional pieces, made of the cheapest wood, badly finished, and sprayed with a cheap veneer to give the impression of age.

One of the older workers looked up and caught Kella's eye. He was a Guadalcanal man with a helmet of snow-white hair above a craggy, distinguished face. He saw the police sergeant's disapproving expression and shrugged hopelessly. Kella nodded. There weren't many jobs for the old in the Solomons; there weren't a lot for the young, either. He could understand the Guadalcanal man's shame at turning out such cheapjack wares. As he stared at the old man, the latter's hand moved nervously to a drawer in the desk before him. Kella moved forward and pulled the drawer open. It contained a number of assorted carved shell trinkets.

The door at the end of the shed opened and Joe Dontate hurried in. 'Kella!' he shouted. 'This is private property. Get the hell out!'

'I wanted to see you, so I left you my calling card,' Kella told him. 'You didn't have to run to get here. A sharp walk would have done.'

Dontate scowled and walked to a door leading to an office at the far end of the shed. Kella followed him in. There was a table and two chairs in the windowless room. Dontate sat behind the table. Kella took the chair in front of him.

'Well?' asked Dontate.

'Something's going on here in the west,' Kella said. 'I'm not sure what, but I think it's big. Nothing goes off in the Roviana area without you knowing about it. So what is it?'

'You're making a mistake,' said Dontate. 'How would I know? I'm a respectable businessman.'

'No you're not,' Kella said. 'Piece by piece you're taking over crime in the Roviana Lagoon. The trouble is, this time you're in danger of getting in over your head.'

'Kind of you to care,' Dontate said.

'What makes it dangerous,' said Kella, 'is the fact that this goes outside the Solomons. This is international. I think we've had two lots of foreign agents here already.'

'Fascinating,' yawned Dontate, pretending to be absorbed in some plans on the table before him.

'There's just one way to get foreigners safely into the country,' Kella said. 'That's as tourists. At the moment, the only tourist party we've got in the Protectorate is the one you're guiding. Eight of them flew home a couple of days ago and one was murdered at Marakosi Mission. That leaves the three who have signed up with you for a personalized tour of the islands visited by John F. Kennedy in 1943.'

'You're out of your mind.'

'Those three agents are looking for something to do with John F. Kennedy when he was a PT boat commander in the lagoon. They're concentrating on matters that might discredit Kennedy.'

'Why the hell would they do that?'

'I don't know.'

'Is what they are doing illegal?'

'Not as far as I'm aware, no.'

'Are you asking me to turn down a substantial fee to guide a group of Yanks round the lagoon?'

'It might be better if you withdrew your services.'

'Go and stuff yourself sideways!' said Joe Dontate. 'Is there any point to all this as far as I'm concerned?'

'It's bad enough you making efforts to be Mr Big in the lagoon, but I can put up with that as long as you don't come near Malaita. What worries me is the way you're getting involved with whitey. You're too tough and too streetwise to be bothered by the local hoods, but if you invite expatriates into the area, sooner or later they'll take over from you. You may think that you can control them, but you can't. These guys will chew you up and spit you out, Dontate. Then I'll have to come over and clear up the mess.'

'Have you come here to deliver a sermon?' asked Dontate.

'I was hoping that you would tell me a few things. In the first place, why was Ed Blamire murdered?'

'How would I know? I guide them, I don't listen to their confessions.'

'But you were at the Marakosi Mission open day?'

'Every bugger and his dog was there. By lagoon standards, that afternoon came under the heading of "quite interesting". Look, you're wasting your time and mine.'

Kella stood up. 'Very well,' he said. 'I was only trying to help you.'

'That'll be the day!'

'Some time ago,' said Kella, 'when Johnny Cho and his Chinatown boys were trying to kill me, you came to my assistance. Before that, you helped me on Malaita once.'

'We all make mistakes.'

'Because of that, I owe you a couple, Dontate. This is my attempt at payback. Don't have anything else to do with Imison and the other Americans. This isn't some inter-tribal blood feud. It's a big-time operation and you're getting sucked into it.'

'I go where the money is, Kella. Don't you think you might be biting off more than you can chew yourself? After all, what are you? You're just a witch-doctor-policeman and you don't have any friends in this district.'

'Just the one,' said Kella. 'Just the one.'

He stood up and left the office. He noticed that Dontate had not moved. By his standards, the islander was almost looking concerned.

TWENTY-ONE

Three of the nuns were sitting around the table in the senior sister's office with Kella. The fourth, Sister Brigid, had been invited to attend but had declined. Kella had arrived at the mission by canoe a few hours ago. He had refused a meal and a bed for the night, and had requested that Sister Conchita convene a meeting. He had been lowering and silent since his arrival and had made no mention of the senior sister's letter to him.

'It's time for us to pool our knowledge and to do what we can to solve the two problems that have been presented to us,' the policeman said calmly after Sister Conchita's introductory remarks. 'I refer to the death of the American tourist Ed Blamire and the attacks at the Alvaro logging camp.'

'You thought they weren't connected,' Sister Conchita could not help saying.

'I never said that. I wanted to follow the pattern of the logging mystery first and see where that led me. In my culture there are no coincidences. All things that happen were meant to happen. It's a matter of studying them and picking out the salient facts, and seeing where they intertwine. The attacks on the island of Alvaro led me to the Roviana Lagoon. After years of peace, something has put the karma of this area out of joint. The only unsettling event in the lagoon this year has been the arrival of a group of tourists. If there have been two crimes immediately following the presence of the Americans in the Western Solomons, then somehow the tourists are connected with both events.'

'There's no proof that the Americans were responsible for either crime,' said Sister Johanna, 'except of course that poor Mr Blamire lost his life while he was in the lagoon.'

'That is true. There are only three tourists left in the area now. They appear to be interested solely in what happened here during the war in 1943, specifically in the events surrounding the sinking of PT-109 under the command of John F. Kennedy.'

'What does that mean?' asked Sister Jean Francoise, who seemed to be enjoying one of her lucid intervals. The French nun was resting her chin on her hands on the long table and leaning forward eagerly.

'I believe,' said Kella, 'that the turbulence of the last few days is all part of a much longer line of events, going back to 1943. The trouble in the lagoon didn't end when the fighting finished, it just submerged for a couple of decades. Now it has come back to the surface because it is time to bring it all to an end, so that the spirits of the lagoon will be satisfied at last.'

'Closure,' said Sister Conchita. 'And are we meant to bring that closure to the deaths and violence?'

'I think so,' said Kella. 'But this is not my area. I have no power or authority here. I am only a policeman. I must do my duty, but I will need help.'

'What sort of help?' asked Conchita.

'Yours,' said Kella.

The nuns looked at one another uneasily.

'What sort of help can we provide?' asked Conchita. 'We are foreigners here too,'

'I need your faith,' said Kella. 'Sister Brigid has the key to these events, going back seventeen years, I am sure of that. She became involved in something that happened in the search for John F. Kennedy in 1943. She won't tell us anything about it. I think that is because at some time when she was searching for the crew of PT-109, her faith came into conflict with the spirits of the lagoon. There was a struggle and she has never been able to talk about it since. Her faith was vanquished by a stronger one. Unfortunately she will not talk about what happened.'

'Nonsense!' said Sister Johanna. 'Sister Brigid was – is – a Christian nun!'

'Operating on her own in a pagan area,' said Kella. 'She did not have enough help. Her *mana* was not strong enough.' He looked at Sister Conchita. 'You know that this can happen,' he said. 'You had experience of it yourself when you met the dream-maker on Mount Austen once.'

Conchita paid no attention to the looks directed at her by the other two sisters. She remembered the occasion when Father Pierre had sent her up into Mount Austen on Guadalcanal to test her faith against that of the dream-maker. It was only a few months before, but now it seemed so long ago.

'What are you trying to say to us, Sergeant Kella?' she asked.

'The troubles of the war in the lagoon have not yet ended,' he said. 'But it will soon be time to put a finish to them, if we can find the truth.'

'Whose truth?' asked Sister Jean Francoise, and giggled.

'What do you want of us?' Conchita asked.

'As I said, my spirits do not operate so far from Malaita, but yours do. Your mission has been in the west for most of the century. Sister Brigid did not have your strength of mind. She allowed herself to be defeated by the Roviana spirits. You might be more successful if you come with me, Sister Conchita.'

'You want me to travel with you on your investigations?'

'I must have someone with me who has power, to make up for my own lack of it outside my home island. There will be times when I will need someone with a strong faith to combat the water spirits of the lagoon. Will you travel with me in search of the truth, Sister Conchita? It is a lot to ask, I know.'

'It's out of the question,' said Conchita. 'I have my own work here at Marakosi.'

'Rubbish!' said Sister Johanna. 'You were sent here to call us to order. Well, you've done that. Now do something really useful. Go with the sergeant, put an end to the evil that has come to Roviana. Release Sister Brigid from the invisible bonds that have bound her for so many dreadful years.'

'There must be a Christian missionary present in any attempt to restore good in the lagoon,' agreed Sister Jean Francoise. 'Johanna and Brigid are too old, and my mind is not attached firmly enough any more.'

'You're too old as well,' Sister Johanna sniffed. 'It has to be Conchita.' She stood up and walked over to stand next to the young nun. 'You were prepared to combat three old women at the mission,' she said gently. 'Are you not also ready to face the wild spirits out there, armed with your faith? After all, it's only a matter of degree.'

Conchita tried to marshal her thoughts. On the face of it, what she was being asked to do seemed absurd. If the church authorities knew that she was even accepting the existence of the local spirits, they would order her back to Honiara at once. If they suspected that she was contemplating going out to match her faith against that of the lagoon devil-devils, she would be sent back to the USA immediately. Yet Ben Kella was asking her to do just that, and the police sergeant had never asked anything of her before, no matter how dangerous his situation. Another thought struck her. He was almost too openly anxious. Was it possible that he had another agenda altogether? Could it be that he had been alarmed at the attempt on her life when the boulder had been dislodged on Kolombangara? Was he taking her under his wing again, as he had done once before? Or was it part of his plan to strengthen her position at Marakosi Mission? By publicly expressing his dependence upon Sister Conchita, he had impressed the other nuns with her importance in the scheme of things at the station. Was he only doing that to make her position in the mission more secure? She realized that the French nun was talking.

'There comes a time,' said Sister Jean Francoise, 'when we have to learn to do what our heart tells us is right, even if our head thinks that it is foolhardy. Besides, it's time somebody from the mission went out into the world again and made some sort of impression on it.'

'Of course,' warned Sister Johanna, 'we're not the best people to be advising you. Jean Francoise and I have been regarded as having gone native years ago – no offence, Ben. Sister Conchita, you might share that fate if you leave the mission with the sergeant. Sisters who spend too much time reacting to local conditions, or even recognizing them, are labelled mavericks. On the other hand, if you are successful in this mission, you might be able to bring dear Sister Brigid back to us from the hell she has been living in all this time. Half a dozen bishops haven't been able to do that.' She paused and looked at Kella. 'By the way, that rock that rolled down on us on Kolombangara, was that a deliberate attempt to kill us?'

'It was a warning for you to keep away from the island,' said Kella. 'If they had wanted to kill you, they could have thought of a dozen better ways. If you go back, they will.'

'So what does that tell us?' asked Conchita.

'That part of the answer to our problem probably lies on Kolombangara.'

Conchita had made her decision. She stood up. Whatever the reason for Kella's request, she was being given a chance to play a part in the investigation of Ed Blamire's death. 'Very well, Sergeant Kella,' she said, trying to expunge the nervousness from her voice. 'Where do we start?'

TWENTY-TWO

'Just how many policemen are there in the Solomons?' asked Sister Conchita of Sergeant Kella's broad back.

'Two hundred and seventeen,' said Kella. He had studied the subject for his promotion-to-inspector examination, which he kept on putting off. 'There are seven gazetted officers, five sub-inspectors and two hundred and five other ranks.'

'That's to cover almost a thousand islands occupying an area of ten thousand square miles, where over seventy different languages are spoken? No wonder you never seem to get any help when you need it.'

'It involves a certain amount of multi-tasking,' agreed Kella. 'Anyway, I always have you. You seem to make a habit of popping up and getting in the way.'

He was in the prow of the mission canoe, steering it along the coast of Munda. They had left Marakosi Mission over an hour before in the late afternoon and were passing the village of Kia, a mile from the airstrip.

'They call that the tin town,' said Kella.

Kia consisted of a collection of huts a hundred yards back from the beach, sheltered by palm trees. Incongruously, a huge rusted assemblage of American and Japanese aircraft parts seemed to sprout from the ground amid the trees, towering over the village. Almost all the huts had utilized items of the wreckage for domestic use. An enormous shell casing suspended from a chain replaced the traditional drum to summon villagers to meetings. Scrubbed petrol tins were in use to store water. Fishing nets sprawled across the beach to dry were attached to lengths of cable as sinkers. The wing of a Zero was hoisted on struts to provide shelter from the sun for the old men of the village. Primitive outdoor kitchen ranges had been constructed out of flat pieces of salvaged metal. A rusted Zero propeller was being utilized as a roasting spit. A copra-drying shed had been thrown together from the sides of a tank.

'That's the American Dump,' said Kella, indicating the heap of wreckage. 'It's even in the tourist guides. The villagers are making good use of the junk on it, so they won't let scrappers come ashore here to remove anything.'

He headed the canoe towards the airstrip. Ten minutes later, he cut out the engine. For some time he sat studying the coastline.

'What's the matter?' asked Sister Conchita.

'It's very quiet,' said Kella.

'If this was a movie, I could say "too quiet",' suggested the nun. 'I've always wanted to play the part of a cowboy hero's sidekick.'

'Gabby Hayes or Andy Devine?' asked Kella.

'I was thinking more along the lines of Dale Evans,' said Sister Conchita. 'She inherited Roy Rogers' fortune after he died.'

'Whatever happened to your vows of poverty?'

'Even a nun can dream! Mind, I don't know what I'd do with the stuffed body of Trigger.'

Kella grunted. Sister Conchita seemed to know her Western movies. Why didn't that surprise him? Not for the first time, he wondered what she had done before she had become a nun. She never talked about that period of her life. He picked up a paddle and began steering the canoe towards the shore. Soon they were pulling the craft up on to the sand by the rest-house. There were still no signs of life. Presumably no charter flights had been booked for the day. There was talk of a small local internal air service being established in the Solomons over the next eighteen months, linking the major islands, but until that should happen, there were no regular internal flights, which meant that the airstrip, over a mile in length, constructed during the war by the Japanese for bombing raids, often lay dormant for weeks at a time. Sister Conchita and Kella walked up to the sprawling rest-house.

'Wait here,' said Kella, and went inside.

There were a dozen small bedrooms leading off the corridor next to the lounge and kitchen. Only one of them showed any sign of being occupied. All the guests seemed to have moved out and taken their luggage with them. The only bedroom in use was larger than the others. It contained Mary Gui's clothes and books. She had been sharing the room with a man. The bed was unmade. Kella went through the clothes discarded by the man and thrust into a brimming laundry basket. There were several T-shirts bearing the inscription *Sydney Stadium*. Kella had seen Joe Dontate wearing similar tops. He threw the T-shirts back into the wicker basket. He wondered how long Dontate and Mary had been sleeping together. Western girls had a reputation for cheerful promiscuity, which was why so many European seamen had deserted in the area during the nineteenth century. Why should Mary Gui be any different? Kella certainly had no claim to her. It looked as if his brief liaison with the rest-house keeper could definitely come under the heading of a one-night stand. Somehow the thought saddened him.

Sister Conchita was waiting for him outside when he returned. 'The place seems deserted,' she said. She saw the look on the sergeant's face. 'What's the matter?' she asked.

Kella shook his head. 'Stay close to me,' he said. 'Something's wrong.'

They walked round to the back of the rest-house. A lean-to kitchen was attached to the main building by a sloping thatched roof. They could hear the sound of sobbing before they turned the corner. Mary Gui was sitting on the ground, with her back to the wall. A large kitchen knife was in her hand. Tears coursed down her frightened face. She scrambled to her feet and raised the knife threateningly when the pair approached her. When she saw who the newcomers were, she dropped the knife to the ground with a groan of despair.

'Joe's gone!' she sobbed. 'I think something bad has happened to him.'

'Joe Dontate?' asked Kella. 'What happened?'

'He had a row with Imison and the other Americans this afternoon,' said the girl breathlessly. 'He went to tell them that he wasn't going to help them any more. I was in our bedroom. I could hear them quarrelling, so I went to the door of the rest-house. Then Joe ran down the beach and jumped into a canoe and paddled away across the lagoon. Ten minutes later, the Americans left. They started up the launch and set out in the direction Joe had taken. I think they were looking for him. I've been waiting here for hours but he hasn't come back.'

'You poor girl,' said Sister Conchita, putting an arm around Mary's shoulders.

'Why did Dontate tell the Americans he wasn't going to help them any more?' asked Kella.

'You know why,' sobbed the girl. 'You talked him into it. You persuaded him to stop helping them. That made them angry.'

'I never thought he'd pay any attention to me,' said Kella, half to himself.

'Joe thinks a lot of you. He would never let you know that, but he often said that you were the only policeman in the islands worth a damn. He never liked the Americans anyway; he was only helping them for the money. When you spoke to him in the shell house and told him that he shouldn't get mixed up with the foreigners, it made a big impression on him. Joe pretends to be very modern, but he's as traditional as any other islander at heart. He pays a lot of attention to custom. When he came back to the rest-house after he had seen you in Gizo, he said that the Solomons didn't need the Americans, and that it had been a mistake getting involved with them in the first place.'

'And he tried to break away,' said Kella. 'Why didn't he just wait until the Americans had left?'

'That isn't Joe's way. He had to tell them to their faces.' The girl sniffed. 'He even gave them their money back.'

'Perhaps he paddled away to fetch help,' suggested Sister Conchita.

'Perhaps,' said Kella. 'Tell me, did he go straight to his canoe after he had left the Americans, or did he go somewhere else first?'

Mary frowned in concentration. 'He stopped off at the kitchen,' she said. 'Then he ran down to the canoe.'

'Was he carrying anything?' asked Kella.

'I'm not sure,' said Mary.

Kella started looking round the small kitchen. He picked up a basket of clams. 'Could he have taken some of these?' he asked.

'I don't know,' said Mary. 'It's possible.'

Kella started to move away. 'I think I may know where he went,' he said. 'Look after Mary for me, will you, Sister Conchita? When she feels better, take her over to Gizo. Tell the District Commissioner what happened here this afternoon. Get him to radio Police Headquarters in Honiara to send a launch and half a dozen armed policemen to the lagoon to pick Imison and the others up.' He looked at the still shaking Mary. 'Have you any idea where the Americans might have gone?'

'Olasana,' said Mary Gui. 'They kept talking about Olasana. They visited Kasolo but they said that it was too small. They wanted a bigger island visited by the survivors of PT-109.'

'They will have stopped off somewhere else first,' said Kella. 'Do as I ask, Sister. I won't be long.'

'Where are you going?' asked Sister Conchita.

'To find Dontate,' Kella said. A thought struck him and he turned back. 'I suppose it was Dontate who knocked me out in the bush village on Kolombangara?'

Mary nodded guiltily, biting her lip. 'He said that you were getting too close,' she confessed. 'He'd come up to the village to keep me company when I had the custom tattoos.'

'How did he get me back down to the coast?'

'Some of the bushmen helped him carry you down. Joe didn't want to hurt you, honestly he didn't. He just wanted you out of the way for a week.'

'But I didn't know anything! I still don't.'

'Joe thought you did. He was sure that you'd seen something in the village. He wouldn't tell me what.'

Kella shook his head in exasperation. He left the two women and went back to the mission canoe on the beach. He filled the tank from a tin of diesel kept in a shed on the sand. Then he pulled the canoe back into the water, started the engine and set off across the lagoon. It was a fine, cloudless morning. On his way he passed fishing canoes out searching for shoals of the multicoloured crayfish, tuna, kingfish and bonito that abounded in the local waters. Dolphins swam lazily alongside him before getting bored and veering off.

Kella thought of the first time he had met Joe Dontate. It had been ten years ago on Malaita. He had been a young constable accompanying a district officer on a tour of the saltwater villages. At one fetid, evil-smelling spot among the mangrove swamps, a headman had arrested a young villager for murder. The district officer had held a preliminary court in the village square, to determine whether the accused should be taken back to Tulagi to stand trial.

The accused was plainly guilty; he had stabbed to death in plain sight a man from another family in the village, as payback for a long-running blood feud. The district officer had decreed that the killer would be dispatched to the administrative centre as soon as a government vessel visited the area. Kella had been standing next to the young villager, guarding him in the witness place, when the islander had produced a knife, smuggled into the court hearing by a *wantok*, and attempted to stab the policeman before escaping into the bush.

Fortunately for the young constable, a Chinese trading vessel had put in at the village earlier that day, and its crew had seized the rare opportunity for a little relaxation and entertainment by sitting in with the villagers at the open-air adjudication. One of the deck hands had been Joe Dontate. Although he was only about twenty, he already bore the facial scars of the successful amateur boxer he was becoming. His reflexes had been better than anyone else's present as well. As the accused man swung the knife at an unprepared Kella, Dontate, sitting in the front row of the crowd, had swayed to his feet, caught the islander's knife arm with one hand and thudded his free fist into the villager's kidneys, sending the man choking and writhing to the ground.

Afterwards a sheepish Kella had tried to thank the western deck hand. Dontate had waved aside his attempts at gratitude.

'Do me a favour and don't ever tell anyone that I helped one of whitey's policemen,' he had growled.

Their paths had crossed on a number of other occasions in the decade that had passed since that day. On several occasions Kella had arrested Dontate for drunkenness and other minor offences, but soon the islander had become much too shrewd to attract official notice. He had never taken offence on any of the occasions that Kella had closed in on him, and over the years the policeman had developed a considerable unofficial liking for the taciturn, straight-forward and extremely brave miscreant. He was not looking forward to what he thought he might see before the morning was over.

Half an hour after leaving Munda, Kella steered past the island of Parara. He cut out his engine as he approached a much smaller island a few yards away. He jumped out and pulled the canoe up on to a narrow strip of coral.

The island was flat, less than fifty yards long and not as wide. Trees grew right down to the water's edge, leaving no room for a beach. A well-trodden track led into the trees. Kella began to walk down it. He exercised care. He was on the notorious Kundu Hite, more commonly known as Skull Island. For centuries it had been used as a shrine for the skulls of priests and the leaders of the headhunting expeditions that had flourished in the adjoining lagoons of Roviana and Vonovana. The bodies of prisoners taken on such raids were buried beneath the ground and blessed by the priests, called *hiamas*, who prayed that the accumulated *mana* of the dead warriors would be transferred to their conquerors. Not only might there be guards stationed on the island, but there would be the spirits of the dead headhunters to contend with as well. He almost wished that he had brought Sister Conchita with him. It would have been interesting to see how strong her *mana* was among the dreaded malevolent ghosts that haunted the island.

A few minutes' walk took him to a sandy mound in the centre of the islet. Triangular open-fronted stone and wooden shrines revealed hundreds of human skulls piled high in gruesome towers. Offerings of shell money on long strings of vine decorated some of the shrines. Decaying stone axes, some of great age, had been discarded on the ground as a reminder of the place's bloody past.

Carefully Kella trod among the shrines until he saw what he had come for. Lying in front of one of the larger stone monuments was the body of Joe Dontate. There were three bullet wounds in the front of his bloodstained shirt. Kella bent over to examine the body. Four or five empty clam shells lay on the ground. Stones had been placed over the dead man's eyes. The ex-boxer had not been dead long. Presumably the Americans in the launch had tracked him down and killed him. They would have had no trouble in making him out across the flat, open waters. In any case, Dontate would not have been trying to avoid being seen. The islander would have made no attempt at concealment or even resistance. Knowing that his death was inevitable once he had spurned the Americans' offer, he had come to Skull Island for two reasons: to draw the Americans away from Mary Gui, and to reach the traditional resting place of western chiefs, so that he would at least die among his peers.

Kella heard someone moving behind him and turned, clenching his fists. Three islanders in loincloths were standing on the path. Two were young and had picked up axes from the ground. Standing in front of them was a tall, dignified islander in his fifties.

'Youfella luuai bilong Kundu Hite?' asked Kella.

'I look after the skulls,' said the older man in English, nodding. 'I am Tapi. It will cost you ten dollars to land on Skull Island.'

As custodian of the skulls, Tapi would know the lineage of every chief in the lagoon area. Kella reached into his pocket and produced a note, and handed it to the tall man. The two younger men relaxed a little. Kella took out another ten-dollar note and gave that to Tapi as well. The younger men's eyes widened at the sight of so much money. Both banknotes vanished into the older man's skimpy loincloth with a celerity born of long practice. The islander would have perfected his English on the tourists who occasionally visited the lagoon. He opened his mouth to go into his introductory address. Kella forestalled him.

'Do you live on Kundu Hite?' he asked.

Tapi shook his head and indicated the adjoining island. 'On Parara,' he said. 'I only come across when we have visitors.'

'Did you hear gunshots this afternoon?' asked Kella

'Three,' answered Tapi. 'We thought the spirits of the chiefs were fighting among themselves. We saw a canoe on the shore and a bigger ship with an engine anchored off the island.'

'But you didn't come over to see what was happening?'

'As I said, it was a matter for the ghosts. There are many of them on Kundu Hite. Mortals do not get involved in matters of the gods.'

And another killing on the island would only add to its macabre reputation and provide more tourist money for the custodian, thought Kella.

'When the big ship left, which way did it go?' he asked.

'That way,' said the custodian, pointing south.

'How many men were on board?'

'I saw three.'

Kella pointed at the body. 'Do you know this dead man?' he asked.

'Of course; he is Dontate, a big man in the lagoon. He comes from a bloodline of warrior chiefs. He went out into the world, some say to be a warrior among the whiteys. Then he returned, with much gold. It is sad that he has died so young. One day he might have become a chief of chiefs in Roviana. He was of the bloodline of Chief Ingava of Nusa Roviana, who worshipped the great rock that looked like a dog.'

'I'll send someone over to take Dontate's body back to Gizo,' said Kella.

'No, we will bury him here,' said Tapi firmly. 'Dontate was a big man; it is fitting that he should lie with the other warriors. He knew that and travelled here when he knew that his time had come. We shall put his skull in an honoured place in one of the shrines.'

Chief Joe Dontate would have liked that, thought Kella. There was nothing to gain by taking his body away. As far as Kella was aware, he had no relatives, and once she got over her shock, the pragmatic and calculating Mary Gui would soon find another man. The authorities in Honiara would regard the hasty burial as irregular and premature, but Dontate would have been long under the coral before they heard about it. Tapi would be discreet about the matter. The custodian had been lying when he had said that he had not witnessed the murder. He had probably been hiding on the island when the Americans had landed. Only an islander would have had the consideration to place stones over the dead man's eyes to prevent their being pecked out by scavenging birds. But Tapi would never give evidence in a white man's court. He was a keeper of the secrets. Every tribe had one.

'Very well,' Kella said to the three islanders. 'See that it is done.'

Sister Conchita was waiting for him on the beach at Munda when he grounded his canoe.

'I thought you were taking Mary over to Gizo,' he said disapprovingly.

'I got her a lift in a United Church canoe that put in for diesel,' Conchita said. 'Don't worry, she's a bright girl and can look after herself. She'll alert the District Commissioner and then the police in Honiara. Did you find Mr Dontate?'

'He's dead,' said Kella. In a few words he told Sister Conchita of his experience on Kundu Hite. The nun crossed herself.

'How did you know he would be on Skull Island?' she asked.

'I guessed that when I saw the basket of brown *derasa* clams in the kitchen,' he said. 'They were eaten by the Roviana warriors as a *vavolo*, the death feast they dined on before going into battle against insurmountable odds. Dontate knew that he was going to die. He just wanted to draw Imison and the others away from Munda, so that Mary Gui and any other innocent bystanders wouldn't get hurt as well.'

'He was a brave man,' said Sister Conchita.

'A warrior,' agreed Kella. 'So why didn't you go with Mary?'

'I thought I might be needed.'

Kella frowned. 'Suit yourself,' he said. 'But I'm going to be busy for the rest of the afternoon.'

He found an axe and a sharp knife in a toolbox in the rest-house and spent several hours amid the trees at the far end of the runway. He cut a dozen branches each about a foot in length and sharpened them into deadly stakes, with points at both ends. Then he went deeper into the bush until he found a *kwilla* tree. This possessed some of the strongest and heaviest wood of all the trees in the Solomons. He cut off a substantial branch several feet in diameter and three feet long. Carefully he sharpened one end of the branch into a point. Then he carried all the shaped pieces of wood and put them into the bottom of the canoe, together with some lengths of creeper and the knife he had been using. For good measure he fetched a spade from the tool shed and added it to the pile.

Sister Conchita carried across two plates of boiled rice and tinned corned beef from the supply of food she had brought with her. They sat on top of an upturned canoe and ate.

'I'm coming with you,' said the nun.

'Definitely not,' said Kella. 'It's going to be dangerous.'

'I may be useful. You said you would need someone with her own *mana* to help protect you so far from home.'

Kella ate in silence for a few minutes. Then he said: 'That's not the real reason why you want to come, is it?'

'No, it's not.'

'Why then?'

'Because,' said the nun, 'you're heading for Olasana for the wrong reasons. You're going to the island for revenge because the Americans killed Joe Dontate. What do you call it in pidgin?'

'Payback.'

'You're going there for payback. You mustn't! You're a lawman twice over, Sergeant Kella. You're a policeman and the *aofia*. You've sworn two different oaths in two separate cultures to administer justice.'

'My kind of justice,' said Kella. 'And yours, come to that. An eye for an eye . . .'

'No,' said Sister Conchita, shaking her head emphatically. 'Vengeance is mine, says the Lord.'

They both started eating again. Then Kella put his plate down on the ground. 'There are three of them,' he said. 'They've got rifles and they know how to use them. They've gone to Olasana either to look for something or to leave something there, I'm not sure which. They haven't got much time left. They'll have to get away from the Solomons fast before they're arrested for the death of Dontate. By the time they reach Olasana, they'll only have a few hours of daylight left. They won't be able to leave tonight because they can't navigate the reefs and get out of the lagoon in the dark. They'll probably wait on Olasana overnight and go first thing in the morning. That means I've got to get there this evening soon after dark. If you come as well, you'll only get in my way.'

'That is my intention,' said Sister Conchita. 'I shall get in your way in every conceivable manner if I believe that you are only going to Olasana to kill three men. If you won't take me there in what, I have to say, is my canoe, or at least the mission's, then I'll find some other way of crossing the lagoon to Olasana. If I drown on the way, and I may well do that, the blame will quite rightly be laid at your door, Sergeant Kella. The spirits of the lagoon will want payback.'

'You can be a considerable nuisance,' said Kella.

'So I've been told,' said Sister Conchita.

TWENTY-THREE

It was three o'clock in the morning when Imison first thought he heard someone moving on the track leading down to the shore. He had been standing outside the fishermen's hut for several hours, cradling in his arms an M1 Garand semi-automatic rifle of the type used in the Korean War. Baxter and Lopez were sleeping inside the thatched hut. Like an experienced fighter relaxing between rounds, Baxter was breathing deeply, getting all the rest he could. Lopez, on the other hand, was sleeping only fitfully, whimpering and sometimes crying out. It was time Imison woke one of them up to take his place on guard duty, but he scorned the thought. He did not expect either of them to do a professional enough job. Baxter was competent but unimaginative, while Lopez was just a snivelling kid.

He scanned the moonlit sky for some signs of daylight, willing a rescuing dawn to arrive. Now that they had accomplished their mission, as soon as he could see to navigate the launch anchored off the coast, they would board it and head for Bougainville, eighty miles away. On his way to Olasana, he had transmitted an encoded message on the ship's transceiver to a Chinese trading store on Bougainville. They could be out of the Protectorate's waters in a couple of days, long before an efficient search could be mounted for them, even if Joe Dontate's body was found. A light aircraft, usually used for smuggling gold nuggets to Australia, would be waiting to take the three of them from Buin to Port Moresby in

Papua New Guinea. From there a scheduled airline flight would carry them to Fiji, where they would be issued with new passports. You had to hand it to the Agency; it was good at rescuing its operatives from screw-ups. Maybe it had had plenty of practice.

Imison was accustomed to getting out of tight corners in a hurry. He had been doing that for almost twenty years. He had not served in the campaign in the Solomons, as his cover story stated, but he had seen his share of clandestine action. As a young lieutenant, not long out of an undistinguished Midwestern law school, he had joined the Special Operations Branch of the Office of Strategic Services. After a brief period of commando training at Milton Hall in Britain, in 1944 he had been parachuted into France as the executive officer of one of the notorious three-man Jedburgh teams, charged with the task of joining up with the French Resistance and causing havoc behind the German lines in the run-up to the Normandy D-Day landings.

Imison had enjoyed his time in France. The combination of violence and intrigue had appealed to him. His natural talent for conspiracy and the remorseless infliction of death, noticed by his recruiting superiors in Washington, had stood him in good stead in the freebooting campaigns in which he was soon bloodily engaged. He had particularly enjoyed his contacts with the French Underground, an organisation so riddled with rival factions, collaborators and traitors as to resemble the court of a medieval Italian city-state in full conspiratorial flow. In addition to guiding nocturnal arms drops from Allied aircraft and participating in raids on isolated German positions, the self-righteous and calculating Imison had taken a particular delight in rooting out and killing those members of the Resistance surrounding him whom he had suspected of being paid by the Germans. Disregarding the need for evidence, the young lieutenant had relied entirely on his own intuition. He had been ruthlessly efficient at this self-imposed task, until one night he had gone too far and stabbed to death a French radio operator he had suspected of being a collaborator. Unfortunately, not only had the radio operator been young and comparatively blameless, if inclined to be a blabbermouth; he had also been closely related to a high-ranking officer in the Free French Army.

After the invasion of Europe, the newly reinstated general in question had wasted no time in launching an investigation into the death of his favourite nephew. Imison's cold, withdrawn and correct manner had secured him few friends amongst the American and French saboteurs with whom he had been working. Only nominal efforts were made to protect him, and for a time it looked as if the lieutenant might even face a court-martial. Fortunately he was flown back to the safety of a Stateside desk job at the last moment, but the episode was deemed potentially sufficiently explosive to ruin his coveted chances of a transfer in 1945 to the CIA, the natural peacetime successor to the OSS.

Instead Imison had been snapped up as a field agent by the more pragmatic but ever-expanding FBI, looking for men of his calibre, with iced water in their veins and the ability to render total and unquestioning obedience to their superiors. He had achieved notice following an enjoyable period as a field agent interrogating hapless Puerto Rican suspects after the nationalist group Los Macheteras had shot up the House of Representatives in Washington in 1954 and wounded five of its elected members. His zeal for the task, merciless interrogation technique and transparent exultation after the accused nationalists had been given minimum sentences of seventy years apiece had led to his appointment as legal attaché, responsible for liaison with local law-enforcement agencies, in the political and criminal free-for-alls of Mexico and Brazil and a number of similar wild areas of the world. His willingness to leave his desk in the US embassies in these countries and get his hands dirty, or even bloody, allied with his dubious wartime record, had, on the orders of the Director himself, also secured him a number of clandestine missions like the one upon which he was currently engaged.

Again Imison heard the rustling of leaves on the track leading to the beach. He started to go down to check, but restrained himself. Baxter and Lopez were not much, but they were the best he had and probably, although not certainly, better than nothing. They were also, as far as he was concerned, highly expendable. He walked softly into the hut and kicked both agents methodically as they lay huddled uncomfortably on the ground in their sleeping bags.

'Get up!' he muttered. 'Somebody's outside.'

At once the two men hauled themselves to their feet and reached automatically for their Garands. Around their shoulders they put slings containing eight-round clips of ammunition. Then they looked to their leader for instructions. Imison had not worked with either agent before their present excursion. The team had been put together at extremely short notice in response to an emergency situation. Lopez was the youngest of the trio, in his twenties, the communications specialist. He could operate a radio, but Imison was prepared to bet money that the boy's future as a field agent was as limited as that of a snowball in a warm place. Not only was Lopez nervous, he was also unlucky. To add to his misery he was transparently afraid of both of his companions on the mission. Baxter, dark-chinned and taciturn, was tougher, but as far as Imison was concerned, he possessed the damning trait of ambition. Baxter saw covert grey operations of this nature as a short cut to preferment in the Agency. Imison had news for him as explicit as that of a town crier: any kudos from this mission when it was over was going to its head honcho.

'Who's out there?' asked Baxter, checking his weapon.

'How the hell do I know?' snapped Imison. 'We'll go down the track a way and see.'

They emerged into the clearing. The hut they had been using had been erected by itinerant fishermen intending to spend the night on this deserted corner of the island. The narrow track to the beach had been slashed out roughly with bush knives and was already in danger of becoming overgrown again. The surrounding trees were so tightly packed that it was impossible to enter the bush area without sustaining painful abrasions.

'Lopez, you take point,' ordered Imison.

'Why me?' whined the youth. 'I ain't no soldier boy.'

'If there's anybody there, he's going to come at us out of the bush from the sides,' said Imison. 'Baxter and I will be marking those. For Christ's sake, can't you do anything right? All you've got to do is lead us down to the beach. Surely you can handle that chore?'

'Take point,' said Baxter, jostling the younger agent with the butt of his rifle and putting an end to the discussion.

Lopez muttered mutinously to himself but did as he was told. He had not known Imison and Baxter long, but he had been present when they had followed and shot Dontate, the tour guide, the previous day. He knew that both men were utterly ruthless and implacable, and that if he did not do as he was told, the likelihood of his ending up lying dead on some forgotten island at this arse-end of the world was higher than a hawk. If that eventuality ever came, he told himself, trying in vain to bolster his spirits, he would not just sit with his back to a mound of skulls and wait for the end like Dontate had done.

The three Americans made slow progress along the track. The branches of the trees formed a canopy overhead. Every time one of them thought he heard something he would come to a halt, and the other two would stop walking as well while the three men checked out the situation. Lopez was aware of the caution being deployed by his experienced companions, and this only increased his nervousness. Unconsciously he increased his pace. Soon he was a few yards ahead of the other two. Both Imison and Baxter noticed this. Neither called the youngest agent back, taking satisfaction in the knowledge that if Lopez should be stupid enough to trample unheedingly through unknown terrain, then he would be the first to encounter any hazards, making it all the safer for the other two.

Only a few minutes passed before Agent Lopez, as the other two had half-expected, ran into serious trouble. His baby face and scrawny knuckles torn and bleeding, he blundered forward, peering warily ahead of him. Unwittingly he passed between two stakes that Kella had earlier stuck into the ground on either side of the track. A length of vine, concealed like the stakes beneath mounds of leaves, joined the two pieces of wood. Lopez's boot tripped the flimsy rope. Another piece of the creeper ran from the vine on the ground to loop over the lower branch of a tree, where it was attached to the heavy spear of *kwilla* wood that Kella had sharpened at Munda. The action released the weapon, which hurtled down through the concealing creepers towards the unsuspecting Lopez below. The young agent did not even hear the projectile falling through the branches. It missed Lopez's head but smashed into his shoulder with agonizing force. The American screamed and fell writhing to the ground.

Imison and Baxter threw themselves on to the track, bringing their rifles up to their shoulders. Neither of them fired. There was no sign of any attacker. Nothing moved in the bush. After a few minutes they crawled cautiously over to the groaning Lopez. The heavy spear had shattered the young agent's collarbone and the point had than embedded itself deeply in his back. He was whimpering and beginning to lose consciousness.

'We can't carry him to the shore,' said Baxter. 'We'd be sitting ducks if anyone's waiting for us there.'

'What do you mean "if"?' said Imison. 'Drag him back to the hut. We'll leave him there.'

Roughly the two agents pulled Lopez's body back along the overgrown path. The journey was an arduous and bumpy one, but by this time the young man had lost consciousness and made no complaint. The two other men got him back to the clearing and hauled his slight body inside the fishermen's hut.

'Take the door,' said Imison. 'If you see anyone, blast him!'

'He ain't going to show himself,' said Baxter. 'Whoever he is, this guy ain't no novice.'

Baxter edged open the door and stared fixedly across the clearing, taking care to keep his body out of any line of fire. Imison heaved Lopez on to a sleeping bag and tore the young agent's shirt off. Lopez groaned. Imison examined his wounds. Then he walked across to Baxter at the door.

'How is he?' asked Baxter.

'He'll live. No way he's going to walk as far as the beach.'

'We'll have to leave him here, then.'

'I'd already figured that out.'

Imison walked back to the recumbent agent and leant over him while Baxter resumed his vigil at the door. Lopez's eyes flickered open.

'Am I dying?' he asked.

'You're going to be just fine, kid,' said Imison impatiently. 'Now listen to me. We're going to clear the way down to the beach. Then we'll come back for you. Have you got that?'

'You won't leave me here, will you?' asked Lopez.

'Of course not,' lied Imison. He had abandoned agents before. If the worst came to the worst, even a green novice like Lopez would probably know enough to keep his mouth shut until the Agency could figure out a way of extracting him.

'Stay loose, kid,' he said perfunctorily, and rejoined Baxter.

'I figure there's only one of them out there,' said Baxter, staring ahead. 'Any more and they would have stormed us by now.'

'Maybe,' said Imison. 'If he is on his own, he knows what he's doing. He fixed up that booby trap just a few yards from where I was standing and I didn't hear a thing. Then he deliberately made a noise to spook us and get us all out of the hut.'

'How do you want to play it?' asked Baxter. 'Shall we try to get out through the trees? My guess is the guy ain't armed, else he would have shot us full of holes by now.'

'No, that's what he wants us to do,' said Imison. 'This man's a jungle fighter and we're not. I say we stick to the path as long as we can. It's only thirty yards to the beach, and he shouldn't have had enough time to fix any more booby traps. Once we get into the trees, he can pick us off one at a time.'

'All right,' said Baxter reluctantly. 'At least we can look out for each other on the track.'

'Especially you looking after me,' said Imison. 'I can navigate the launch, and you can't. Remember, you need me more than I need you, buddy boy.'

Baxter threw Imison a look of unadulterated hatred, but nodded. The two men waited a moment. Then Baxter threw open the door and the two men ran zigzagging across the clearing to the edge of the track. They reached it in safety and began to shuffle uneasily along the path. They passed with particular care the tree from which the spear had descended upon Lopez, and started to edge forward through the overhanging tentacle-like branches. Imison came to a sudden halt.

'Wait!' he said.

He sank to his hands and knees and groped at the carpet of leaves on the ground before him. The surface started to yield. He shuffled quickly through the leaves. Soon he came to a latticework covering of long thin branches over a shallow pit. At the bottom of the hole, a dozen sharpened bamboo poles had been stuck into the ground. Anyone walking across the branches would have fallen through the frail covering on to the deadly wooden spikes below.

'That's it!' snarled Baxter. 'The bastard's probably booby-trapped the whole length of the path. I'll take my chances in the trees!'

Sister Conchita waited, cold, tired and hungry, on the beach. She listened to the waves pounding monotonously on the reef like the blows of a mighty hammer on an anvil. As soon as they had landed from the mission canoe on Olasana four hours ago, Kella had ordered her to wait there and not move, while he prepared the track from the shore to the fishermen's hut. He had then left her carrying a spade and a number of sharpened stakes. Conchita had seen no sight of the police sergeant since. She wondered if anything could have happened to him. After all, even with his local knowledge, he was up against odds of three to one, and the Americans were armed.

Conchita decided that she could wait no longer. She had to know what was going on in the interior of the island. She also wanted to get close to Kella, in case he was still determined to exact vengeance on Imison and the other two. She prayed that his resolve would have slackened by now. If she could only get near to him, she might be able to exert some sort of restraining influence on the possessed Malaita man. It was certainly her duty to try. Placing one foot carefully in front of the other, she started to walk inland through the trees and undergrowth, parallel to the track.

It was hard, laborious going, with even the pale moonlight blotted out by the branches and vines around and above her, but the nun continued doggedly forward. She had read that John F. Kennedy and his crew had kept to the south-east tip of the island when they had been sheltering there, in case there were Japanese troops already on Olasana. They had slept huddled together on the beach. If Imison and the others were intent on retracing Kennedy's steps for their own reason, they would not be far away from this area.

Half an hour later, her flesh lacerated in a dozen places, her habit stained and torn, she emerged in the clearing. From the hut on the other side she heard the sound of groans. She tiptoed across the intervening ground and peered cautiously in through the open door of the hut. The figure of a man lay on top of a sleeping bag. He was twisting and turning violently, obviously in pain. The nun entered the hut. It seemed to have been occupied recently. In addition to three sleeping bags on the ground, there were several holdalls, some tins of food and a small cardboard box.

Conchita hunted through both holdalls. In one of them was a small flashlight. She switched it on and approached the man groaning on top of the sleeping bag. He was young and scrawny, his ribs prominent as he lay stripped to the waist. Sister Conchita could see that one of his shoulders was twisted and contorted and that his back was bruised and bloody.

She went through the holdalls again but could find no sign of any medical supplies. Fortunately the young man, whom she recognized as one of the tourists in Imison's party, seemed to be drifting off into increasingly long periods of sleep. His cries and moans were becoming muffled, and eventually ceased altogether as he relaxed and began breathing deeply on top of the sleeping bag.

Conchita looked round the hut. She yielded to her curiosity and picked up the cardboard box. It seemed to be the same box that she had seen one of the Americans carrying ashore on Kasolo some days before. She took off the lid. The box contained half a dozen carved pieces of turtle shell. They were all the same. Each piece of turtle shell was stuck to a larger white flat seashell. On the central turtle shell was carved a rough facsimile of a frigate bird.

Conchita examined one of the shells. There was no doubt about it. It bore a strong resemblance to the carved shell she had taken from the tree house of Teiosi, the magic man she had found dead on Kolombangara. The headman there had implied that the magic man had taken the token from Kakaihe, the murdered guide who had conducted Sister Brigid on her ill-fated search for John F. Kennedy. The shells in the box seemed to be crude copies of the original.

Contentedly Kella could hear the two Americans blundering through the bush in the darkness. They were trying to get to the shore, but they kept being forced to make long detours around spectacularly large trees or avoid banks of particularly thorny undergrowth. This sometimes disorientated them, and they would start heading off in a completely different direction to the one they had originally been taking. All the same, throughout it all, the two men still kept together, a sign to Kella that they had undergone some form of military training even although obviously it had not been in bush conditions of this nature.

He kept close to the men, waiting patiently for them to grow tired. Once they did that, they would start drifting apart. Then would be the time for him to move in on Imison's companion. From what he had seen so far, the older of the two Americans was far sharper and more alert than the dark-chinned one. Kella would take out the second man and then concentrate on the leader of the expedition.

For the time being he contented himself with shadowing the Americans, moving through the bush close to them, sometimes to one side and then the other. Now and again he would drop some way behind them. He could always hear them moving and knew that he could catch up with them whenever he wanted to.

It would be as well for him to keep changing his position. Every so often, one or other of the two men would lift his rifle and fire blindly into the bush. The action had no effect other than to disturb birds nesting in the trees or to send an alarmed wild pig snorting through the bush. By now they were on the edge of a tidal mangrove swamp close to the sea. The warm salt water lapped at their ankles.

Finally the gap between the two Americans grew wider. Kella continued to hang back. Another ten minutes passed. By now the two men were out of sight of each other. To make matters better for Kella, Imison had turned in a full circle and was dragging himself back in the direction of the clearing and the hut. The sergeant let him go. He could track Imison whenever he needed to.

Silently he moved through the bush towards the second man. He could see his shadow flitting against the boles of the trees. He glided past the American and waited behind a tree. He picked up a substantial fallen branch and muttered the Lau incantation of revenge, '*The lightning flashed, why did the thunder not follow?*' The man staggered past him. Kella stepped out and brought the branch down as hard as he could on the back of the American's head. The branch broke but the man went sprawling forward into the undergrowth, dropping his rifle. Kella stooped and picked it up. The fallen man squirmed round and peered helplessly through the gloom at his assailant. Kella thought of Joe Dontate waiting resignedly for his death on Skull Island. He lifted the Garand. He also remembered Sister Conchita's entreaties. With no change of expression, he fired two shots.

The FBI agent screamed as two searing rounds went into his leg. His body jerked convulsively. Blood pumped out through the wounds. Ignoring the man, Kella hurried away through the trees, looking for signs of Imison's progress. He soon picked up his tracks. He was surprised to see that the American definitely seemed to be heading back to the clearing. Kella slowed his pace to let Imison reach the hut.

A quarter of an hour later, he was standing behind a tree on the edge of the clearing. There were signs of activity from the hut thirty yards away. Then the door was flung open, and Imison came out, pushing someone before him. Kella could see that it was Sister Conchita.

'I know you're there,' shouted Imison across the clearing. 'Come out, or I'll kill the nun!'

TWENTY-FOUR

'I mean what I say!' shouted Imison. 'Come out of those trees before I pull the trigger!'

There was a long pause, and then Kella came watchfully into the clearing. He was carrying the Garand of the agent he had shot in the bush.

'Put that rifle down and come over,' said Imison, pushing Sister Conchita forward so that she was standing between him and the policeman.

Kella placed the Garand on the ground and then walked steadily over towards the hut. From within, Lopez could be heard sobbing in pain.

'That's far enough,' said Imison when Kella was a few yards away. 'Who are you anyway?'

'I'm Sergeant Kella of the British Solomon Islands Police Force. I'm here to arrest you for the murders of Joe Dontate on Skull Island and Ed Blamire at Marakosi.'

Imison laughed mirthlessly. 'You've got a nerve,' he said. 'What happened to Baxter? I see you've got his rifle.'

'He's back in the bush.'

'Dead, I suppose?'

'No,' said Kella. 'As it happens, he's still alive.'

'Thank God!' said Sister Conchita, feeling inexpressibly relieved. 'You only wounded them.'

'That's no use to me,' said Imison. 'They're both out of action.'

'Another ten minutes and I would have got you too,' said Kella regretfully.

'Is that supposed to reassure me?' asked Imison.

'I'm sorry,' said Sister Conchita miserably. 'It's all my fault.'

'Most of it is anyway, I'd say,' agreed Imison. 'Don't worry. You certainly did me a favour. I came back to the hut for some more ammunition and I found the sister ministering to the sick. It just shows you that no good deed ever goes unpunished. Just when I was wondering how I could get off this island, too.'

'Let her go,' said Kella. 'You've got me as a hostage. You don't need her any more.'

'What the hell are you talking about?' asked Imison. 'Are you crazy? I don't want hostages. All I need is a way to get back to the launch without being shot, and now I've got it, thanks to the sister here.'

'You won't get the other two on board,' said Kella with subdued satisfaction. 'They can't walk, and they both need medical help.'

'Whose fault is that?' asked Imison. 'I never liked either of them anyway. Yes, I have to say that you've sadly depleted my crew. Luckily I can handle the steering by myself.'

'It was the *knap knap*, wasn't it?' asked Sister Conchita suddenly. With a pang of shame, she realized that even at a moment when the lives of both Sergeant Kella and herself were in danger, she still felt impelled to get to the root of what had been happening. Imison also seemed to recognize the incongruity of her enquiry.

'What?' he asked irritably.

'That's why you're here in the Solomons. Somewhere you heard a rumour about the islander guide Kakaihe and his taking an offer of safe conduct to Lieutenant Kennedy and the other survivors from PT-109 as long as they surrendered to the Japanese, and you came here to check it out. When you couldn't prove anything, you got Joe Dontate to manufacture some replicas of the *knap knaps* at his Gizo shell factory. You scattered some of them on Kasolo, the first island Kennedy landed on, and now you've come to Olasana to do the same thing here before you leave the Solomons. If you ever want to tarnish Mr Kennedy's reputation, you can arrange for someone to find one of those carved shells one day, and all the old rumours will start circulating again. That's a disgraceful act!'

'You catch on quick,' said Imison.

'I saw those frigate bird *knap knaps* in the hut Mary Gui was sharing with Joe Dontate in the bush village on Kolombangara,' said Kella. 'So that's why Dontate knocked me out and had me put on the trading vessel. He had been on the way to deliver the fake *knap knaps* to you, Imison. He left them overnight in Mary's hut and was frightened that I had seen them and would recognize their significance. He overestimated me. I didn't even catch on when I saw some more of the shell frigate birds in Dontate's Gizo shell house.'

'It would all have gone fine if it hadn't been for Dontate,' said Imison. 'He supplied the *knap knaps* and was well paid for them. The he started getting scruples and said that he wanted to pull out.'

'So you shot him,' said Kella. Desperately he tried to think of something else to say to retain the American's attention. For the past few minutes he had been aware of a figure scurrying across the clearing behind Imison. He tried to look everywhere except in the direction of the hut.

'Who sent you?' he asked. 'Who wants to blacken Kennedy's reputation? I suppose it's somebody who doesn't want him to become president?'

'You know I can't tell you that,' said Imison. 'All I can say is that it was a sweet little scheme, before it started going wrong, sweet as a nut. We can't waste any more time. Sister, you go and stand next to the sergeant. It'll be light in an hour and I must be getting on my way.'

Slowly Sister Conchita walked over and stood next to Sergeant Kella. Kella tensed to leap across at the American, although he knew that he would surely be shot down before he had covered even half of the distance between them. A swarm of fireflies danced delicately across the clearing. This was a bad omen; fireflies were regarded as the ghosts of men killed in battle. Kella wished that he could have some indication from the ghosts of what was going to happen. The previous day, after his return to Munda from Skull Island, he had forced himself to sleep for an hour, in the hope that his *ano*, his soul, would leave him as he rested and wander freely, to return later and tell him what it had seen across the lagoon. There had been no such visitation.

He commended his soul to the safe keeping of his ancestor Sina Kwao, the war god known as Shining White because of the light colour of his skin, who had journeyed to the artificial island of Sulufou from far over the seas. Then he prepared to launch himself at the American.

It was then that the apparition struck from the shadows of the hut. As Imison shifted the position of his rifle, the figure sprang forward, a knife raised in its hand. Imison heard a sound, but before he could turn, his attacker was on him, striking fiercely at his neck and back. Imison screamed and fell to the ground. The figure toppled over on top of him and struck savagely twice more. Imison lay still. The figure stood up.

'This is the second man I have killed on Olasana,' he said sadly, hurling his knife as far away from him as he could into the trees. 'The dreaded gods of war must assuredly follow me here to torment me.'

It was the dignified patrician politician Welchman Buna.

TWENTY-FIVE

'Lieutenant John F. Kennedy came from a wealthy and influential family,' said Welchman Buna, as if reciting the bloodline of a much-respected traditional chief. 'After his ship had been sunk by the Japanese in the Roviana Lagoon, there were all sorts of rumours. Some claimed that he and his crew must have been asleep not to see the Japanese destroyer bearing down on them that night. Others said that he narrowly avoided a court-martial afterwards.' The politician paused. 'And there were stories that Kennedy and his men were so upset that they had not been rescued quickly, that they were even contemplating surrendering to the Japanese.'

'And these were all lies?' asked Sister Conchita.

'Of course, but there are always those who are prepared to think the worst of the privileged.'

They were sitting in the refectory at Marakosi Mission. Around the long table were the four sisters of the mission, Sergeant Kella and Welchman Buna. Several days had passed since Buna had attacked Imison and saved the lives of Sister Conchita and Kella. During that time, a police launch had arrived at Olasana and taken on board the stricken bodies of the American FBI agents. All three men had been taken to Pilgrim Hospital in Honiara, the capital. A cryptic radio message to the mission, which would have meant nothing to outsiders listening in, had informed Sergeant Kella that the Americans were expected to live. Sister Conchita, Kella and Buna were waiting for a government vessel to arrive some time over the next few days to take them all to Honiara to attend a series of meetings about the events in the Roviana Lagoon over the last two weeks.

'How did you get involved in the affair, Mr Buna?' Kella asked.

Buna looked across the table at Sister Brigid. The elderly nun seemed a different person since the politician had arrived at the mission. She had greeted his arrival first with incredulity and then with transparent joy. Since then the pair of them had spent much time wandering around the island deep in conversation. They seemed to have arrived at some sort of agreement, because the nun was now almost beaming as she looked proudly across the table at the islander.

'It started in August 1943,' said Buna. 'The coast-watchers were sending every man who could be spared to search for the missing seamen from PT-109. I was only a young man then, but I had already helped look for a number of downed US pilots in the lagoon. On this occasion I had just finished searching a small island called Nisi when Sister Brigid and her guide Kakaihe also landed there.'

'I had picked up Kakaihe on Kolombangara,' said the nun. 'I had never met him before, but he seemed eager to take part in the search. We stopped off at Nisi for water.'

'We were to find out why very soon,' said Buna. 'The three of us agreed to join together because it would make searching the islands easier. Next we paddled to Olasana.'

'So you actually found Lieutenant Kennedy and his men?' asked Sister Conchita.

'Not quite, although we came very close, as you will hear,' said Buna. 'It was night by the time we landed on Olasana. We were very quiet because we weren't sure if there would be Japanese on the island. As it happened, there were no Japanese there.'

'But Lieutenant Kennedy and his men were sleeping on another section of the beach round a headland,' said Sister Brigid, who was growing quite animated by her standards. Little red spots of excitement burned on her pale cheeks.

'We didn't know that, of course,' said Buna. 'We decided to sleep on the beach and search Olasana the following morning. Sister Brigid rested in a small tent she had brought with her, and Kakaihe and I slept in the open on the beach a short distance away.'

'A few hours after we had all retired, I heard the sounds of a struggle on the beach,' said the elderly nun. 'Mr Buna and Kakaihe were fighting one another over a knife. It was a dreadful sight in the moonlight.'

'I had returned from attending to a call of nature,' said Buna with some embarrassment. 'When I did so, I found Kakaihe examining something on the beach. He seemed to be making preparations to leave. He tried to hide what he was looking at, but I demanded that he show it to me. He refused, so I took it from him and examined it. It was a frigate *knap knap*.'

'A signal of safe passage,' frowned Conchita. 'But . . .'

'Or a sign of surrender,' said Buna. 'It was then that I guessed what had happened, of course. Kolombangara was occupied by many Japanese soldiers at the time. Some of the villagers on the island were on quite good terms with the Japanese, and would scout for them and perform other services, like looking for coast-watchers and reporting on their whereabouts.'

'Kakaihe was working for the Japanese?' asked Conchita.

'It was uncommon, but it did happen,' said Buna. 'Kakaihe was young and not very bright. In addition, his tribe was engaged in a blood feud with some of the villages that were supporting the Americans. I believe that he was using the *knap knap* to gain safe passage among all the islanders in the lagoon, while he looked for the stranded American sailors. If he found them, he would report their presence to the Japanese on Kolombangara.'

'So he was a traitor,' said Conchita.

'Let us say that he had no particular allegiances,' said Buna. 'After all, with a few exceptions, most of the British in the Solomons had fled to Australia as soon as the war had broken out. That dented the confidence of some islanders in the invincibility of the white men.'

'Could you prove that he was working for the Japanese?' asked Kella.

'Oh yes, I had my suspicions confirmed in a most violent manner that night,' said Buna drily. 'When I saw the *knap knap* and had guessed what it was, Kakaihe suddenly produced a knife and attacked me with it from behind. We struggled on the sand. It was then that Sister Brigid came out of her tent. I'm afraid that what she witnessed must have horrified her. I was bigger and stronger than Kakaihe. I managed to get the knife from him and stabbed him with it. When I examined his body, I saw that he was dead.'

'What did you do?' asked Sister Johanna.

'I thought it best to get off Olasana as quickly as possible, in case there were Japanese on the island and we had aroused them with the noise of our struggle. Sister Brigid was in a state of considerable shock by this time.'

'I had never seen a man killed before,' said the elderly nun.

'I paddled Sister Brigid and Kakaihe's body back to Kolombangara,' said Buna. 'Then I made myself scarce. I knew that the villagers would bury Kakaihe and see to it that Sister Brigid was taken back to her mission. Soon after that, two other islanders came across Lieutenant Kennedy and his men and escorted them to safety. All in all, a most satisfactory conclusion to the affair, except that ever since, rumours have persisted that John F. Kennedy and the survivors of PT-109 were preparing to surrender to the Japanese, which was a total and complete lie, of course.'

'But I don't understand why Mr Imison and his two friends came to the Solomons,' said Sister Johanna.

'It's complicated,' said Buna vaguely.

The politician would say no more. A few minutes later the meeting broke up. Buna indicated with an almost imperceptible nod of his head that he wished to speak to Conchita and Kella. The three of them gathered in a small group in a corner of the room. Buna waited until the other sisters had left before he spoke.

'I think I owe you both a further explanation,' he said. 'Shall we go for a stroll?'

It was a warm evening on the beach, with just a soft breeze coming in from the lagoon. Buna led the way along the sand, fastidiously skirting the rocks and small pools.

'That night when I killed Kakaihe changed my life,' he began abruptly. 'I reported back to Lieutenant Evans, the coast-watcher, and he sent me to see some American officers at their headquarters on Tulagi. They questioned me closely about what had happened. They seemed very pleased that Lieutenant Kennedy had got back safely with his men and that I had inadvertently prevented his falling into the hands of the Japanese.'

There was a rustling among the trees, and the nocturnal invasion of coconut crabs began in the cool night air. They were huge creatures, around five or six pounds in weight, three feet long and with a leg span of thirty inches. They burst out of their burrows containing beds of packed coconut fibre beneath the outer ring of trees, and began swarming over the area in their search for food, providing a living brown carpet of heaving movement. The two men paid no attention to them, but Sister Conchita, captivated, stopped to watch.

'It would have been a feather in their cap if the Japanese had captured somebody as well connected as John F. Kennedy,' said Kella.

'No doubt! Anyway, I was passed from one officer to another on Tulagi and Guadalcanal, repeating my story again and again. Each one seemed to have more braid on his shoulders than the one before. The war in the Solomons was almost over by this time. I didn't know it, but the Americans were starting to plan for the post-war period when they would have to hand the islands back to British colonial rule. They wanted to have their own carefully selected islanders in place for the day when independence would be granted.'

Some of the crabs were already hauling themselves up the trunks of coconut palms, using their massive claws to gain a purchase on the wood, looking for edible leaves and using their pincers to nip off coconuts and send them crashing to the ground below.

'Sleepers,' said Sergeant Kella. 'People like that are called sleepers, because they have to lie dormant for a long while. You were one of those?'

'If you say so, Sergeant, although I was ignorant of the word you have just used. I was given a regular weekly salary and told to make my way to the new capital, Honiara. I was to build upon my mission-school education, and also to take the opportunity to enter local politics. Any expenses I incurred would be reimbursed, as long as I made my way up the political ladder. As I was suddenly financially independent, I did not have to work and could devote all my time to studying and voluntary public service, and eventually enter the Administrative Council and nurse my constituency in the Roviana Lagoon.'

The orange-red coconut crabs on the ground were still massed together. They did not venture more than thirty yards from the holes in which they spent their daylight hours. Two of them were fighting savagely for possession of a dead fish on the sand. Both creatures were emitting a clicking sound and stretching their legs to a tiptoeing position. If they were hungry enough, they would kill and eat one another. Guiltily, Conchita ran lightly along the beach to catch up with the two islanders.

'The Americans would have asked around,' said Kella, 'and discovered that you came from a good bloodline, had an outstanding educational record and were well thought of on your own island. You were a potential vote-gatherer. In addition, they would have known from the way that you dealt with Kakaihe on Olasana that you were also brave and resourceful.'

'Presumably; it is not for me to say. For their part, the Americans continued to pay me but otherwise made no attempt to contact me for seventeen years, until a few months ago.'

Sister Conchita looked back over her shoulder. One crab was hauling a length of seaweed across the sand, out of the way of the others, so that it could pause to examine the potential source of food at its leisure. During the war, coconut crabs had invaded the trenches being occupied by American marines at the height of the fighting in order to steal their provisions.

'What happened then?' asked Sister Conchita, returning her attention to the men.

'It seemed,' said Buna thoughtfully, 'that the devil-devils of 1943 were returning to haunt the Roviana Lagoon again. My contact alerted me to the fact that a group of FBI agents was coming to look for evidence that Lieutenant Kennedy and the rest of his crew had considered surrendering to the Japanese while they were on Olasana. Needless to say, if that turned out to be true, then Mr Kennedy's chances in the forthcoming election would be negligible.'

'Why would the FBI be interested?' asked Sister Conchita.

'It was not so much the organization as its director, Mr J. Edgar Hoover. Apparently Mr Hoover likes to keep tabs on all influential Americans, in case he may be able to use that information to his advantage one day.'

'Herbert's secret files,' said Sister Conchita. 'I've read about those.'

A number of the crabs had discovered fallen coconuts lying on the ground. They bowled them over with their pincers, looking for cracks in the husks that would enable them to gain a purchase on the nuts and tear them open with their claws.

'It's in all the newspapers,' went on Conchita. 'Apparently he even has ones on Albert Einstein and Mrs Eleanor Roosevelt. That's not very nice. I can't think why he does it.'

'Simple,' said Buna. 'It makes him a very powerful man. It is said that none of the last four American presidents has dared sack him because he knows where too many bodies are buried. The same might have applied to Mr Kennedy if Hoover's agents had been able to prove that he showed cowardice in action.'

'Which they couldn't,' said Kella. 'So you're saying they deliberately planted evidence in the shape of the *knap knaps*? Incidentally, how do you know all this?'

'The construction of the US government organization is not unlike like that of the feuding headhunting tribes of the nineteenth-century Solomon Islands,' said Buna. 'It is a matter of constantly shifting alliances and antagonisms. The FBI, the CIA, the Secret Service, the State Department and a dozen other agencies all live in a constant state of armed neutrality. As I understand it, I am employed by the State Department. This institution keeps a wary eye on the others. It heard that Mr Hoover was sending a small team to investigate John F. Kennedy just before the presidential election, and asked me to keep an eye on the team when it arrived, and report back to my paymasters.'

Conchita noticed that already the crabs had denuded the ground and were lumbering back contentedly to their holes. They were confident in the knowledge that they had no natural predators on the islands and that at Marakosi Mission not even the humans bothered to hunt them. That's the problem, she thought, we haven't been proactive enough.

'So you knew all about Imison's schemes,' said Sister Conchita.

Welchman Buna shook his head. 'I had been briefed. I knew they were gathering information on Mr Kennedy, hoping to file it in case it came in useful for the FBI one day. I knew nothing about the *knap knap* scheme. You discovered that, Sister Conchita. The credit belongs to you. When Mary Gui arrived in Gizo yesterday and told the authorities about the murder of Dontate, it was plain that Imison and the other two would have to act quickly before leaving the Protectorate. While the District Commissioner waited for help from Honiara, I paddled a small canoe to Olasana and came ashore farther along the coast. I was alerted by the sound of rifles being fired and made my way to the hut in the dark. The rest you know.'

'Thank goodness you did!' said Sister Conchita.

'Yes, indeed,' said Kella. 'But where does Ed Blamire, the tourist who was murdered, come into this?'

'I don't know,' said Buna. 'Perhaps my employers do, but they have not shared that information with me.'

'Then why did Imison and the other Americans kill Mr Blamire at the mission on open day?' asked Sister Conchita.

Welchman Buna looked surprised. 'They didn't,' he said. 'That isn't possible.'

'What do you mean?' asked Sister Conchita.

'The Americans certainly did not harm Mr Blamire,' said Buna. 'Acting on my instructions, I was watching Imison and the other FBI agents all the time that afternoon at the mission open day. None of them went anywhere near the church. You can take my word for it: they did not kill Ed Blamire!'

'And I thought we had solved the murder,' sighed Sister Conchita unhappily.

An hour had passed. Welchman Buna had gone to his bed in the guest quarters of the mission, expressing profusely his courteous and pained regrets at having ruined their theories about the murder of Ed Blamire. Sister Conchita had gone to the kitchen to prepare sweet potatoes for the next day's main meal. Kella had followed and was helping her.

'It looks as if we're back to the beginning,' he said.

'Almost everybody in the district seems to have been at the open day,' Conchita said. 'Most of them had the opportunity to kill poor Mr Blamire.'

'He knew somebody was after him,' said Kella. 'You saw him waiting in the church and sensed that he was worried about something. He couldn't get off the island and was trapped there. He was expecting someone to kill him. He knew that he had antagonized someone dangerous.'

'And he had claimed sanctuary in the mission church,' said Sister Conchita. 'That's what grates on me.'

'It would almost be easier,' said Kella, pursuing his line of thought, 'to work out who *wasn't* at the mission that afternoon.'

The door opened and Sister Jean Francoise came in. She was carrying several tuna fish wrapped in banana leaves.

'I bought these from some fishermen who put in at the reef,' she said. 'I'll store them in the fridge and we can eat them tomorrow.'

'They look good,' said Sister Conchita.

'At least they'll be better than the ones that poor boy ate,' said Sister Jean Francoise, opening the door of the generator-powered refrigerator and depositing the tuna inside. She closed the door. 'It's a wonder he wasn't poisoned.'

'What boy?' asked Conchita. She wondered where Sister Jean Francoise's wandering mind had taken her on this occasion.

'You know, the nice one you brought to the clinic a few days ago,' said Sister Jean Francoise, dusting her hands on the front of her habit. 'What do you call them – VSOs.'

'Do you mean Andy Russell?' asked Conchita. 'What does he have to do with eating fish?'

'That's why you brought him to the hospital, wasn't it?' asked Sister Jean Francoise. 'He'd made himself ill eating some dreamfish. I know the signs. I thought you realized.'

'The *gnarli* fish?' asked Kella, suddenly alert. 'The boy had made himself ill by eating *gnarli*? Are you sure?'

'Of course I'm sure,' said Sister Jean Francoise. 'I can recognize the symptoms of eating dreamfish when I see them. It was very naughty of the boy. I suppose some of the islanders told him about it. They picked the habit up from Japanese soldiers during the war, of course. Good night.'

'What were you both talking about?' asked Conchita after the other nun had left the kitchen. 'And what does it have to do with Andy Russell?'

'Let me try to get this straight,' said Kella. 'You didn't know that Russell was suffering from food poisoning when you brought him to the mission from Kasolo?'

'Why, no, I thought he'd been out in the sun for too long, left alone on the island like that. What is this dreamfish Sister Jean Francoise was talking about?'

'The *gnarli* is a small fish with a stripe running along the side of its body. It's not eaten in the Solomons because it doesn't taste very nice. But if it's cooked the right way, it causes hallucinations in the person eating it. The Japanese stationed in the west used to catch them for just that purpose. It was their equivalent of taking drugs, sitting around a campfire.'

'Then Sister Jean Francoise was right. Andy was very naughty to experiment with such things, especially when he was all alone on the island,' said Sister Conchita. 'Perhaps it was all a mistake. He was hungry and might not have known the effects the dreamfish would have on him.'

'There's more to it than that,' said Kella. 'You've got to cook and eat just the right amount of the *gnarli* to induce hallucinations. If you have too much, then you go into a coma that can last up to thirty-six hours.'

'The poor boy,' said Sister Conchita vaguely. 'On top of everything else on that wretched island, he suffered from food poisoning as well.'

'Unless,' said Kella, 'he did it on purpose.'

'Surely not?' said Sister Conchita. 'Why on earth would he want to do that?'

'To provide himself with an alibi,' said Kella. He warmed to his proposition. 'We've been discarding Andy as a suspect in the attacks on the logging camp because he was in a coma when you brought him to the hospital. Suppose it was a self-induced coma? He was on the island. He waited until the fishermen landed, then as a bonus you came by. He had already caught the dreamfish and recognized what they were, so he had cooked them in advance. Just before any visitors arrived, he ate them.'

Sister Conchita remembered the remnants of charred fish on the fire by the VSO's tent on Kasolo the day she had found him lying gibbering in his sleeping bag.

'When I arrived, he was incoherent,' she said.

'That would be the first hallucinatory effects of eating the fish,' said Kella excitedly. 'But Russell had deliberately eaten too much. As you and the fishermen loaded him into the mission canoe, he went into the second stage – a deep coma. You assumed that he had been drifting in and out of unconsciousness for days and therefore couldn't have left Kasolo, so he wasn't a suspect in any wrongdoing. In reality, there had been nothing wrong with him until a few minutes before you arrived on the island.'

'Good heavens!' said Sister Conchita.

Kella frowned. 'Wait a minute,' he said. 'How could he have got off the island? He was stranded there.'

Sister Conchita concentrated. Half-formed images of her two visits to Kasolo began to run jerkily though her mind, like an old and flickering film being exposed in slow motion.

'Not necessarily,' she said, racking her brain. 'There were things that I noticed and stored but didn't think about at the time.'

'What sort of things?' asked Kella.

'The first time I visited the island, I followed the fishermen along a track to a clearing where Andy was lying.'

'What did you notice?' asked Kella, who had reason to have considerable faith in the nun's powers of observation and retention.

'The first time I was there, I noticed that the grass along one side of the track had recently been crushed flat by a heavy object about six feet long and half as wide.'

'Like a canoe?' asked Kella.

'Exactly. Yet when I returned to Kasolo a few days later, and met Imison and Dontate, all the grass had sprung up again and there was no sign of any indentation.'

'And your inference from this?' prompted Kella.

'That the grass sprang back into place quickly once any object placed on top of it was removed. Almost certainly the impression I saw on the grass earlier had been caused by a canoe only recently, although Andy claimed to have been stranded alone on the island with no form of transport for almost a month.'

'It sounds as if young Mr Russell has been telling lies,' said Kella.

'There's something else,' said Sister Conchita. 'When I first saw Andy on Kasolo, he was at the hallucinatory stage after eating the dreamfish. He was rambling. He said something in pidgin.'

'What?'

'He said *painim aut*. What does that mean?'

'It means "to find out",' said the sergeant slowly. His eyes locked with Sister Conchita's.

'Somebody had discovered him and his canoe on the island, when he was supposed to be stranded there without transport,' said the nun.

'Ed Blamire?' suggested Kella. 'He borrowed a canoe and left Munda to look at the islands where Kennedy and his crew had hidden. Andy Russell knew that Blamire could break his alibi.'

'What are we going to do about it?' asked Sister Conchita.

'I think the best thing would be to have a chat with the lad,' said Sergeant Kella.

TWENTY-SIX

'We've got to find Andy Russell and Mary Gui,' said Kella. 'Andy no longer has an alibi to prove that he wasn't at the mission open day, and I don't think Mary has told us everything she knows.'

'You find Andy while I look for Mary,' said Sister Conchita.

'Why that way round?' asked Kella.

'Because I don't think you would be totally impartial if you were to question Mary,' said Sister Conchita bravely. Oops, she could have put that better, she thought as she saw the sheepish expression on the sergeant's face. She determined to stick to her guns. Knowing Kella, as she was beginning to, there was likely to be some sort of history between him and the attractive rest-house proprietor. She was aware of the sergeant's reputation for fully appreciating the young women he met in the course of his official duties, and this particular western girl was not only intelligent and sophisticated, but also very beautiful and spirited.

'You don't like Mary, do you?' asked the sergeant unexpectedly.

'She is one of God's creatures and as such is to be cherished,' replied the nun. Kella's sceptical gaze did not leave her face. 'No,' she said. 'I'm sorry, but I believe Miss Gui has an eye to the main chance and that her ambition exceeds her regard for her fellow men and women. There, I've said it, and I'm not sorry!'

'Hmm!' said Kella drily. 'Obviously I've seen another side of Miss Gui. However, speaking as a policeman, I have to admit that you're right. Mary knows where she's going, even if she's not sure who's going with her. Go ahead, see if you can find her.'

They were standing on the wharf at Gizo in the early-morning sunshine. They had dragged the mission canoe up on to the beach. It lay a few yards away from them, tilted on its side. Inland, the district centre looked as somnolent and neglected as usual. Those few islanders and expatriates who were already around were moving slowly and without any great sense of purpose. Kella nodded to the nun and started walking along the wharf, past the moored vessels.

Sister Conchita was both shrewd and observant, he thought. She had certainly summed Mary up dispassionately. If he had not been so attracted to Mary, he wondered if he would even have liked her. Yes, he would, he told himself. That evening in the Mendana Hotel she had showed herself to be both brave and difficult to subdue, even by a gaggle of middle-class expatriate women. There was a lot to Mary Gui, and he was not thinking exclusively of her undeniable physical assets.

There were a few battered trading vessels with shallow draughts moored to the wharf, taking on board cargoes of copra and fruit and vegetables, as well as tins of diesel fuel. They were made to appear almost spanking new by a decrepit private yacht lying next to them, with several rake-thin, sun-blackened, heavily bearded expatriates sprawled exhaustedly on its deck. Probably another would-be round-the-world effort in the throes of disintegration, thought Kella. It would come to an end as soon as the disillusioned young crew abandoned the effort and wired home for money, or sank ignominiously and ingloriously among the reefs somewhere offshore.

He continued his progress along the wharf. With half a dozen inter-island trading vessels waiting to leave, the odds were that at least half of them would be crewed by Malaita men, and of these crews, a large proportion would come from the Lau area. He found who he had been looking for two-thirds of the way along the jetty.

As it happened, they were not seamen. A wizened elderly islander was sitting on an upturned box, smoking a clay pipe. There were half a dozen other Malaitans around him, all stevedores living in Gizo, whose job it was to load and unload visiting vessels. Kella could see from the tribal markings on the old man's face that he came from the Lau lagoon area. The policeman nodded respectfully and squatted on the deck next to the old man, politely making sure, as a sign of the deference due to age, that he was at a lower level than the other islander.

'*Maani koba ana uta*,' he said. 'May you be warmed by the sun.'

The old islander nodded. He took his pipe from his mouth and gave the traditional title of respect to the *aofia*. '*Lau talo inao*. The first to take up a shield in battle.'

'I am looking for a young white man,' went on Kella in Lau after a further leisurely exchange of compliments. 'His name is Andy Russell. He is tall and thin and does odd jobs for the government. Do you know him?'

The old man pointed with the stem of his pipe. 'Sometimes he works at the canoe village, half an hour's walk along the beach,' he said.

It was a pleasant morning as Kella left Gizo and walked in the direction indicated by the old wharf labourer. The sand was warm beneath his feet. Small hermit crabs, alarmed by his approach, scuttled out from beneath the shells littering the beach and ran in all directions. It did not take long to leave the district centre behind him. When he reached it, the canoe village was no more than a hamlet of four huts clustered a hundred yards in from the beach, on the bank of a stream running down to the sea. On the sand between the huts and the beach were a number of canoes in various stages of construction. They ranged from simple dugouts to a half-completed ornate replica of a war canoe, complete with a fierce Nguzunguzu figurehead representing the god of war. Isolated pieces of half-completed hand-carved accoutrements lay scattered on the ground waiting to be fitted into place, including outlines of ribs, gunnels, thwarts and stem pieces. A fire containing burning tongs had been kept alight so that the interiors of some of the canoes could be burnt out when the time came.

Next to the canoes on the sand were thirty or forty wet logs drying in the morning heat, each about twenty feet long, of good-quality wood, already stripped of their branches and planed to a rough finish.

Four men were working on the canoes. They toiled with the confident air of men comfortable in their own physicality and secure in the knowledge that they were good at the work they did. One was in his fifties. The other three were younger, presumably the sons of the older man. They looked at Kella with hostility, but did not at once stop working. Finally one of the younger men put down his adze and walked over to the sergeant. He was slight but muscular, with the bunched shoulder muscles of a paddler. He was not overtly aggressive, but neither was there any trace of humility in his attitude.

'What does the white man's policeman want here?' he said in good English. 'We keep the law and mind our own business.'

'I'm looking for the young white man called Andy,' said Kella. 'He is a VSO. I am told that he works here.'

'Sometimes,' said the islander. 'He is not here today.'

'How does he help you?' asked Kella.

'We are teaching him to become a canoe-maker,' said the islander. 'The whiteys give him nothing to do and he is bored.'

Kella nodded. 'Is that the only way that he helps you?' he asked.

The young islander did not answer. His brothers and father had stopped working and were looking on suspiciously. Kella ignored them and walked past the canoes under construction to the line of logs just above the high-water mark on the beach. He examined the tree trunks, taking his time, aware of the gaze of the canoe-building family. The work on the canoes was of good quality. The men of the village were craftsmen and so would be doing very nicely for themselves at a time when the prices of canoes ranged from a few Australian dollars for a simple dugout to ten times that amount for one seating six people.

'You do good work,' he said, walking back to the group of men. 'But you are lucky to find such fine-quality wood on an island like this.'

'It is driftwood,' said the young islander quickly. 'We find it floating in the sea after storms and drag it ashore.'

'Driftwood consisting of the finest kauri trees, ready-trimmed to be sent to factories in Australia?' asked Kella, raising a sceptical eyebrow. 'Truly the sea gods have been good to you and your line, canoe-maker. You do not need to pray when you are so well treated by the sacred ones.'

'That's just the way it happened,' said the young islander sulkily.

'I wish I could believe you,' said Kella. 'Unfortunately, I don't. Nobody could be that lucky. Do you know what I think has happened? I think somebody has visited the logging camp at Alvaro when it was dark. That somebody removed the wooden boom from a pool of treated logs in the lagoon, waiting for the next transport ship to be sent overseas. With the boom gone, the logs floated out into the main lagoon. There were people waiting in canoes in the dark for that to happen, people from a family of canoe-builders, perhaps. These men steered as many logs as they could back to their village on Gizo island and pulled them ashore. Then, if anyone asked, they could say that the logs were driftwood, saved from the sea. But we know better, don't we, brother? We also know that it's illegal. The whitey in charge at Alvaro will surely bring the police in if he finds out that someone has been stealing his best wood. Perhaps someone will tell him this.'

'You would betray another islander to a whitey?'

'I would do my duty as a police officer,' said Kella.

Without another word, the young islander turned and walked back to his waiting father and brothers. He spoke urgently to them.

They replied at length in undertones in their own language. He nodded and walked back to Kella. Kella guessed that he had received permission from his family to talk freely. After all, the canoe-builders owed no loyalty to the white youth. He was right.

'What do you want to know?' the young islander asked resignedly.

Joe Dontate's home village was a series of hovels on one of the foothills behind Gizo. The hamlet was too close to the district centre to be more than a caricature of an island community. It looked as if most of the detritus from Gizo had been hurled contemptuously up the hill by giant hands and had come to rest among the squalid assemblage of thatched huts. Scattered about the village square were discarded iron baths, the chassis of an ancient truck, holed pots and saucepans and various items of shattered furniture, suitable only for firewood. Scrawny chickens pecked their way amid the rubbish, and dogs yapped mournfully. No wonder Joe Dontate had been willing to take up the hardest sport of all if it had presented the opportunity of fighting his way out of this squalor, thought Sister Conchita.

Some flustered young island sisters of the Roman Catholic church, in the district centre, surprised to see the white nun, had told her that Dontate's pathway sending was to be held in his village that morning, and that Mary Gui had announced her intention of attending. It was a sign of the lack of character of the village that it did not even have a name. It had taken Conchita forty-five minutes to climb the hill. Behind her sprawled the dull vista of Gizo itself, and then the beautiful languid lagoon dotted with islets. On the far side of the village, the rate of ascent grew steeper. The central hills of the island suddenly rose starkly against the cloudless sky like alarmed sentinels called to arms.

Conchita could not help comparing the tawdry nature of her

surroundings with the loveliness of the mission she had just left. She felt a sense of despair. Perhaps Marakosi was too beautiful. It represented a shelter, which its sisters were unwilling to leave. Had she done anything in the month she had been there to bring them closer to reality? Was she the right person to try? Had she failed in the project handed to her by the order? She had certainly made a complete muddle of her investigation into the death of Ed Blamire in the mission church. All that she had emerged with was a suspicion that a nice, apparently ingenuous young VSO had been deceiving her. Andy Russell could have been present at Marakosi at the mission open day, and if he had a canoe, he could also have made the attacks on the Alvaro logging camp at night and returned before dawn. But why would he do such things? It seemed out of character with his affable personality. Surely the boy was not a murderer?

The sound of ragged chanting came from one of the huts. A few minutes later a line of men and women straggled out into the cluttered village square. Sister Conchita saw that Mary Gui was among the twenty islanders who had been praying indoors. Conchita knew nothing about the pathway-sending ceremony except that it was designed to send the soul of a dead leader to the island he had chosen, where his spirit could roam freely during the everlasting afterlife. In reality, Dontate's body was now mouldering on a leaf bed on a treetop on Skull Island. When the appropriate time came, it would be taken down and buried, but not before his skull was added to the cache of great Roviana chiefs there.

The mourners stood in a straight line facing the custom priest. Only the women were singing, expressing their loss and asking the spirits what would happen to them now that their protector had gone. When they fell silent, an old man stepped forward and began talking in a reedy voice. No one had made any attempt to wear custom dress. Even the priest wore only a pair of shorts and a singlet.

'On behalf of the village, that old man is asking the gods for protection, support and guidance now that Joe has gone,' said a familiar voice at Conchita's side. 'These were all the things he gave to his line while he was alive.' Mary Gui had slipped away from the line of mourners to join her. 'Some of the men have gone into the bush to cut down an almond tree in his memory. Then there will be a feast. After that, Joe's friends and relatives will stay in his hut for three nights, praying for his spirit. Will you stay for the feast, Sister? You are welcome to do so.'

'No, I'm afraid that I must be leaving,' said Conchita. 'Actually, I came up here because I was hoping to find you. May I talk to you for a few minutes?'

Mary looked across at the village square. The islanders were making preparations for the feast. A pig had been killed and roasted on a spit. There were piles of fruit and vegetables on banana leaves on the ground. The rest of the villagers were beginning to assemble.

'As long as I'm back in time for the three mourning nights,' she said. 'No one will miss me at the feast. I'm a stranger to most of the villagers anyway. I seldom came up here when Joe was alive. Between you and me, it's a dirty, unhygienic place. Let's walk down the hill and get away from it.'

'I'd like to ask you about Andy Russell,' said Conchita as they started strolling back down towards Gizo. 'What can you tell me about him?'

'The VSO?' asked Mary. 'I hardly knew him. I've only been back from Australia for a few weeks, if you remember. He seems quite nice.'

'Didn't he help you with the independence party?' asked Conchita.

'Not really,' said Mary. 'He might have come to one or two meetings. I don't remember. He hardly ever said anything if he did come.'

'That's strange. I had an idea that he helped you with the administration, writing letters and so on. Didn't he even have anything to say about the logging operations?'

'I don't know; I can't remember if he did.'

'If you don't mind my saying so,' said Sister Conchita, 'I find that hard to believe.'

'Are you calling me a liar?' asked Mary with a flash of anger.

'I think,' said Sister Conchita in neutral tones, 'that you are a pretty and charming young lady who has discovered quite early on in life how to adapt these attributes to her own advantage. In short, Miss Gui, you know how to use people.'

'That's a dreadful thing for a nun to say,' said Mary.

'You used Joe Dontate because you thought he would have the power in the west to help you fulfil your own ambitions, whatever they may be, and I suspect that somehow or other you have also used Sergeant Kella because you thought he might also be of help to you one day.'

'I don't know what you're talking about!'

'But most of all,' said Sister Conchita inexorably, 'you have seduced and used a young boy in Andy Russell, again for your own selfish ends.'

'This is all rubbish,' said Mary, stopping. 'I won't listen to any more!'

'I've almost finished,' said Sister Conchita. 'You set up this spurious organization called the Solomon Islands Independence Party and you persuaded a few of the disgruntled local islanders to join it, but you have really been using it as a front for your own ends.'

'What ends?'

'I'm not sure yet, but you played on the enthusiasm of a credulous young man like Andy and persuaded him to make a couple of efforts to sabotage the logging company on Alvaro island, convincing him that it was in the interests of the people of the Solomons.'

'How could I possibly do that?' asked Mary.

'As I said, you have a talent for making the most of people and situations. The local District Commissioner, who I am afraid is a lazy and inefficient official, sent Andy to Kasolo for some work experience, and then forgot all about him, in effect stranding an inexperienced young boy on a small uninhabited island in the lagoon.'

'That doesn't have anything to do with me.'

'No, it doesn't. But you, on the other hand, did realize that Andy had not returned to Gizo. You asked around and discovered that he had been sent to Kasolo. You went there by canoe on your own and found him in a state of some distress and extremely resentful at the way he had been treated by the authorities. With your particular talent for turning events to your own advantage, instead of taking him back to Gizo and looking after him, you persuaded him to remain on the island, knowing that this would give him a cast-iron alibi if anything untoward were to happen anywhere else. You had a potentially lethal weapon on Kasolo, and in Andy's current state of simmering resentment, you were able to launch him practically anywhere you chose.'

'Ridiculous!' snapped Mary. 'Why would I send the boy to destroy timber on Alvaro of all things?'

'I'm not sure yet,' said the nun. 'Neither do I know how this led to the death of Ed Blamire, but I'm sure it did.'

'I hardly know the VSO,' repeated Mary.

'I think you had more to do with him than you claim,' said Sister Conchita. 'He's a normal, susceptible eighteen-year-old and you led him on. You got him involved with the Solomon Islands Independence Party and persuaded him to wreck some of the timber at the logging camp. He let me have some writing paper with the SIIP's heading on it. I think you had been encouraging him to write to the logging people complaining about their activities on Alvaro. Then, when they ignored him, you suggested that he launch raids on the island as a form of protest, since he had the alibi of being stranded on Kasolo.'

'Can you prove any of this?' asked Mary. 'Because if you can't, I would be very careful, Sister Conchita. You are a guest in the Solomons. If you start making accusations against innocent islanders, you could find yourself in very serious trouble. I should take care if I were you. Now, if you will excuse me, I must return to mourn the man I loved!'

Sister Conchita watched the girl walk angrily back up the hill. The nun did not move. She felt inexpressibly sad. She had no right to talk to Mary as she had just done. Her unwavering pursuit of the truth had made her go too far again. She was using the authority of her office to follow what was little more than a private hobby. If the church authorities heard what she had just done, she would be in trouble once more. Even so, she had felt impelled to harass Mary Gui in an effort to get something out of her. She had certainly stirred the girl up. Who knew? It might lead to something.

She resumed her progress back to Gizo, hurrying this time. Sergeant Kella would probably be cross with her when she revealed the forthright approach she had just taken with Mary Gui. He was waiting impatiently for her by the canoe on the beach. He forestalled her when she tried to tell him what had happened after the pathway-sending ceremony.

'Talk to me about it on the way,' he said, pushing the canoe into the water and starting the outboard engine. 'We've got to get to the logging camp in a hurry. I'm afraid that Andy Russell might be about to do something silly!'

TWENTY-SEVEN

'Well, don't keep me in suspense. What did you hear about Andy?' asked Sister Conchita as the canoe bumped across the lagoon, its engine opened to capacity.

'They told me at the village that he had borrowed a canoe an hour ago and said that he was going to the logging camp,' said Kella, his eyes fixed on the coastline of Alvaro as it grew closer. 'Apparently he had business to finish there.'

'I hope he's not going to do anything silly,' said Sister Conchita.

'The point is,' said Kella, 'what silly things has he already been doing over the last couple of weeks?'

The policeman was looking uncharacteristically sombre. Sister Conchita had never seen him so tense and on edge.

'Whatever it is, he's probably been egged on by Mary Gui,' she said. 'Just like she talked Joe Dontate into joining up with Imison and his friends. That girl has a genius for preparing bullets for other people to fire, if she thinks it will do her any good.'

'You're entitled to your opinion,' said Kella.

Conchita's instincts told her that this would be a good time to keep quiet. 'I can't believe that Andy murdered Ed Blamire,' she heard herself saying. 'What reason would he have?'

The beach was only a few yards away. Kella cut out the engine, jumped over the side and dragged the canoe out of the water. He ran up the slope to Jake Michie's office, with Sister Conchita at his heels. Work seemed to be going on as usual around the camp, although one or two of the Melanesians threw curious looks at the police sergeant and his companion as they hurried past. At the beginning of the coral road leading inland, a large truck with a cargo of logs had been driven into a ditch, jettisoning its load. Kella ignored it and ran across to the company office. He threw the door open and they went in.

Andy Russell was standing being supported by the two Australian security men. His head drooped dispiritedly. When he looked up, Conchita saw that there was a livid bruise on his right cheek, and that his nose and mouth were bleeding. Jake Michie, the logging boss, was sitting behind his desk.

'Let him go,' said Kella, indicating Andy. At first the big Australians merely glowered at him and did not move. The sergeant advanced on them. 'Let go of him now, or I'll arrest the pair of you for assault and obstructing a police officer in the course of his duty,' he said. 'I don't think either of you'd fancy six months in an island prison, and that would be before your trial even began!'

Michie growled something at the Australians. Reluctantly the security men released their grip. Sister Conchita took Andy by the arm and led him over to a washbasin against the wall. She filled the basin with water, soaked a corner of her habit in it and started bathing his damaged face. Andy submitted dazedly to her treatment. All the fight seemed to have drained out of him.

'The kid went crazy,' protested Michie, standing up. 'He came running up the beach and tried to get in one of the giant trucks with a load of timber on it. He was going to turn it over and block the road inland. It would have taken us days to get it right, and the silly sod could have killed himself. Luckily he only drove it into a ditch. Mitch and Quincy here dragged him out before he could properly get started. I want him arrested. I'll press charges.'

'Did they have to beat him up?' asked Sister Conchita, glaring at the Australians.

'Too right they did!' said Michie. 'We had to subdue him. The kid went berserk when we got him out of the truck.'

'You're ruining this island, you and your kind!' said Andy defiantly. His nose had started to bleed again. 'You cheated the islanders out of their custom land and you've ruined the habitat! Somebody's got to try and stop you.'

'You two can leave now,' Kella said to the security guards before anyone else could speak. 'Don't go far away. I haven't finished with you yet.'

The two Australians slouched disconsolately out of the office. Kella looked at Andy. 'Do you deny that you trespassed on this island at night on two separate occasions, and damaged supplies of logs here by setting fire to them?' he asked.

'No, I don't,' muttered Andy, holding a reddening handkerchief to his nose. 'I'd do it again, too!'

'Who put you up to it?'

'Nobody,' said the VSO. 'It was all my idea.'

'Like hell it was,' said Kella. 'This was all part of Mary Gui's plan, wasn't it? She talked you and Joe Dontate into helping her.' He did not look at Sister Conchita, who suppressed a smile. The sergeant had not been completely blinded by lust, then.

'This is how I see it,' went on Kella. 'When she discovered that you were stranded alone on Kasolo, apparently without transport, she realized that this would provide you with an alibi if you raided the logging station. You could hardly be a castaway *and* a saboteur at the same time. She provided you with a canoe, so that you could land on Alvaro twice at night and set fire to the logs. She even put you up to crapping on the beach to make it look as if it was an old-time custom raid undertaken by a group of local freedom fighters.'

'But what was the point of damaging the logging operations?' asked Sister Conchita.

'Mary knew how ingenuous Andy was, and that he was upset by the way in which the Alvaro Company had ruined this island. She also knew that he was young and foolish enough to take risks to put an end to the company's operations.'

'So it was all part of the Solomon Islands Independence Party's campaign?' asked Sister Conchita.

'There is no Solomon Islands Independence Party, and there never has been any campaign,' said Kella, shaking his head. 'All Mary had was a few pieces of headed notepaper printed up to fool someone as credulous as Andy and make him think that he was striking a blow for the freedom of the islands. All the talk of meetings and motions being passed was just a smokescreen, the SIIP is a phantom, a figment of Mary Gui's imagination.'

'How can you be sure?' asked Sister Conchita.

'When I was in Gizo, I went to see the one man who would know,' said Kella. 'His name is Raesohu. He works at the radio station. If ever there is an uprising in the Western District, he will be behind it. He had never heard of the SIIP, and neither had four other leading independence fighters I questioned in the district centre.'

'This is all very interesting, but I've got a company to run,' said Michie suddenly. 'If you'll excuse me, I'll just go and see how much damage Little Lord Fauntleroy here has really done.'

The logging boss lumbered towards the door. For a moment Sister Conchita thought that Sergeant Kella was going to stop him, but the policeman thought better of it. He followed Michie outside. At a loss to understand what was going on, but with implicit trust in Kella and determined not to miss a moment of what was going to happen, Sister Conchita went after them. Still dabbing at his nose, Andy brought up the rear.

The small party walked across the compound to the coral road. At the sight of the logging boss, those Melanesians in the area bent studiously over their tasks. Michie gave a grunt of exasperation and started examining the wrecked truck.

'So what was the point of Mary Gui claiming that there was an independence party?' asked a bewildered Sister Conchita.

'Money,' said Kella. 'Isn't that right, Mr Michie?'

Michie stopped checking over the truck and turned back to the others. 'How the hell would I know?' he asked.

'Because you were in on it with her,' said Kella.

'Now what are you talking about?' asked Michie warily.

'Mary Gui had the original idea, but she needed someone on the inside of the company to help her. Mary always needed a man for her operations. You were the only man on Alvaro in a position to help her. She discussed her plan with you, and you fell in with it.'

'I've never heard so much garbage,' said Michie.

'Using the guise of the SIIP, Mary Gui wrote to you claiming that the freedom party would destroy the logging camp unless a donation was made to its funds,' Kella went on. 'To underline the point, she had persuaded Andy to make his raids. You were able to contact your head office and inform them that it was your considered opinion that unless they released the money to pay off the SIIP, the freedom fighters would step up the intensity of their attacks and slow down the production of logs. You told me once that the company would do almost anything to ensure that their operation here kept going. A couple of thousand dollars to keep the local independence movement off their backs would be nothing to such a wealthy company. They were probably making similar payments out of petty cash all over the world. You knew that it wouldn't be long before you were replaced with by a local logging boss, so you thought you'd make a little extra cash while you could. They authorized the payment, and you and Mary Gui split the money between you. You used Andy, the pair of you.'

'That's a load of balls!' protested Michie.

'I don't think so,' said Kella. 'I discovered over a thousand dollars in a box in Mary Gui's hut. She would never have saved that sort of money as a student in Australia. That was her share of the extortion money you persuaded your company to part with. I imagine that if I search hard enough, I shall find a similar amount in your possession somewhere.'

'Prove it!' said Michie.

'I'm getting there. The part that really troubled me was where Ed Blamire came into all this. What did he do to merit being killed?'

'I suppose you're going to accuse me of that as well,' said Michie.

'Oh yes,' said Kella. 'You murdered Blamire in the mission church on open day and threw his body on the bonfire. Neither Andy nor Mary would have had the physical strength to do that.'

'You were certainly at the mission that day,' said Sister Conchita, casting her mind back to the day of the killing. 'I saw you supervising the logging exhibition. You could have slipped away from the demonstration at any time and gone to the church. You found poor Mr Blamire there and killed him!'

'Do any of you want to tell me why I would kill a man I didn't even know?' asked Michie.

Suddenly matters became clear to Sister Conchita. 'You didn't have to know him,' she said. 'He knew you. He was hunting you down. Ed Blamire worked for the Alvaro logging company, didn't he? He had been sent here to investigate the threats against their operation. I remember now. While he was talking to me in the church just before he died, he told me about the different jobs he'd had. One of them I didn't understand at the time. He said that he had been a tree-hugger. I suppose that was his way of saying that he was working for the logging company.'

Kella cast a glance of approval at the nun. 'Exactly,' he said. 'That was the conclusion I came to as well. Blamire was an investigator sent in the guise of a tourist to check up on the sabotage attempts. Unfortunately for him, he was also a political supporter and admirer of John F. Kennedy. While he was here, he hired a canoe and paddled it to Kasolo to see for himself where Kennedy and his crew had landed after PT-109 had been sunk. When he arrived, he found Andy hiding on the island – with a canoe, which meant that he could go anywhere in the Roviana Lagoon. It didn't mean anything to Blamire at the time, but unwittingly he had destroyed Andy's alibi of being stranded on Kasolo and unable to leave the island. I suspect that Andy told Mary Gui or Joe Dontate what had happened, and that one of them informed you, Michie.'

Everyone looked at Andy. The VSO shuffled his feet and said nothing. Kella continued his story.

'That meant that without knowing it, Ed Blamire had a vital piece of the jigsaw. By this time he was beginning to close in on you as the instigator of the extortion attempts, Michie. He knew that there would be vital evidence in the anonymous letters that you and Mary Gui had written on behalf of the SIIP demanding money in return for stopping the raids on the logging operation – if such letters existed. He even went to the District Commissioner and asked if Maclehose had the authority to perform arrests. At the time, he said that if he discovered some letters, he would return with them as proof. That's where I got it wrong. I thought he meant letters that Imison and the other Americans had received from the FBI referring to the rumours about Kakaihe being involved in Lieutenant Kennedy debating surrendering to the Japanese.'

'I'm sure that if we contact the authorities in Honiara, they will have discovered by now that Ed Blamire was a private detective working for your company, Mr Michie,' said Sister Conchita. 'When they hear what has been going on, Alvaro will send half a dozen investigators here to look at your books. They'll soon unearth anything illegal.'

'You jokers are out of your minds,' said Michie. 'Have you got just one piece of evidence to support these allegations?'

'I think I might have,' said Sister Conchita, remembering the day when Sister Jean Francoise had come hurrying excitedly out of the bush after her search for *kava* roots. 'We've found the war club you stole from the mission and used to kill Mr Blamire. It was right in the heart of the undergrowth on Marakosi. One of the nuns found it by chance. The police will be able to examine it for fingerprints. No one wears gloves in the Solomons. You probably wiped it down when you got rid of the club, but if you've left just one trace on it, it will be found.'

Michie sighed. Suddenly he started running. He headed away from the coral road, towards the shore, moving with surprising speed for such a big man. The Melanesian labourers gaped at him as he passed. Kella cursed and set off in pursuit. Sister Conchita and Andy exchanged worried glances and followed at a slower pace.

'He's trying to get to the launch!' said Andy.

Michie reached the beach. He hesitated. Kella was gaining on him. Abruptly the logging boss changed direction. He ran towards the fenced-off enclosure containing the latest consignment of logs waiting in rows in ten feet of water. There was a stiff breeze coming off the lagoon, stirring the tightly packed tree trunks so that they jostled hard against each other in the gurgling water.

'Don't be a fool!' Kella shouted, coming to a halt.

Michie ignored him. Balancing precariously, his arms held out on either side of him, the big man started running across the slippery logs towards the anchored launch on the far side of the pen. Several times he tottered and almost fell, but he kept moving. Kella hesitated, and then started across the logs after him. The trunks were as slippery as glass. Michie looked back over his shoulder and increased his pace. He was almost halfway across the pen before he lost his balance. One of the logs revolved beneath his feet. The Australian danced grotesquely, his arms waving. Then he went sprawling across the heaving tree trunks. For a few moments he lay semi-conscious on top of the timber. A gap appeared between two of the logs. The Australian tried to cling to the glistening surface, but his clawing fingers lost their purchase. The trunk began to spin around. With a muffled shout, Michie slipped off the top into another gap appearing momentarily in the phalanx of timber. Then, as the logs smashed together again above his head to form a huge, immovable swaying wooden raft, he disappeared from sight.

TWENTY-EIGHT

'What will happen to everyone?' asked Sister Brigid.

'Not a great deal, to be frank,' said Sister Conchita. 'Mr Michie is dead, so he can't stand trial for the murder of Ed Blamire.'

'But what about Mary Gui? According to what Ben Kella said, she was responsible for the whole dreadful business. She planned to extort money from the logging company by threatening to sabotage its equipment and involved Michie in the plot in return for a share of the proceeds. Then she seduced young Andy into making several raids on Alvaro and trying to make it look like an old-time custom attack, so that Michie could tell his head office that the threats were genuine and they would have to pay up if they wanted to keep the operation working.'

'Oh yes, Mary was the ingenious guiding light behind it all,' agreed Sister Conchita. 'We're sure of that. But we can't prove anything.'

'Surely Andy Russell—'

'Andy won't say a word against Mary Gui. He's too besotted with her,' said Sergeant Kella with some feeling. 'All the lad wants to do is go home and take up his university place. He won't betray Mary, that's for certain. They say you never forget your first love; you probably don't shop her to the police, either. Anyway, if Andy told his side of the story, he would have to admit to setting fire to the timber on Alvaro island. I don't suppose the Cambridge authorities are very keen on arsonists.'

'Fancy a girl like Mary having such an effect on men,' mused Sister Brigid.

'I suppose some would say don't knock it until you've tried it,' said Sister Conchita, looking meaningly at Sergeant Kella. With a pang of glee, she thought she saw the policeman blush beneath his brown skin.

'Well I never,' said Sister Brigid, at a loss. 'So Mary will get away with everything?'

'I daresay there will be a few unattributable comments added to her secret files in Honiara,' said Conchita, 'but nothing official will be done, I'm sure. After all, she may become the first indigenous prime minister of the Solomon Islands one day. If that happens, some expatriate civil servant will have to sit up all night destroying the files on local politicians, so there will be no record at all before long. The logging company is willing to draw a line under the whole affair as long as it's allowed to continue its profitable operations on Alvaro.'

'And those three dreadful Americans who killed Joe Dontate?'

'I daresay much the same will happen to them. Or won't happen, to be more exact. There were no witnesses as to what occurred on Skull Island. They will be extradited back home as soon as they recover in Pilgrim Hospital. After the debacle on Olasana, I dare say their FBI careers will be permanently stalled, but apart from a series of postings to Albuquerque or somewhere similar, they'll probably get away scot free.'

'Albuquerque,' said Sister Brigid with a shudder. 'Punishment enough, if you ask me.'

The two nuns and the police sergeant were standing on the beach at Marakosi Mission early in the morning. The area was much busier than usual. A group of islanders with a concrete mixer and several wheelbarrows were putting down a base for the planned boarding school. Sister Jean Francoise was vigorously hoeing the half-acre of vegetable garden she had carved out of the bush to feed

the imminently expected new intake of residential students. Outside
the mission, Sister Johanna had stripped down the old generator and
was reassembling it.

'Don't say we never do anything for you,' said Sister Brigid.

'I'm overwhelmed,' said Conchita. 'Really I am.'

'Don't be silly,' said Sister Brigid, putting a hand on the other
nun's arm. 'It was the least we could do after all you've done for us.
Especially for me.'

'It was such a noble effort on your part,' said Sister Conchita. 'For
all those years you never said a word about Welchman Buna killing
Kakaihe on Olasana.'

'Welchman stabbed Kakaihe to save Lieutenant Kennedy and his
men from betrayal to the Japanese,' said Sister Brigid. 'If I had
spoken about it, he would have been involved in a lifetime of blood
feuds with Kakaihe's line. He couldn't afford that. Even then,
anyone could see that Welchman Buna had a considerable career
ahead of him. I reported what had happened to the coast-watcher,
Mr Evans, and left it at that.'

The government ship *Bellama* was anchored a hundred yards off
the shore. It had arrived to pick up any passengers booked from the
mission for Honiara. A dinghy rowed by two seamen was already
pulling for the shore. 'Will you start visiting the islands again?' asked
Sister Conchita.

'I shall do my best,' said Sister Brigid. 'I don't suppose it will be
easy, but I've been cooped up at Marakosi for too long. Thank you
again, my dear. I'm quite looking forward to getting out and about
again.'

'It was Welchman Buna's soul that you took responsibility for,
wasn't it?' asked Conchita.

'In a way. Welchman killed Kakaihe on the beach at Olasana
because he was fighting in the white man's war. He was young and
had never killed a man before. He was in a terrible state afterwards.
I felt that I had to do what I could for him.'

The elderly nun squeezed Conchita's arm and hurried back to the basket of yams she had been sorting through for that evening's meal. Kella nodded, picked up his knapsack and walked down to the wharf, where he joined the waiting Welchman Buna.

The dinghy reached the wharf. A tall, thin young man in the robes of a priest stepped out and walked along its length. Several islanders picked up his luggage and followed him across the beach towards the house. Sergeant Kella and Welchman Buna stepped down into the dinghy. The seamen started rowing them out to the *Bellama*. Sister Conchita walked across the sand to welcome the priest to his new home.

There were a number of passengers from Gizo already on the deck of the *Bellama* when Kella and Buna climbed up the swaying rope ladder from the dinghy to the government vessel. One of them was Mary Gui. The girl smiled dazzlingly at the sight of them. She walked over and put her arm through that of the politician.

'Hello, Welchman,' she said. Her smile faded a little, like a flickering light bulb, as she turned to the police sergeant. 'Sergeant Kella, how are you?'

'Hi,' said Kella. 'Where are you going, Mary?'

The girl looked at Buna. 'Is it all right to tell people now?' she asked, squeezing his arm.

'Of course,' smiled the politician. 'Your posting has been officially announced in the Solomon Islands' *Gazette*, my dear.'

'Posting?' asked Kella.

Mary laughed affectedly. 'I really don't know whether I'm coming or going,' she said. 'I have been appointed the Protectorate's representative at the South Pacific Commission in Noumea for the next three years. Aren't I lucky? Of course I owe it all to dear Welchman here.'

So Buna was calling in a few of the debts now owed him by the

British and American governments. The South Pacific Commission was financed by a number of European nations to sponsor the economic and educational development of countries in the area. It was a prestigious, well-paid appointment with the opportunity to make influential contacts. It would serve the ambitious Mary well as she prepared to enter politics. It should also get her out of Buna's hair for the next three years, and remove a possible cause of unrest from the islands, so everyone ought to be happy. Uncharitably, Kella wondered how hard Mary had had to work on her back to get the politician's all-important sponsorship. Then he felt ashamed of himself. After all, Mary Gui had lost Joe Dontate. She could not be blamed for looking for another protector, even if her period of mourning had perforce not been a lengthy one. As for Buna, there was no doubt that he had saved the lives of Kella and Sister Conchita on Olasana. If the determined Mary had fallen into his middle-aged lap, probably almost literally, he could not be blamed for taking advantage of the situation.

'Let's go and look at the dolphins,' suggested Mary, almost overdoing her skittishness, leading Buna away towards the ship's rail. She glanced cursorily back at the policeman and winked. 'Take care, Sergeant Kella. Don't get into any more scrapes in the Mendana Hotel!'

Sergeant Ha'a saw Kella standing on his own and ambled over. He had been dispatched with a squad of policemen to scour Kasolo and Olasana for any remaining frigate bird *knap knaps*, and was on his way back to Honiara with his men.

'You're needed back on Malaita,' said the rotund policeman abruptly.

'Why, what's gone wrong there?' asked Kella, his heart sinking. After all, he had only been away for a couple of weeks.

'It was on the SIBS news last night. Timothy Anilafa's up to his tricks again.'

'Who?' asked Kella. Then he remembered. 'You mean the old man who built the ark? What's he done?'

'You know that a couple of Emperor Rats took up residence in his ark. It gave his cause a lot of credence.'

'Yes, I was there at the time. So what? One pair of animals doesn't constitute a mass migration.'

'You're out of date. Make that two pairs,' said Ha'a. 'A district officer on tour in the area reported last week that two ground boa snakes had moved in as well.'

'You're joking!'

'I'm not even wearing a funny hat,' said Sergeant Ha'a. 'The best way the DO could figure it out, the ark is so dark, damp and dangerously unhygienic, it's likely to attract all sorts of creatures over a period of time. Besides which, the old man keeps stockpiling food supplies for them in it. Anyway, our Timothy has taken advantage of the situation.'

'How so?'

'He's announced that he's formed a new religious denomination called the Lau Church of the Blessed Ark. Any of the local villagers who don't make a donation of shell money to its funds will be doomed to spend a period in hell when they die, where they will be gnawed by animals rejected for the ark. It's causing a bit of a stir among the saltwater villages.'

'I bet it is,' said Kella. 'You're right. It's time I was getting back home.'

On the shore, Father Johnson, the new priest, was fussily supervising the transfer of his luggage from the wharf. Sister Conchita walked over to him.

'Welcome to Marakosi, Father,' she said. 'I'm Sister Conchita. I hope you'll be happy here.'

'I haven't come here to be happy, Sister,' said the young priest censoriously. 'I believe, indeed I know, that there is a great deal of work to be done, and I am anxious to get on with it quickly. I hear that this mission has fallen into a considerable state of disrepair, both physically and spiritually.'

'The sisters are working very hard,' said Sister Conchita protectively. 'Would you like to meet them?'

'Time enough for that later,' said Father Johnson. Suspiciously he watched the Melanesians carry his bags up to the mission house. 'I believe that you have been here just to keep matters ticking over, Sister Conchita. You won't have had time to put your imprimatur on the mission. I intend to stay much longer and carry out a root-and-branch revision of all that goes on, or does not go on, here.'

'Yes, Father,' said Conchita humbly, suppressing the answer that rose to her lips. The priest was young and inexperienced and could not be expected to establish himself at the mission first. He would have to make his own mistakes and invent the wheel for himself, just as she had. For his sake she hoped that it would not be too painful a process. She took a deep breath.

'I could delay my departure and stay on for a few more weeks if it would help,' she offered.

'No need, no need,' said the priest, transparently anxious to be rid of her. He extended a limp hand. 'Goodbye, Sister; I hope that your brief sojourn at Marakosi was an enjoyable one, even if you didn't have time to accomplish a great deal.'

'Oh, it was,' said Sister Conchita, but the young priest was already scurrying away purposefully up to the house. Engrossed in his shining plans for the future, he did not look round.

The dinghy was making the return journey from the *Bellama* to pick her up. Conchita picked up her holdall. Sister Brigid, Sister Jean Francoise and Sister Johanna hurried over to the young nun to hug her and say their tearful goodbyes. Conchita looked at the slim, unbowed form of Father Johnson as he entered the mission house, busily shouting orders to the carriers. Then she turned back to the three elderly, innocuous-looking nuns. She wondered what lay in store for the energetic young priest in his new life. She was rather afraid that she knew.

'Be gentle with him,' she said.